P9-DWM-926

A
Just Clause

Berkley Prime Crime titles by Lorna Barrett

MURDER IS BINDING

BOOKMARKED FOR DEATH

BOOKPLATE SPECIAL

CHAPTER & HEARSE

SENTENCED TO DEATH

MURDER ON THE HALF SHELF

NOT THE KILLING TYPE

BOOK CLUBBED

A FATAL CHAPTER

TITLE WAVE

A JUST CLAUSE

Anthologies

MURDER IN THREE VOLUMES

A Just Clause

Lorna Barrett

BERKLEY PRIME CRIME
New York

BERKLEY PRIME CRIME
Published by Berkley
An imprint of Penguin Random House LLC
375 Hudson Street, New York, New York 10014

Library of Congress Cataloging-in-Publication Data

Names: Barrett, Lorna, author.
Title: A just clause / by Lorna Barrett.
Description: First edition. | New York : Berkley Prime Crime, 2017. | Series: A booktown mystery ; 11
Identifiers: LCCN 2016059528 (print) | LCCN 2017006111 (ebook) | ISBN 9780399585913 (hardcover) | ISBN 9780399585920 (ebook)
Subjects: LCSH: Miles, Tricia (Fictitious character)—Fiction. | Women booksellers—Fiction. | Murder—Investigation—Fiction. | BISAC: FICTION / Mystery & Detective / Women Sleuths. | GSAFD: Mystery fiction.
Classification: LCC PS3602.A83955 J87 2017 (print) | LCC PS3602.A83955 (ebook) | DDC 813/.6—dc23
LC record available at https://lccn.loc.gov/2016059528

First Edition: June 2017

Printed in the United States of America
1 3 5 7 9 10 8 6 4 2

Cover art by Teresa Fasolino
Book design by Laura K. Corless

PUBLISHER'S NOTE: The recipes contained in this book are to be followed exactly as written. The publisher is not responsible for your specific health or allergy needs that may require medical supervision. The publisher is not responsible for any adverse reactions to the recipes contained in this book.

To Amy and Steve Hart.
Thanks for your friendship.

Cast of Characters

Tricia Miles: owner of Haven't Got a Clue mystery bookstore

Angelica Miles: Tricia's sister, owner of the Cookery and the Booked for Lunch café, and half owner of the Sheer Comfort Inn. Her alter ego is Nigela Ricita, the mysterious developer who has been pumping money and jobs into the village of Stoneham.

Pixie Poe: Tricia's assistant at Haven't Got a Clue

Ginny Wilson-Barbero: Tricia's former assistant; wife of Antonio Barbero

Mr. Everett: Tricia's employee at Haven't Got a Clue

Antonio Barbero: the public face of Nigela Ricita Associates (NRA) and Angelica's stepson

Grace Harris-Everett: Mr. Everett's wife

Steven Richardson: thriller author

Grant Baker: chief of the Stoneham Police Department

John Miles: Tricia's and Angelica's father

Sheila Miles: Tricia's and Angelica's mother

Mary Fairchild: owner of the By Hook or By Book crafting/bookstore

Jim Stark: Tricia's contractor

Fred Pillins: Pixie Poe's fiancé

Russ Smith: owner of the *Stoneham Weekly News*

Nikki Brimfield-Smith: owner of the Patisserie; wife of Russ Smith

Lois Kerr: Director of the Stoneham Public Library

Carol Talbot: Plays darts against Tricia at the Dog-Eared Page

Brad Shields: Carol's neighbor

Ellen Shields: Carol's neighbor

Marshall Cambridge: owner of Vamps magazine shop

A
Just Clause

ONE

Tricia Miles almost always felt a thrill to host a book signing at her mystery bookstore, Haven't Got a Clue, especially when it involved a favorite author. Tonight that author was Steven Richardson, known for writing *New York Times* and *USA Today* bestselling thrillers. Stacks of his latest hardcover, *A Killing in Mad Gate*, sat on a table at the front of the store. The weather was perfect for a signing: drizzling and gray. Now all she needed was for the guest of honor to arrive.

Tricia's assistant, Pixie Poe, checked the big pink watch on her left wrist. "He's late," she sang. To honor the author, Pixie had chosen a fuchsia floral dress that had been made at least six decades before, and, despite her rather chunky frame, the dress not only fit as though it had been made for her, but was actually quite flattering, giving her an hourglass figure that she seemed to enjoy flaunting.

This month, she was again a blonde, and when she smiled, her gold canine tooth flashed. She'd been smiling a lot that evening—every time she glanced at the modest diamond solitaire on her left hand. Her newly minted fiancé, Fred Pillins, was a nondescript kind of fellow who matched Pixie in years—about fifty. He stood near the back of the store, camera in hand, trying to look inconspicuous—except that his fond gaze rarely strayed from Pixie. He seemed to enjoy the view. He must have taken at least a dozen candid shots of her since his arrival some twenty minutes before. That was when the signing was supposed to have begun.

In addition to the Tuesday Night Book Club members, nearly two dozen of Tricia's customers from a fifty-mile radius had shown up to welcome the author. Tricia was glad she'd not only ordered a cake with the book's cover printed in edible ink from the Patisserie but a big plate of assorted cookies to go along with the sparkling punch she'd made from her sister Angelica's recipe.

Angelica approached, looking stupendous in a tailored ivory suit with matching stilettos, holding a paper cup filled with punch. "Your author *was* aware of the time of the signing, wasn't he?"

Tricia sighed. "Yes. But he was driving up from Boston. Thanks to the rain, who knows what the traffic is like. I'm sure he'll be here soon—and if not, I hope he'll at least call me." Tricia squinted at her sister. "Remind me again why *you're* here?"

"*Moi*?" Angelica practically cooed.

"*Oui, tu*. You're not exactly a thriller reader."

Angelica sighed patiently. "I want to see if there are sparks!"

"Sparks?"

"Yes, between you and Steven."

Tricia eyed her sister coolly.

"He kissed you on the *Celtic Lady* cruise."

Tricia frowned. "I have kissed three men since then."

"Daddy, Antonio, and Mr. Everett don't count," Angelica said, citing her stepson and Tricia's elderly employee and friend.

"There will be *no* sparks."

"She said in denial," Angelica muttered.

Tricia's frown deepened to a glare. "Instead of sparks, you might see my temper explode."

Angelica shook her head. "It's never going to happen, my dear sister. You don't *have* a temper."

"I'll consider getting one."

The bookstore's door opened, the little bell overhead tinkling cheerfully, but it was not Richardson who entered. Instead, it was someone well known to Tricia and Angelica.

"Oh, dear," Angelica muttered, taking in the man dressed in an outrageous—for him—pink aloha shirt and holding a big black umbrella with a couple of broken ribs. Again, Tricia sighed and, despite a pang of dread, forced a smile. It had been five all-too-very-short months since she'd last seen her father, John Miles.

"Daddy! Whatever are you doing back in Stoneham?"

John struggled to close the soaked bumbershoot. "I came to visit my two best girls, of course."

Angelica's smile was even more rigid. "What a pleasure."

It wasn't.

Still, once he'd closed the umbrella, the sisters leaned in to give John a kiss on each cheek.

To say John had outstayed his welcome back in January was an understatement. Not only had he left the village owing money to nearly half the Chamber of Commerce's members—which Angelica had had to reimburse—but he'd left the Sheer Comfort Inn without notice and apparently with his suitcases filled with a number of the antiques that had decorated the place. Their father's deadbeat behavior had not only been unexpected—but unprecedented. That he'd left with no explanation was just as surprising.

Before the sisters could ask even the most basic of questions—like

"When are you leaving?"—the bell over the door tinkled once again, this time admitting the long-awaited author, looking decidedly damp around the edges.

"Tricia!" Richardson called. He sounded winded.

"Steven—at last!" Tricia excused herself, leaving Angelica to deal with their father. She joined the author. "Are you okay? I was getting worried."

"I just ran from the municipal parking lot. Sorry I'm so late. The traffic outside of Boston was abominable, and then there was a wreck near Nashua that backed everything up for miles."

"I figured as much."

"Do you still want me to give a reading?"

"I think your fans would be disappointed if you didn't speak—but if you'd prefer to do a Q and A instead, I don't think anyone would object."

He nodded and pointed toward the table piled with his latest novel. "Shall I?"

"Yes, please," Tricia said, and gestured for him to stand beside it. She joined him to face her customers, who were mostly talking among themselves and scarfing down cookies and punch. "May I have your attention!" she called, but without much impact. "Excuse me; we're ready to start!" Her efforts weren't attracting much attention.

Pixie moved to stand beside her. "I'll take care of this." She raised her right thumb and index finger to her lips and let loose with a shrill whistle that was as effective as nails on a chalkboard for silencing the room. Tricia winced as everyone turned in attention, while Pixie studied her hand. "Damn. Now I've got to go freshen my lipstick."

Tricia plastered on a smile. "Ladies and gentlemen, won't you please take your seats? It's my pleasure to present a man whose books are well known, and loved, by all of us here tonight—"

"Not me," muttered a female voice from somewhere in the store, but Tricia had no clue who said it.

Momentarily rattled, she launched back into her introduction. "Author Steven Richardson."

A smattering of applause followed, and then there seemed to be a mad dash as everyone sought a seat at the front of the room, which had been rearranged so that the comfortable upholstered chairs of the reading nook faced the front of the store, with metal folding chairs set up in rows behind them.

It took another minute or two for the murmur of voices to quiet, then Richardson spoke.

"It's great to see such a welcoming crowd here at Haven't Got a Clue. Before I tell you about my latest book, *A Killing in Mad Gate*, I'd like to tell you a little about myself."

"Don't bother," came the same rude voice. Tricia searched the faces of the women that populated the small audience, but still wasn't sure who'd spoken. It definitely wasn't Grace Harris-Everett, who sat primly next to her husband, Mr. Everett, nor could it have been Mary Fairchild, her neighbor and owner of the By Hook or By Book craft store. Tricia wasn't as familiar with the rest of the ladies.

She circled back to the table that held the goodies, where Angelica was again ladling punch into her cup. "This really is good!" she whispered.

"Who's being rude to Steven?" Tricia asked.

Angelica took a sip. "No idea. Why would someone come to a signing if they didn't like the author?"

"I just hope there isn't going to be any unpleasantness."

John had ditched his soggy umbrella, and he sidled up to the table, grabbing a napkin and taking a couple of the cookies. "We should probably talk," he said, and popped one of the butter cookies into his mouth, chewing. He jerked a thumb in the direction of the back of the store.

Tricia wasn't sure she wanted to engage in conversation with her not-so-dear old dad. It was nearly seven thirty. Was he about to beg for a bed to stay the night? Luckily, she wasn't in a position to offer him one—thanks to the state of her home, which had been torn apart for the renovation of the second and third floors of the building she now owned, as evidenced by dust that had accumulated on the baseboards and had escaped Mr. Everett's lamb's wool duster. Unbeknownst to most of the village of Stoneham, Angelica owned not only the Sheer Comfort Inn, but the Brookview Inn. After he'd pulled a disappearing act, Tricia was pretty sure her sister wouldn't be issuing an invitation for their father to stay in either location. Angelica had been pretty steamed to have to not only clean up after him but come up with a reasonable explanation for his boorish behavior.

Still, he *was* their father.

The sisters followed John to the back of the shop.

"Daddy," Angelica began, and Tricia recognized that no-nonsense tone. "You left rather suddenly back in January, with many unpaid bills."

Instead of looking embarrassed, John actually grinned. "Now, that's not quite right—"

"Yes, it's definitely right," Angelica insisted, keeping her voice low. "I know, because I had to come up with excuses for many of the merchants in the village as to why you disappeared without a trace. You didn't even let Tricia and me know you were leaving the area."

"I was offered a wonderful business proposition—but it was time dependent, and I simply had to leave. But now I'm back and prepared to make restitution."

"*Full* restitution?" Angelica asked.

"Of course. Although there seems to be a little resentment from some of the local merchants. They said they had no rooms at both the Sheer Comfort Inn *and* the Brookview Inn, and yet the parking lots for both establishments were nearly empty."

Tricia knew Angelica had provided the staffs of both properties with a picture of John Miles and a warning to them *not* to give him a room should he ever show up again.

"Would I be able to stay with either of you?" John asked.

Tricia shook her head sadly. "My loft is undergoing a massive renovation. I'm not even staying here right now."

"Really?" John asked, sounding skeptical. "And yet I see no trace of work being done."

Tricia wasn't about to point out the dust. Instead, she jerked a thumb over her shoulder. "There's a twenty-yard Dumpster behind the building, just through that door."

John turned to Angelica. "I have a one-bedroom loft."

"I'd be perfectly willing to sleep on the couch."

"I'm sorry, Daddy, but it's out being upholstered," Angelica lied without batting an eye.

John's jovial features began to sag. "Where am I to stay? I have no other friends or relatives in the area."

"Why aren't you with Mother?" Angelica asked, rather pointedly.

"Ah, I hate to be the bearer of unhappy news, but . . . your mother and I have separated."

Tricia gave her sister a sidelong glance. This really wasn't surprising news. Not that either of them had heard a word about it from their mother after their ill-fated visit to Bermuda to see her five months before.

"Has she gone back to Rio?" Tricia asked.

"Uh, initially yes. As you know, things aren't quite as nice as they once were in Brazil. When we last spoke, she told me she had packed up and was moving back to Connecticut."

"When was this?" Angelica asked.

"About a month ago."

"And where were you at the time?" Tricia asked.

"In Las Vegas." John's good-humored smile had returned once more.

"Gambling?" Angelica guessed.

"Just for fun," John admitted. "Unfortunately, the business deal I spoke of only moments ago fell through."

"And that's why you're back here?" Tricia guessed.

"Er, yes. A man can always depend on his loving children in a time of crisis."

"What's the crisis?" Angelica asked, none too kindly. "You said you came back to make full restitution to the area merchants."

"Well, yes—"

"It's not a health scare, is it?" Tricia asked, and this time she was concerned.

"Oh, nothing of the sort."

"That's good," Angelica said, but her gaze was still sharp.

"Why don't we go over to the Dog-Eared Page and get a drink and talk things over," John suggested.

Tricia nodded toward the front of her store, where the author talk was still in full swing. "I've got a business to run."

"And I'm helping her," Angelica said.

Actually, Pixie was helping Tricia run the event, but she didn't contradict her sibling.

"I could go over and wait for you both, but there's a tiny problem. The proprietress doesn't seem to want to serve me."

So, his first stop after being refused accommodations *hadn't* been to seek out his darling daughters.

"That's because you left the village with a very large tab," Angelica said.

"What's a few dollars?" John said, shrugging.

"A few *thousand* dollars," Angelica corrected him. "Surely you didn't think the people you owed money to wouldn't come asking Tricia and me about your whereabouts and expecting to be paid."

"It's all a big misunderstanding," John insisted.

"I'm listening," Angelica insisted.

But before John could explain, the group of people at the front of the shop broke into enthusiastic applause.

"I've got to get back to work," Tricia said. "If you'll excuse me."

"And I've got to help her," Angelica insisted, and followed in her sister's wake.

By the time Tricia made it to the middle of the shop, Richardson had already taken his seat at the book table with pen in hand, while Pixie readied the books, handing them to him open at the title page, ready for him to sign.

"I'll take care of the cake," Angelica said, and marched around the goodies table. "Do you want me to wait until Steven has his picture taken with it before I cut it?"

"Let's not bother." The hands on the clock were already marching toward eight. "I'd better go man the register." Tricia turned, but Mr. Everett was already stationed behind the sales desk, waiting for the first customer.

She hurried over to him. "Oh, Mr. Everett, it's your night off. I'll take care of the sales."

"I saw that you were engaged, Ms. Miles, and I thought it best to cover all bases."

"You're a dear. Angelica's about to cut the cake. Why don't you get a slice for yourself and Grace?"

"I will, thank you."

Tricia watched her friend stroll over to the goodies table, but saw that her father was already there—stuffing his pockets full of cookies and speaking to one of the store's customers—Carol Talbot. The fifty-something woman's heavily lined features no doubt were the result of years of heavy tanning and reminded Tricia of an angry bulldog, which matched her personality. It was her body that was the envy of women decades younger. This evening she'd dressed in a form-fitting pink floral sundress with a bolero jacket, accented by a string of faux pearls around her neck. A cutthroat darts player, Carol had often played against Tricia on tournament nights at the Dog-Eared Page. Carol wasn't one of Tricia's favorite people, nor a regular customer, so it was surprising she had made the effort to attend the signing.

"I'd like to check out now, please," said a woman in a floral top with dark slacks.

"I'm sorry. I'd be glad to help you," Tricia said, then rang up the sale, adding a few of the bookmarks that had been dropped off by other mystery authors. By the time she'd finished with her first customer, two more stood in line. She looked back to the table where Angelica was serving cake and noticed that John and Carol had moved to one side, apparently engaged in animated conversation—at least her father seemed in great spirits. Tricia rang up another two sales before she had another opportunity to look up—only to see Carol raise her hand and deliver a hearty slap across her father's left cheek. Then, she turned on her heels and stalked toward the front of the store.

Richardson was no longer sitting at the signing table. Tricia saw him standing outside the store's display window and under the awning, smoking a cigarette. Funny, she hadn't known he was a smoker. Carol barreled through the door, turned, and ran straight into the author. Another customer set down a copy of *A Killing in Mad Gate*, as well as another couple of vintage mysteries, and Tricia busied herself taking care of that sale, too. When she looked up again, she watched as—once again—Carol raised her hand, slapping Richardson's cheek, as well.

Angelica hurried over to the register, leaving the cake duties to Pixie. "What's with all the slapping?" she whispered, and placed the books into a bag, then plastered on a smile. "Thanks for shopping at Haven't Got a Clue!"

"We'll talk as soon as we finish all these sales," Tricia muttered, and turned back to her work.

Richardson returned to the shop, and Tricia wondered what he'd done with his cigarette butt, hoping he hadn't tossed it on the sidewalk. His left cheek bore a red blotch where he'd been struck, and he gave her a pained smile as he passed by the cash desk, making his way over to the cake table, where he stopped to speak with several of his readers.

Ten minutes later, the shop had pretty much emptied, and at least thirty of the fifty books Tricia had ordered for the signing had been sold—as well as another twenty or thirty paperbacks. It had been a very good signing indeed.

"That was a good night's worth of sales," Angelica said, echoing Tricia's thoughts.

"I'm ready for a martini."

"What are we going to do about Daddy?"

"I don't know. But I'd like to find out why Carol Talbot slapped him—and Steven."

"Isn't that the woman who you always beat at darts in the Dog-Eared Page?"

Tricia nodded. "And also one of my not-so-favorite customers. The only other time she came in, we had a register jam and couldn't give her a proper printed receipt. Mr. Everett patiently wrote out a receipt by hand, and she made him add up the numbers three times just to make sure he hadn't made an error."

"Poor Mr. Everett. I can't imagine anyone questioning his—or your—honesty."

"Is there really no room at either of the inns?" Tricia asked.

Angelica shook her head. "Not for Daddy."

"I suppose we could put him up at the Motel 6 on the road to Nashua. At least there he can't steal much more than the towels."

"I wouldn't bet on it," Angelica muttered.

But when Tricia looked around the store, she saw only Pixie and Fred, who were tidying up the food table, and Richardson, who'd returned to the table to sign the rest of his books.

Angelica elbowed her sister. "You should invite Steven to accompany us to the bar—where I promise I'll make a discreet exit so you two can get to know one another better."

"You're right, I should invite him—but I'm not sure I *want* to get to know him better. At least not tonight. I'm pooped. It's been a long day. And Miss Marple"—Tricia's cat—"has been alone for almost twelve hours back at the bungalow."

Angelica, in her Nigela Ricita role, had invited Tricia to stay at one of the Brookview Inn's bungalows for a deeply discounted rate after it had been made clear to Tricia that a work zone—her loft—was detrimental to her (and her cat's) nerves and peace of mind. She'd been bringing Miss Marple to work, but because of the signing, she'd left her back at the Brookview for the day.

"I'm game for one drink, then I'm going to my temporary home." She frowned, looking around. "And where did Daddy go?"

"I don't know. I didn't see him leave. Maybe Pixie or Fred did. I'll ask. You go invite Steven." And with that, Angelica gave her sister a mild shove in that direction.

Richardson was just finishing signing the last book with a flourish when Tricia approached. He closed the cover.

"It was a great signing," Tricia said. "Thanks so much for coming all the way to Stoneham. Will you be driving straight back to Boston?"

"I have some other business here in the village. I've booked a room for the night at the Sheer Comfort Inn. I've got a meeting set up in the morning, but I'm free for lunch. How about you?"

"That would be very nice. In fact, I was going to invite you across the street to the pub for a drink."

"I'd love to—but it's been a long day. I'm beat. How about we have one at lunch tomorrow?"

"Sounds lovely. The Brookview Inn, not a mile from here, has great cuisine."

"I'll pick you up here at noon tomorrow."

"Great. Thank you."

Richardson picked up one of his books, rose, and came around the table. "Can I bum a copy off you? I've got an interview scheduled tomorrow and my publisher didn't send the reporter a copy."

Publishers sent authors a certain number of free copies of their books for just that kind of situation, but Tricia hid her annoyance behind a smile. "Sure." She hurried to get one of the store's bags so that the book wouldn't get ruined by the rain. She handed it to him, and Richardson leaned forward, planting a pleasant kiss on Tricia's lips.

"Until tomorrow, then."

She smiled, then watched as he left the store.

Once the door closed on his back, Pixie began to sing, "Tricia and Steven sitting in a tree; k-i-s-s-i-n-g . . ."

Tricia turned. "Pixie!"

Pixie blushed. "Love is in the air!"

Hardly.

What was left of the cake was back in its box. Pixie had previously negotiated for the leftovers to go home with her and Fred. She held it while Fred collapsed the table. "Shall I put this in back?"

"Yes, please," Tricia said.

Fred nodded and hauled the table away.

"Pixie didn't see Daddy leave, either," Angelica said. She held a plastic bag containing the leftover plastic cups and cutlery.

Tricia sighed. "I'm sure we'll hear from him before too long." She turned to her assistant. "Would you and Fred like to join Angelica and me for a drink across the street?"

"We'd love to—but, uh"—Pixie eyed her groom-to-be—"we've sort of made other plans." She lowered her voice. "If you know what I mean." She waggled her eyebrows à la Groucho Marx. Love certainly *was* in the air.

Fred returned, heading for the other table.

"Don't worry about that, Fred. Pixie and I will put everything to rights in the morning."

"Are you sure?"

"You two lovebirds run along," Angelica said, sounding besotted herself.

"We don't mind hanging around a few more minutes," Pixie assured her.

Tricia shook her head. "I'm going to turn out the lights and lock up. I'll see you in the morning."

"Good night," Fred called, and held the door open for his bride-to-be.

"Good night!"

The door closed, the bell over it tinkling cheerfully.

"I'll just get my purse and umbrella, and then we can go to the pub," Tricia said.

Less than a minute later, the sisters crossed the darkening street, heading for the Dog-Eared Page, where several cheerful neon signs glowed in the windows, brightening the gloom.

"What a soggy night," Tricia said.

"But you're going to have a beautiful day tomorrow—starting with lunch with Steven."

"Oh, don't start on that. We're barely acquaintances."

"And that's why you're having lunch together—to become friends. And perhaps friends who become lovers?"

"You're pushing!" Tricia chided her.

"Just a little nudge," Angelica admitted, and reached up to close her umbrella before entering the pub, where they could hear music and laughter.

"Wait a second, Ange. Do you see that?" Tricia said, craning her neck.

"See what?"

"Down the street. There's something lying on the sidewalk at the end of the block by the Armchair Tourist."

That something looked like an open hardcover book, its pages fluttering in the light breeze—which meant it hadn't been there long enough to get soaked.

Tricia charged down the sidewalk, hoping that whoever owned the book had either put their name in it or had pasted in a bookplate. She stooped to pick it up: a brand-new copy of *A Killing in Mad Gate*. She opened it to the title page—and sure enough, Steven's looping signature adorned it.

"What is it?"

"Someone who was at the signing must have dropped it." Tricia passed the book to her sister, then looked around. Almost instantly, her breath caught in her throat.

"What is it?" Angelica asked.

There, nestled at the side of the three-story brick building's empty brick patio, was what looked like a bundle of wet rags. In the dim light, it was hard to see exactly what it was, but Tricia had a pretty good idea. She dug in her purse, pulled out her cell phone and switched on its mini flashlight. She ventured forward and nearly slipped. She bent down and picked up what looked like a pearl. Waving the flashlight's beam across the brick patio outside the Dog-Eared Page, she saw more of the beads scattered before her. "Uh-oh."

"Oh, please don't tell me you've found another—"

Body.

Yes.

Tricia aimed the narrow beam of light on the now-smooth features of Carol Talbot's face.

TWO

"Don't you ever get tired of this?" Stoneham's chief of police, Grant Baker, asked Tricia. His voice was weary. *He* looked weary in the glow of the flashing blue lights from his cruiser and those of the Stoneham Fire and Rescue Unit's truck, the visor of his hat beaded with droplets.

"Yes. Especially when it means that not only don't I get to go home to bed but I didn't get my reward for the day in the form of a lovely gin martini." Tricia sat in the backseat of a Stoneham patrol car, which she shared with an impatient Angelica.

"I'll second that," Angelica groused, inspecting the faux leather upholstery that looked none too clean—no doubt wondering if something on it would stain her ivory suit. "I do hope we can wrap this up soon, because now I *really* need a drink."

"Let's go over it again," Baker said.

Tricia sighed. "When Carol left my shop, she wasn't holding a copy of *A Killing in Mad Gate*."

"Are you sure?"

Tricia thought about it. "Definitely."

"Did you sell any copies of the book before this evening?"

"Maybe half a dozen, but they weren't signed like the one you're holding."

"Could one of those customers have come to your store this evening to have the author sign it?"

"Possibly. I didn't sell any of those copies, but Pixie or Mr. Everett may be able to answer that question." Tricia knew what she needed to tell the chief next, but she felt like a bit of a tattletale doing so. "We did have an incident just after the signing."

Baker's brow furrowed. "Oh?"

"Yes. Carol and Steven Richardson apparently had words, and she slapped him."

Baker's eyes widened. "What brought that on?"

"I don't know. Steven apparently stepped outside the store to smoke a cigarette, and when Carol left, she stopped to speak to him. I don't know what was said, but Carol looked extremely angry and"—Tricia waved her hand in the air for dramatic flair—"slapped him across the cheek. It must have hurt. She left a mark."

"And what did Richardson say about it?"

"Nothing."

"And you didn't ask?" he pressed.

"I didn't want to embarrass him."

Baker looked decidedly unhappy. He opened the book to the title page once more. Richardson had signed the book, but only with his name—it hadn't been personalized. "At these signings," he began, "doesn't the author usually write more than just their name?"

Tricia shrugged. "It depends on the author. Many times customers will buy a book and read it, then give it as a gift. Also, when it comes to the secondary market, a personalized book isn't worth as much as one with only a signature. These books are first editions. They're always worth more than those from additional print runs."

"If you say so."

Tricia bristled. "If you don't want to know the facts about publishing, don't ask."

"I didn't say that at all."

"Your tone was dismissive."

Baker opened his mouth to reply, then seemed to think better of it. "Never mind."

"Chief," Angelica said, her own tone mirroring Tricia's pique, "when can we leave?"

"When I'm satisfied you've told me everything I need to know."

Angelica's gaze hardened. "We walked up the street, saw the book, and then found Carol. There's not much more to tell."

"I'll be the one to determine that," he said, then slammed the book shut and stepped away from the patrol car.

Angelica stuck out her tongue at his back.

"Oh, Ange," Tricia chided.

"He's punishing us."

"What for?"

"Because you dumped him."

"I didn't dump him," Tricia said emphatically. "I chose to no longer go out with someone who wasn't ever likely to make a commitment."

"And now it seems you feel the same way."

"I do not."

"Then why are you so prickly when it comes to dating Steven Richardson?"

"I'm not prickly. I am going to lunch with him tomorrow, although as far as I'm concerned it's definitely not a date."

"Well what would you call it, then?"

"Lunch!"

"You're going to lunch with him?" Baker asked.

When had he returned? Had he been eavesdropping?

"Yes, tomorrow. I'm assuming you'll want to speak with him. He's staying at the Sheer Comfort Inn, at least for tonight. He said he was going there straight after the signing. He said he had other business in the village tomorrow morning, too—talking to Russ Smith." The owner and editor of the *Stoneham Weekly News*.

"Thanks. I'll be sure to track him down."

"And *now* can we leave?" Angelica asked, sounding just a little desperate.

"Yes, you can go. Although I may have more questions for you at a later time."

"You know where to find us," Tricia said, and eased her legs out of the backseat. Baker gave her a hand to get out, but then turned away, apparently uninterested in helping Angelica. Tricia opened her umbrella and then stepped forward to give her sister a hand. Baker's indiscretion had not gone unnoticed.

"There's one cop who won't be getting a donation in his name to the policeman's benevolence fund," Angelica groused as she tottered to stand on her stilettoes. "Can we still stop in at the Dog-Eared Page? After this little interlude, I dearly feel the need of a libation."

"Me, too," Tricia agreed, and the sisters turned in the direction of the pub, sharing Tricia's umbrella.

It had been at least ninety minutes since they'd found Carol's body, and while there was a small crowd of rubberneckers standing on Main Street's sidewalks, from the sound of the music and laughter inside the tavern, not many of its patrons had bothered to check out the excitement.

Then again, when the sisters entered the cozy bar they were hailed with a not-so-welcome greeting of, "Found another stiff, eh, Tricia?"

"That was uncalled-for!" called Michele Fowler, the manager, from behind the bar. "I'm sorry, Tricia."

"Maybe I should just go home," Tricia muttered, already turning for the door, but Angelica grabbed her arm and pulled her farther into the pub.

"Oh, no you don't. I'm getting my drink—or else!"

"You can have a drink—but you don't have to have my company."

"Well, I *want* it. And I usually get what I want."

Tricia knew it didn't pay to argue with her older sister, so she let herself be dragged to the first empty booth. Once they were settled, Michele appeared. "I'm sorry about Marshall," she said.

"Oh, was *that* who was so rude," Angelica said and rolled her eyes.

Marshall Cambridge was new to Stoneham. Despite his short tenure in the village, he'd no doubt heard about Tricia's penchant for finding lifeless bodies and her being branded the local jinx.

Though the man's name seemed rather lofty, his vocation bordered more on the vulgar. Just two months earlier, he'd opened a shop just over the village line—not far from the highway—that dealt with old magazines, most of which were pornographic in nature, as well as some true crime periodicals. His shop, Vamps, with its stock and clientele, had not endeared him to a large number of villagers—mostly those of the female persuasion. Tricia couldn't say she knew of anyone who bought such reading (or, rather, ogling) material, but then all his customers left the store with their purchases in brown paper bags.

"Is it true that you found Carol Talbot?" Michele asked.

Tricia nodded.

"Oh, dear. And do they suspect you?"

"Of course not!" Angelica cried.

"I've heard it's happened before," Michele said quietly. She shook her head and glanced at Tricia. "Poor Carol. Her death brings you that much closer to being named Stoneham's ultimate darts champion."

"Of course we're upset about Carol," Angelica began, "but you make it sound as though Tricia might have had a motive to get rid of her."

"Oh, no—I didn't mean that at all. But surely Chief Baker is going to ask about it . . . won't he?"

Tricia was about to refute that statement, but then thought better of it. Even when she and the chief had been in the midst of a serious relationship, he'd suspected her more than once of being involved in a death. That was another reason their relationship had fizzled.

"It's not like Carol and I were going to play against each other anytime soon," Tricia said.

"Didn't you hear? We've been challenged by the Purple Finch pub in Nashua. They're coming to play next Monday. Of course, you'll want to defend your status as one of our best players."

"Of course," Angelica said.

"Wait a minute—maybe I wouldn't. Not if people think I may have whacked Carol to get rid of the competition."

"We both know that's not true—so I don't see what the problem could be."

"The problem is my reputation."

"Which won't suffer—especially if you win." Angelica turned her attention back to Michele. "What's the prize involve?"

"The Finchers don't play for money; they play for honor—and a few rounds of drinks. But because of Tricia and Carol, we've gained a reputation in these parts."

That was news to Tricia. She just liked to play the game. The fact that she'd gotten good at it was as much a surprise to her as it was to the rest of the Dog-Eared Page's patrons.

"You *will* play, won't you Tricia?" Michele asked, not only sounding sincere, but looking awfully darned hopeful.

"What time next week?"

"Nine o'clock, sharp!"

Tricia heaved a sigh. "Only because it would be good publicity for the pub." Yes, that's the answer she would give if anyone else asked. Nobody had to know just how much she'd come to enjoy the game—and especially winning. It was silly, really. She'd been an average tennis player, but she had never excelled in any sport. Okay, throwing darts wasn't exactly an athletic pursuit, but it did require a certain level of skill. Soon after the pub opened, she'd actually ordered a dartboard and darts and practiced in the evenings. Even Angelica hadn't been aware of how much time she'd devoted to the game. It was her little secret. She'd even packed the board and darts and taken them with her to the Brookview so she could practice. Miss Marple seemed to love to watch the darts sail through the air and puncture the board.

"Now, what can I get you ladies to drink—as if I didn't know," Michele muttered under her breath.

"My usual," Angelica said.

"Make it two," Tricia chimed in.

Michele gave a curt nod, pivoted, and headed back toward the old oak bar.

"Do you think she'll bring us some chips or popcorn?" Tricia asked.

"Feeling peckish?"

"I had only half a veggie sub for supper. It tasted great, but didn't stay with me long."

"You could have had some cake or some cookies at the signing."

Tricia wrinkled her nose. "I must admit, I've got a hankering for salty rather than sweet tonight."

"I'd take them both. Wouldn't a salted caramel sundae be good right now?"

"Not with a martini."

Angelica shrugged. "Maybe after? I just so happen to have the makings over at Booked for Lunch. Can I entice you?"

A year before Tricia would have answered with an emphatic *"No!"* These days . . . she just might be persuaded. She shook her head. "Not tonight. I'm pooped. But I'll take a rain check."

That seemed to please Angelica, who smiled. "I'll hold you to it."

They turned at the sound of ice, gin, and vermouth swishing inside a cocktail shaker and watched as Shawn, the bartender, deftly poured the drinks into two chilled stemmed glasses. As hoped, Michele set a napkin-lined basket on a tray, picked up the drinks, and headed toward their table.

"Thank you. You're a mind reader," Tricia said, pleased when Michele set down the bowl of popcorn.

"Not really. I just know what you like."

"Me, too!" Angelica said. "Thanks."

Michele set their drinks on cocktail napkins. "Cheers!"

The sisters watched her head back to the bar before turning to their glasses.

Tricia picked up hers. "What shall we drink to?"

"Your upcoming victory at the darts tournament."

"Don't you start, too."

"No—you're going to win for the honor of the Dog-Eared Page. I'm sure we can get Russ"—editor of the *Stoneham Weekly News*, and another of Tricia's ex-lovers—"to cover the event with his camera."

"I don't need my picture splashed across the front page of the village's weekly rag."

"I wasn't thinking front page, but I'll take it," Angelica said. Unbeknownst to most of the villagers, she not only owned the little retro café, Booked for Lunch, the Cookery bookstore, and a share in the Sheer Comfort Inn, she was also the CEO and owner of Nigela Ricita Associates, which owned not only the Dog-Eared Page, but the Brookview Inn, the Happy Domestic gift and bookstore, and the newly opened Stoneham Salon and Day Spa.

"Why don't we drink to poor Carol. May she rest in peace," Tricia said.

Angelica clinked her glass against Tricia's, but she looked as though she'd have preferred a happier toast.

Before the sisters could even take a sip of their drinks, the pub's door opened and Chief Baker strode inside, making a beeline for them. "Oh dear," Tricia muttered.

"What?"

Tricia didn't have time to answer, because suddenly Baker towered over them. "I thought you said Steven Richardson was heading straight for the Sheer Comfort Inn."

"That's what he told me."

"Well, he isn't there. In fact, they don't even have a reservation in his name."

"Did he use a pseudonym?" Angelica asked.

"No. All their scheduled guests have checked in, and Richardson isn't among them."

"That's strange. I wonder why he lied," Tricia said.

"That's a very good question."

"Well, don't look at us to answer it for you," Angelica said, and reached for a handful of popcorn. "If nothing else, you can speak to him when he picks up Tricia for lunch at noon tomorrow."

Baker glowered. Why was he acting so possessive? They hadn't dated in nearly two years.

"I spoke with Pixie," Baker said. Had he interrupted her romantic evening?

"And?"

"She said Richardson took a signed book with him when he left Haven't Got a Clue this evening."

"Yes, he did."

"Which sounds awfully suspicious."

"Was Carol beaten to death with the book we found?" Angelica asked.

"No. It looks like strangulation."

"Then how can you assume—?"

"I don't assume; I deal in facts."

"And do you deem it a fact that just because Steven had a copy of his book that it was the same one that was found on the ground not far from Carol's body?"

"Since she and Richardson had had words, it's something to consider."

"I sold about thirty copies of the book tonight. I'm sorry, but I don't know the names of all the people who bought copies."

"I assume you have charge receipts."

"Some of my customers paid in cash."

"I'd appreciate it if you'd try to help me with this case."

"Oh, Tricia—how exciting. Now the chief is actually *asking* you to help. Isn't he usually telling you to *mind your own business*?" The last part of that sentence was delivered with a cutting edge.

"I will do all I can to help you, Chief."

"You used to call me Grant."

"Yes, I did." Tricia left it at that.

Baker glowered. "I have work to do. I'll speak with you again tomorrow."

"Until then." Tricia picked up her martini, held it aloft, and toasted him.

Baker's expression hardened, and he turned and stormed for the exit.

Angelica didn't bother to strain her neck to watch him go, and she, too, picked up her glass. She took a sip before speaking. "It just occurred to me that there's something one of us probably should have mentioned to Chief Baker."

"And that is?"

"That Steven Richardson wasn't the only one Carol slapped tonight."

THREE

Cat carrier in hand, Tricia arrived at Haven't Got a Clue the next day just before opening. Thank goodness Pixie and Mr. Everett had already arrived and had not only vacuumed and moved the reading nook's furniture back into place but had erased all signs of the book signing the previous evening—even the baseboard was now dust free. The shop never looked better, although Tricia knew that wouldn't last. Too bad the sound of saws and hammering from the floors above already marred all that perfection.

"Good morning," Tricia shouted above the clamor.

"Coffee's made," Mr. Everett hollered in reply, waving hello.

"I'll put out the leftover cookies from last night," Pixie called.

Tricia stowed her purse under the cash desk, put the cat carrier down behind it, and opened the door, but Miss Marple made no move to exit. The past couple of days had been fairly quiet, but on that bright Wednesday morning it sounded like Jim Stark's entire crew had showed up for work. The noise had definitely had a negative impact on business, which was another reason Tricia had been so happy about the previous evening's sales. It was lucky that the workmen didn't show up on weekends, which was when sales were at their peak.

Mr. Everett met Tricia at the glass case where the cash register stood. "Ms. Miles, I bought a gross of these at the big-box store on the highway. I thought we might offer them to customers." He handed her a package of disposable earplugs. It was a good idea, but she doubted they'd have many takers.

"Thank you. We'll put them here so that any customers who come in have the opportunity to take them. What do I owe you?"

"Nothing. I see it as a public service," Mr. Everett said gravely.

Pixie joined them. "I was thinking," she shouted over the shriek of a power saw. "What if we set up a table outside and featured our sale items? We might actually make a couple of bucks a day that way."

"Good idea. But I might have to get a permit from the village to do so. I'll check with Angelica."

"Would you like me to cull some of the stock, just in case?"

"Great idea."

A loud bang issued from the floor above, giving all three of them a start.

Why, oh why did I ever decide to renovate my home? Tricia thought. The demo had been finished two weeks before. She'd had so much to think about while setting up the signing during the previous days that she hadn't even looked at the progress on her apartment for almost a week. She'd renovated the top floor when she'd first moved into the building. As she'd originally been leasing the place, her modular kitchen was constructed so that it could be moved if she decided to relocate in the future. Of course, now that she owned the building she would have a bigger kitchen and living space, since the top floor would become one large master suite with a comfortable reading nook.

"I'm going to go upstairs to see what I can do about the noise," Tricia said, or, rather, shouted.

Her employees nodded enthusiastically.

She retrieved her cell phone from her purse, pocketed it, and set off.

"I'll get Miss Marple some water," Mr. Everett offered, and followed Tricia to the back of the shop. He continued to the washroom and the tap and she entered the door to the stairwell that was marked PRIVATE—NO ENTRY.

The air-conditioning had already cooled the shop, but as Tricia climbed the steps she could feel the heat rise. At the landing to the second floor, she darted through the plastic barrier that was supposed to keep the dust in the shop to a minimum, but often failed to do so. Tricia took in the five or six workers dressed in T-shirts, jeans, and hard hats. The bones of the living room were starting to take shape, what with the floor-to-ceiling bookcase that was in the process of being installed on the south wall, but it seemed like most of the work was being done in the kitchen. Some of the cabinets had been installed, but most of them were still sitting in the middle of the room. She'd chosen to put down ceramic tile, which had arrived and was piled in the living room. The flooring in that room would remain the original oak—sanded, stained, and finished. When that was scheduled to happen was anybody's guess. Every time she'd asked, she'd gotten the runaround.

"Ma'am—this is a work area. You need to wear this hard hat," said one of the T-shirted guys, who was already sweating profusely.

"Thank you," Tricia called over the din, and put the hat on, then charged for the kitchen, where her contractor stood over the island, its granite surface covered with a heavy canvas tarp to protect it from damage. Pencil in hand, Stark seemed to be going over a set of figures.

"Hi, Jim," she called.

Stark looked up, but didn't smile. Their relationship had suffered the previous August after Pete Renquist's death, but once they'd straightened things out, he'd taken the renovation job and neither of them had mentioned the past. "Hey, Tricia. Come to check on the progress?"

"Yes. Is there a more quiet place we can talk?"

He nodded toward the stairs, indicating they should move to the third level. Leaving his paper and pencil behind, he headed for the door. She followed.

In the old configuration, the stairs led to a landing and a locked door, but the door had been removed. Eventually a wrought iron safety gate would be installed, but for now it was open to the stairwell.

Lengthy steel beams had been installed so that the load-bearing walls could be removed, and the space was now wide open. Tricia looked around, taking in the changes. The tiny bathroom had been gutted and expanded. A refurbished antique soaker tub stood ready to be installed, but the walls were still nothing but studs with just the rough plumbing installed.

"It's shaping up," she said halfheartedly.

"The plumber will be in again tomorrow and we'll get moving on the bathroom. We finished the ceiling," Stark said, indicating that Tricia should look above. Spray foam insulation had been applied and then covered with wood that had been stained. The lighting had yet to be installed, and wires hung waiting for fixtures.

"We'll get the bathroom walls up next week, start on the walk-in shower, and get the new floor in. After that, we'll get to work on the master closet. We should be painting and refinishing the bedroom floor in two weeks."

Tricia nodded, feeling a little heartsick. She'd known she'd be living away from her home for at least a month. Now it was beginning to look like it would be longer.

"What's your estimate on the kitchen and living room?"

"Two to four weeks." He studied her face. "You don't look happy."

"Apart from Christmas, summer is my busiest time. Customers don't stay long when there's a lot of construction noise."

"If I get another job, I can put you off until the fall, but I don't think you really want to do that."

She nodded. "No. I guess it's better to get it over with as soon as possible."

"I know it seems like chaos now, but we're pretty much on schedule, and I'm juggling the trades as best I can."

"I know. It's just hard not having a home—and having all my stuff in storage."

"When we're done, you'll be glad you suffered through the inconvenience."

Having gone through one renovation already, Tricia knew he was speaking the truth.

"Thanks, Jim. I know you and your guys are doing your best."

Tricia's cell phone rang. She retrieved it, saw it was the shop's number, stuffed a finger in her right ear to muffle the continual banging from below, and hit the talk icon. "Yes?"

"Tricia. Chief Baker is here to speak with you," Pixie said brightly.

"Is he angry?"

"You better believe it."

Rats! "Tell him I'll be right down." She ended the call, turned back to Stark and forced a smile. "Duty calls."

"We'll talk again in a few days. Once we get moving on the bathroom, I know you'll feel a lot better."

"I'm sure you're right." Tricia gave him another forced smile and headed for the stairs.

The steps were slick with dust, and with the banister removed to better allow the workers to move stuff up to the second and third floors, Tricia forced herself to step carefully. Okay, she wasn't exactly eager to get a tongue-lashing from Baker, so that may have also caused her to move slower than she might have, but all too soon she opened the door to the shop and nearly barreled right into the angry cop.

"Sorry. I didn't know you'd been standing in the way," she explained.

"I wanted to make sure you didn't hightail it out the back door," Baker said, louder than was absolutely necessary.

"Why don't we go somewhere else to talk?" Tricia said.

"What?"

"I said," she practically shouted, "why don't we go outside to talk?"

Baker grabbed her by the elbow and hauled her toward the front door. Pixie moved to intercept her. "You won't be needing that hat," she said, and snatched the headgear from Tricia.

Once outside, Tricia pulled her arm free. If she hadn't known the chief so well, she might have had a beef about being manhandled in such a manner. "Why don't we go to the village square?"

"Fine." He started down the sidewalk, heading for the intersection and the crosswalk.

"I haven't had my coffee yet," Tricia called, and hurried to catch up with Stoneham's finest.

"This isn't a social occasion," Baker said, his tone none too friendly.

Without her purse, she wasn't in a position to stop at the Coffee Bean to buy herself a cup, and Baker's body language told her it was taking all his will to keep from exploding. She'd just have to wait for her morning caffeine fix.

They waited for Stoneham's only traffic light to change before crossing the street, and then they had to wait again on the other side before making their way to the square. A couple of elderly gentlemen were tossing crumbs to sparrows, and they moved deeper into the square, heading for the grand stone gazebo and one of the benches that sat nearby. Baker gestured for Tricia to sit, but didn't perch beside her.

"So?" Tricia asked, trying to sound cheerful.

"Two things. First, I spoke to Russ Smith. He says he had no meeting scheduled with Richardson."

"Oh. Sorry." Tricia shook her head. "When Steven asked for that copy of his book to give to a reporter, I guess I just assumed he meant Russ. And the second thing?"

"I heard from other sources that you neglected to tell me what else went on last night at Haven't Got a Clue."

"And who would that be?"

"I don't divulge my sources," Baker said belligerently. "Why didn't you tell me that Carol Talbot not only slapped Steven Richardson, but she slapped your father as well?"

"Oh, yeah," Tricia said, feigning innocence. "I'd completely forgotten about that."

She could tell by Baker's expression that he didn't believe her.

"Where can I find him?"

"I really don't know. The last time I saw him, he was in my shop. Then I got busy with customers and didn't see him leave."

"I've already spoken with the clerks at the Brookview and Sheer Comfort Inns. They say he's been banned and didn't stay the night with them. Was he with you or Angelica?"

Tricia shook her head. "Miss Marple and I are staying at one of the bungalows at the Brookview Inn while my apartment is being renovated. I know Angelica told him she didn't have room for him at her place, either."

"Did you three have a falling out?"

Tricia shrugged. "No doubt you—and half the village—heard that when my father left back in January, he left a trail of unpaid bills behind him. Angelica made good on them, but it put us both in a rather awkward position with our fellow merchants. Angelica was extremely embarrassed, because she felt it reflected badly on her, as she's the head of the Chamber of Commerce."

"So you're letting him fend for himself?"

"We talked about getting him a room at one of the motels on the highway to Nashua, but before we could even talk to him about it, he'd left the shop."

"Do you have any idea why Carol Talbot would have slapped him?"

"None at all."

"What was her demeanor during the signing?"

"I was a little preoccupied dealing with Daddy, and then with customers, but someone—a woman—muttered a few disparaging remarks during Steven's talk."

"So, you're on a first-name basis with this guy?"

"Yes. I usually do call authors who sign in my store by their first names. It's a lot less formal that way."

"Go on," Baker said, sounding none too pleased.

"I couldn't tell who spoke, but in retrospect, it was probably Carol—especially since by her actions afterwards, she seemed to have a beef with Steven."

"Do you have his phone number?"

"Back at the store."

"Can I have it?"

"Of course. But as Angelica said, he's supposed to pick me up for lunch at noon. If you don't track him down before that, you should be able to talk to him at the Brookview's restaurant. Just don't take too much of that time. Pixie and Mr. Everett need their lunch hours, too."

He nodded. "I have to go." And without another word, he turned and walked away.

Tricia watched him stalk off toward the police station feeling . . . not exactly sad, but disappointed that now when they interacted there always seemed to be acrimony between them. Sighing, she pulled out her phone and tapped the contacts icon and then Angelica's name. Her sister picked up on the third ring.

"The great and powerful Oz knows all," Angelica quipped in a forbidding tone.

"What?"

"Oh, nothing. Tommy the short-order cook and I were just talking about *The Wizard of Oz*. Every child in the world must have been frightened by those horrible flying monkeys."

"Have you got a minute?"

"Two. Come over to Booked for Lunch. You can test Tommy's latest dessert offering."

"Since I haven't had breakfast, I'll take you up on it. Be right there."

"Right there" ended up being about two minutes later, but Angelica had the coffee poured and sat at the table that overlooked the street. She waved as Tricia approached.

"Sit down and tell me what's going on."

Tricia sat, taking in the wonderful spicy aroma that permeated the little café. Before her sat a piece of dark cake with confectioner's sugar sprinkled over the top—but in a pretty design, like a lace doily. "Smells great."

"Today is National Gingerbread Day, and that's what we're offering for dessert." Angelica picked up her fork and plunged it into the rich cake. She took a bite and swooned. "Oh, happy day. This is delish!"

Tricia did likewise, chewed, and swallowed. "Oh, goodness, you're right. This is excellent. But I never heard of National Gingerbread Day."

"There's a national something-or-other day every day of the year. It's fun. We decided we'd try to feature as much food as we can for our daily specials. It's also National Moonshine day today, but we don't have a liquor license so decided not to mention it."

Tricia wasn't about to complain. She took another bite, then sipped her coffee. "A few minutes ago, I had a not-so-pleasant conversation with Grant Baker."

"I figured you might."

"Why?"

"Well, because I also spoke to him this morning. In fact, I called him. I feel very conflicted, but I told him that Carol slapped Daddy last night."

"Why would *you* of all people tell him that?" Tricia demanded, not exactly sure why she was angry.

"Because . . . I didn't want you to get in trouble with him."

"I'm *always* in trouble with him."

"I figured if one of us didn't come clean it would look like we were trying to hide something."

"You're right," Tricia conceded, and took another bite of cake. "Have you heard from Daddy?"

Angelica shook her head. "He could have at least said good-bye to us before he left your store last night, although he was probably very disappointed in us—primarily me."

"*He* wasn't very nice leaving town and leaving you to clean up after him."

"I know, but I should have handled it better. It's just that—things were a little tense at the time."

"I'll say." Tricia took another bite of cake; she really was enjoying it. "How are we going to track down Daddy? Do you think you should call Mother?"

"I don't have a number for her, either. We didn't exactly part as friends back in January. She may feel that the three of us ganged up on her."

"I did *not* gang up on her."

"No, you didn't," Angelica admitted. "But maybe you should have," she muttered, and cut another piece from her slab of cake.

"Let's not go there. We need to figure out why Carol was in such a slap-happy mood last night."

"You should leave that up to the chief. It's what he gets paid for."

"We have a stake in this: our good family name."

"I'm afraid Daddy forever tarnished that back in January." Angelica ate her cake, looking distinctly unhappy.

"I have a feeling Daddy didn't go far. After all, he didn't get what he wanted last night."

"Which was?"

"Who knows? I'm sure he'll resurface sometime soon, and then we may be sorry he did."

The sisters polished off the last of their cake in silence. Angelica was the first to speak. "Where would we look?"

Tricia looked up. "What do you mean?"

"For Daddy? Do you think he might have hitched a ride somewhere?"

"Maybe. I need to talk to Pixie and Mr. Everett. Maybe one of them saw Daddy leave."

"Good idea. I can send some cake over as a bribe."

"That's not necessary. Pixie already put out the leftover cookies from last night. Believe me, we're good to go for the day—maybe the week and month, thanks to the noise in my shop. I spoke with Jim Stark earlier. He says they're on schedule for the renovation, and that it should only be another month, but right now it feels like forever."

"You'll love your home even more when it's done."

Tricia nodded. She'd barely had time to get used to being back *in* her home after the cleanup from the fire the previous year. It had taken too many months after the fire for the insurance company to come up with a check to repair the damage to her store and home, and then another two months for the work to actually be done. She'd lived in her refurbished home a scant four months before the renovation process started again.

Tricia drained her cup. "Thanks for the coffee and cake. It was just what I needed."

"Are you still going to lunch with Steven?"

"I haven't heard otherwise."

"Good. Call me as soon as you return. I want to hear *all* the details."

"Okay," Tricia said, and sighed. She rose from her seat. "Talk to you later."

"Ta-ta!"

Tricia left Booked for Lunch and paused at the curb. Traffic was actually brisk on that bright summer morning, and she hoped some of the travelers would make a stop at her store. But as she waited for the line of cars to disperse, she wondered about her so-called lunch date. If Richardson hadn't been found at the B and B the previous night, and had no reservation, where had he gone? And more importantly, why had he lied?

FOUR

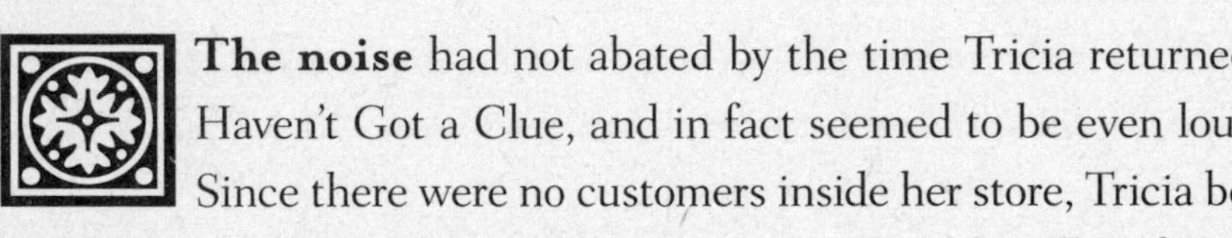

The noise had not abated by the time Tricia returned to Haven't Got a Clue, and in fact seemed to be even louder. Since there were no customers inside her store, Tricia beckoned Pixie and Mr. Everett to join her out on the sidewalk in front for a powwow. Both removed their earplugs so they could listen.

"First, I'd like to thank you both for everything you did to make last night's book signing such a success."

"Just doin' my job," Pixie said.

"It was my pleasure," Mr. Everett said.

"I'm sure you heard about Carol Talbot."

"Uh, no," Pixie said. "Fred and I didn't turn on the TV this morning. We were . . . kind of occupied." She left it at that. "Did she have an accident?"

"A fatal one, I'm afraid," Tricia admitted. "I'm surprised Chief Baker didn't mention it when he called you last night."

"Don't tell me *you* found her?" Pixie asked, in what sounded like disapproval.

Tricia nodded. "Well, Angelica *and* I found her. She wasn't that hard to miss—or at least the evidence someone left on the sidewalk near her body made it rather easy."

Pixie frowned. "No wonder the chief was so pissed at you."

"What do you mean?"

"Just that he—and some of the other citizens here in Stoneham—seem to blame *you* when somebody turns up dead."

"I have noticed that," Tricia muttered. She seemed to be a human divining rod when it came to finding corpses. "I want both of you to give your full cooperation to the chief, because I'm sure he's going to want to speak with you again about what happened at the signing."

"You mean with your Pops and Carol?" Pixie asked.

"Well, yes."

Pixie nodded. "Sure thing."

"By the way, did you happen to notice when my father left the signing?"

"He snuck out the back after he spoke with you and Angelica. I had Fred go after him."

"Did he speak with my father?"

"I don't know. Maybe. He was gone a couple of minutes. I didn't exactly ask. Fred locked the back door when he came back in, though."

"You might want to tell that to the chief. He may want to speak with Fred, too."

"Will do."

Mr. Everett had averted his gaze when Carol's name had come up—it wasn't that he looked guilty, but he seemed very uncomfortable with the topic.

"Is everything all right, Mr. Everett?"

The elderly man pursed his lips. "It's a shame about Mrs. Talbot."

"But?"

He shook his head. "It's not nice to speak ill of the dead."

"I agree. She wasn't always the most pleasant person in the world, but I would like to see the police apprehend the person who killed her."

Mr. Everett said nothing, his gaze fixed on the floor.

Tricia decided not to push it. She knew Mr. Everett would never disparage a living soul—even if they deserved it. Well, she did once see him lose his temper—but it was only once, when he'd first come to work for her and his patience had been pushed beyond reasonable limits.

It was time to change the subject. "Pixie, your idea to hold a sidewalk sale is brilliant. I haven't had a chance to ask if we can do it, but let's go for it. Otherwise, we won't make any sales for the foreseeable future."

"They do say it's easier to ask forgiveness than permission. How much longer are the guys going to be working on your apartment?"

Tricia sighed, heartsick. "At least another month."

Pixie winced, then she shrugged. "Just in time for me and Fred to tie the knot. I still feel guilty about me leaving you in the lurch when we go on our honeymoon."

"Don't you dare worry about it. Mr. Everett and I can handle everything here while you're gone. But I am concerned about the renovations interfering with your bridal shower. I'm going to see if we can't hold it at either the Brookview or the Sheer Comfort Inns."

"Oh, but Tricia—that would be so expensive."

"Angelica has an in with Nigela Ricita Associates. I'm almost certain she can get us a break on the cost." *As in paying nothing.* Of course, the affair would still need to be catered, but that would be part of Tricia's wedding gift to Pixie and Fred. "We can e-mail or phone everyone on the guest list to make sure they know about the change of venue."

Pixie actually blushed. "Aw, Tricia, you're too good to me."

"Nonsense. Now, let's get the folding table and some books out on the sidewalk in time for the afternoon tour bus."

"Yes, ma'am," Pixie and Mr. Everett said in unison, and both scurried into the shop to get started.

While Pixie and Mr. Everett took care of whatever customers wandered up to their makeshift selling area, Tricia took her cell phone and walked back to the park to call the Board of Selectmen's office to see if she needed a permit for her sidewalk sale. She did, and she went and got it, thankful that the current board was made of up business people who understood and made allowances for extenuating circumstances.

By the time Tricia returned to her store, it was nearly noon. She retreated to the washroom, dragged a comb across her hair, and applied a fresh coat of lipstick for her not-a-date with Steven Richardson. With Carol's death, they'd certainly have more than enough to talk about—not that she wanted to dwell on the subject. And she had a feeling that Steven might be averse to being questioned by her about the incident the evening before, too.

Mr. Everett reentered the shop. "Ms. Miles, since you have a luncheon engagement, Pixie and I thought we'd take turns to get our own lunches—with your approval, of course."

"Of course."

"We agreed that I should take the first hour. I will arrive back in time for Pixie to leave at one."

"I'll try not to be too long at lunch."

"Take your time. Enjoy yourself. I know how stressful it is for you being away from your home, and the noise level here is enough to test one's sanity."

"I know it's been difficult for you and Pixie. I completely understand if you'd like to take some time off."

"Nonsense! What would you do without us?"

Tricia smiled. "I wouldn't want to test that scenario."

Her answer must have pleased him; the corners of Mr. Everett's wrinkled mouth rose. "I shall see you after lunch."

"Very good," she said, and she couldn't help but smile as well.

After Mr. Everett had gone, the pounding overhead seemed to abate. A couple of members of the work crew came down the stairs and exited through the back of the building, no doubt heading out for their own lunches.

Pixie returned inside, but kept a watch on the table in front of the big display window. "Peace," she said simply.

"Yes. But every minute they aren't working makes it that much longer until I can move back home."

"Eh, time will fly—faster than if you were in jail," Pixie said, and laughed. She'd spent a couple of stints in the New Hampshire State Prison for Women, thanks to her former career as a woman of the night, but she hadn't had so much as a parking ticket since coming to work for Tricia two years before and no longer had to meet with a parole officer. And now she was getting married. Tricia couldn't have been more proud of her assistant.

Pixie consulted her copper-colored vintage watch that coordinated so nicely with her pumpkin-colored dress and clunky heels. "Your date is late."

"This is *not* a date," Tricia asserted, and part of her wondered why she wasn't more excited at the possibility of their encounter meaning so much more. Maybe it was because Steven lived in Boston and Tricia knew that most long-distance relationships were doomed. Okay, the drive to Boston was only a little more than an hour, but when a girl—woman, she reminded herself—needed a shoulder to cry on, an hour wait just wasn't acceptable.

Then there was the whole idea that a woman without a man could not be complete. Her first real lover, Harry Tyler, had faked his own death to avoid the messy life of his own making. Tricia's ex-husband, Christopher, had left her to go on a soul-searching quest. Russ Smith had been possessive and had stalked her when their relationship had soured. Grant Baker had been unable to make a commitment. Maybe all that heartache—and a desire to stay in charge of her life—had been the reason Tricia had been so open to establishing more permanent roots here in Stoneham by buying the building where she lived and worked and undertaking the extensive renovations to make the place a more welcoming and enduring place for her to reside.

Yes, she loathed the entire renovation process that had forced her and her cat to relocate for what might be two or more full months, but when the job was done, she knew she would love her new digs. It turned out Pixie was a wiz at buying and selling items on eBay and Craigslist—which was how she came to acquire so many of her vintage outfits and accessories. Tricia hadn't yet consulted her assistant, but she was sure Pixie would be willing to help her sell off items she would no longer require and find new things that would make the place feel more like home. She mentally added that to her list of things to do.

Pixie retrieved the store's vacuum cleaner from the storage area out back and attacked the dust that had escaped when the workers upstairs had left for lunch. By the time she put the noisy appliance away, it was twelve fifteen.

Tricia hauled out the latest copy of the *Stoneham Weekly News* to once again consult the tag sale section. Several of the listings mentioned books. Pixie had a good eye for culling such collectibles. Perhaps Tricia would send her out on Friday to evaluate the offerings and buy whatever seemed to be a sure fit for the shop. Pixie loved to be assigned such duties, because she got to play while working. She'd confided that such forays had allowed her to shop for hers and Fred's combined home.

Tricia glanced at the clock on the wall. Richardson was now twenty-five minutes late to pick her up.

Pixie grabbed Mr. Everett's lamb's wool duster and attacked the books along the south wall before joining Tricia at the cash desk. "I know Mr. Everett will just have to vacuum again before we leave tonight, but I just can't *stand* the mess."

"You and me both," Tricia said.

Pixie's gaze moved to the clock and back to Tricia. Still, she said nothing about Tricia's lack of a date—if that's what it was. "I've been rereading Arthur Conan Doyle's *Memoirs of Sherlock Holmes*. Man, what a *great* book."

The two of them weighed the pros and cons of said title for another ten minutes.

The tourist bus arrived early, and Pixie exited the store to greet the potential customers. She was great with them—she spoke their language, and they dutifully trotted inside with their sale items and to check out the rest of the stock. Tricia rang up their sales.

All too soon, the work crew reappeared and the hammering and sawing started anew. Mr. Everett returned precisely at one, and it was Pixie's turn to leave the shop to find sustenance elsewhere.

And still, Steven Richardson had not appeared or called.

Time dragged until Pixie returned at two o'clock. It was then Tricia pulled out her cell phone and tapped her sister's number on her contacts list.

"Hello, baby sister," Angelica sang.

"Any chance I can come over and join you for lunch? I'm starved."

"Don't tell me that bastard stiffed you."

"Okay, I won't."

"Give me ten minutes. The café is still a little crowded."

"Will do," Tricia said, and rang off. She found enough to do to kill time for nearly twenty minutes before she left the store in Pixie's and Mr. Everett's care and crossed the street, heading for Booked for Lunch.

A tall, rather good-looking older male customer held the door open for Tricia. She gave him a cheery "Thanks" and entered. The café still boasted half a dozen customers, but Angelica sat in one of the booths, apparently nursing a cup of coffee, with a stack of computer printouts in front of her. Tricia sat down across from her.

"There you are," Angelica said, sounding pleased. "What are you doing for supper tonight?"

"Nothing."

"Then come and help me try out a new recipe I've concocted. You can chop some of the veggies."

"I'd like that. I like it when we cook together."

One of Angelica's hands flew up to cover her mouth, and her eyes filled with sudden tears. "Oh, Tricia, you don't know how happy you've made me by saying that. Grandma Miles would be *so* pleased."

"I wish I'd started years ago," Tricia admitted. "What are we making?"

"Zucchini casserole. Tommy's growing enough squash to feed half the state and brought in a bushel basket this morning."

"Sounds wonderful. And then maybe I'll take Sarge for a walk."

"We could go together," Angelica suggested.

"I wouldn't mind."

Bev, the waitress, wandered over to the table, and Angelica discreetly turned over her pages. "What can I get you, Tricia?"

"How about the soup and half sandwich special?"

"Egg salad and zucchini soup coming right up. What kind of bread would you like?" Bev asked.

"Do you have seeded rye?"

"Sure do."

"Great. Thank you."

"Make that two," Angelica said.

"Got it, boss."

As usual, Bev didn't write the order on her pad; she was used to Tricia's meal being on the house. Oh, the perks of having a sister who owned a restaurant.

"You're really making use of those zucchinis," Tricia said.

"Waste not, want not," Angelica replied. "So what do you think happened to Steven?"

Tricia shrugged. "I have no idea. Perhaps Chief Baker found him and hauled him in for questioning."

"It would serve him right," Angelica said, and turned her pages over once again.

"What are you doing? Checking on your millions?"

"Yes, actually. It's tedious work. I'd much rather hear what you've got going on. Have you heard anything about Carol's murder?"

"I spoke to the chief this morning. He's not giving out a lot of information at this point."

"I'm surprised you didn't whip out your phone and immediately call Russ over at the paper to see what he's found out."

"I'm even more surprised he hasn't called me—especially after talking to Grant first thing this morning. We have shared information on a death before this."

"Well, you've got your work cut out for you, then."

"I think I'll drop by and see him before I go back to my shop."

Bev arrived with a tray laden with their lunches. Tricia had never had zucchini soup before, so it was going to be an adventure. But, she hoped, not nearly as exciting as what she might learn when she got a chance to compare notes with Russ.

FIVE

A warm breeze blew down Stoneham's main drag as Tricia made her way from Booked for Lunch toward the *Stoneham Weekly News*, hoping its proprietor would be ensconced behind his desk. Come to think of it, lately she hadn't seen him out and about chasing down the news of the day—or rather, the week.

Tricia paused to admire a large poster for the upcoming Stoneham Wine and Jazz Festival that took up space on the Happy Domestic's front display window, where her ex-assistant, Ginny Wilson-Barbero, used to work. Ginny had moved up the management line of Nigela Ricita Associates and was now in charge of their events division. As part of the promotion, Ginny had hired an accomplished artist to do a rendering of a combo playing in the village's quaint gazebo. At the top of the poster was a banner heading spelling out the name and date of the event, and all around were images of people holding wineglasses and toasting. A copy of it would look nice framed and hanging in Tricia's brand-new living room. She'd have to ask to see if she could obtain one. Or, better yet . . . maybe contact the artist and buy the original piece. It was something to think about.

Tricia carried on down the sidewalk to the newspaper's entrance. The bell over the door jingled as Tricia entered the newspaper's offices. It was obviously still lunchtime, as Gloria, who usually manned the receptionist's desk and was in charge of the classifieds section of the paper, was still among the missing. The door to Russ Smith's office was open, and Tricia could see him hunched over his desk eating a sandwich and reading over what looked like news copy.

"Anybody home?"

Russ looked up. "Hi, Tricia. I didn't hear the bell."

"You're probably so used to hearing it that you tune it out when it actually rings. I know I get that way sometimes. Have you got a few minutes?"

He gestured for her to enter his tiny office, where she took one of the two chairs that sat in front of his very messy desk. "What can I do for you?"

"I was wondering what you'd heard about Carol Talbot's death."

Russ shrugged. "Not a damn thing, why?"

"But you did speak with Chief Baker."

"Yeah, but it was *him* asking the questions."

When he said no more, Tricia tried again. "Will you be looking into Carol's death?"

"I hadn't planned on it."

"Why not?"

"What's the point? By the time the paper comes out, the chief—or you—will probably have solved it. As news, it'll be staler than two-day-old bread at the Patisserie."

"That's never stopped you before from trying to get a scoop."

"Scoops are for Lois Lane and Clark Kent. Me? I'm just the owner of a small-town rag with a circulation of about eight thousand—and dwindling all the time."

"Oh, Russ—you sound so pessimistic. Whatever happened to the crusading reporter I used to know?" As he'd once stalked her, Tricia declined to add the words *and loved*. She wasn't sure she'd *ever* loved him, even though they were an item for more than a year.

"That guy no longer exists," he admitted wearily. "He vanished when he acquired a wife and child. It would be negligent of me to ignore my family by pursuing stories that might bring me into harm's way."

"Talking to the chief—or other witnesses like me—is hardly a dangerous pursuit."

"As you recall, there *were* times when I would go above and beyond simple interviews to get a story. Those days are gone," he reiterated.

"Will you be printing *anything* about Carol's death?"

"I've got an obit started, and I'll mention where the police are in the investigation, but other than that it's a dead issue—if you'll pardon the pun."

She wouldn't.

"But if the chief is tight-lipped about the investigation, can I count on you telling me what you know—if only to beef up the obit?"

"At this point, I know very little." And one thing Tricia desperately wanted to do was make sure that her father had nothing to do with the woman's death. Because now that Chief Baker knew Carol had slapped him, he was most certainly one of two suspects in her murder. Then again, Tricia liked Steven Richardson—or she had until he'd stood her up. Still, she didn't want to believe that he might be capable of murder, either.

Russ shrugged. "I know once your interest is piqued, you'll stay on this thing until there's a resolution. Whatever you can share would be appreciated." The words were right, but he almost sounded bored by the conversation.

Tricia nodded. There was really no reason to prolong their chat, so she changed the subject. "How is little Russell?"

Even that topic didn't seem to lift Russ out of his doldrums, as he recited what the pediatrician had said at the boy's last well-baby checkup. She wondered if Russ could be clinically depressed. Tricia supposed it was possible that his wife, Nikki, had laid down the law: no dangerous pursuits because they had their baby's welfare to think about. In that respect, taking no chances made it seem the prudent choice. But there was something dead in poor Russ's eyes. He looked like a trapped animal, and, in the long run, feeling that way could be just as deadly to his family relationships. She didn't envy him.

Russ finally wound down, and Tricia forced a smile and stood. "It's been great to catch up with you, Russ."

"But you haven't said a word about what you're up to."

"I'm living through a massive home renovation, which means that *nothing* is happening in my life."

"Maybe that'll be worth a story when it's finished. Take some during- and post-construction pictures. My readers love that kind of humdrum crap."

Crap? That was hardly an inducement.

"Sure," Tricia said, and smiled sweetly. What was the point in even commenting? She turned for the door. "I'll keep in touch." Not.

"See ya," Russ called.

By the time Tricia got to the door, she turned back to see that Russ's nose was again buried in his boring paperwork. Well, perhaps he deserved it, but it was also sad to see that the passion that had once driven him had been doused like a bucket of cold water on a fire.

One thing was for sure: despite the fact she'd lost a sleuthing ally, Russ was right. She would follow through until she found out who killed Carol Talbot and why.

Tricia hadn't made it to the corner when she heard a familiar voice calling her name. She turned and saw Chief Baker hurrying down the sidewalk to catch up with her. Was she in for another browbeating session?

"Yes, Chief. What's up?" she asked, shading her eyes on that bright afternoon.

"I tried calling the store, but Pixie said you hadn't returned from lunch."

"I was on my way there now. What do you need?" She could be testy with him, too.

"To know if you've heard from your father since last night."

She shook her head. "Sorry, no. But I'm sure he's still around—somewhere."

"And why's that?"

Because he hadn't gotten any money off either her or Angelica. Because he'd been fishing for a place to stay—which meant he probably *had* no money. "He seems to have unfinished business with us."

Baker nodded. "Of course. I heard the rumors after your father left the village back in January."

"Rumors?" Tricia repeated, playing dumb.

"That he'd skipped town owing just about everybody—and that he was a little light-fingered, too."

Tricia felt a blush rise up her neck to stain her cheeks.

"I'm sorry to have to be the one to tell you," Baker continued, "but your father has a rather checkered past."

"How checkered?" Tricia asked, dreading the answer and wishing he hadn't decided to break such news to her on the street where passersby could listen in.

"Petit larceny; mail fraud; racketeering."

Tricia's stomach did a flip-flop, and it was a struggle to remain silent as her eyes filled. She wasn't sure if it was embarrassment for herself or her father. But Baker wasn't finished with his list of bad news.

"His rap sheet is as long as your arm. He's spent some time in jail, but mostly he's had the best lawyers working to keep him from being incarcerated. From what I gather, he's never been gainfully employed, at least not in any honest endeavor."

That could only mean one thing: that Tricia's mother had bailed him out of trouble time after time. After all, how often had she heard about her mother inheriting the Griffith family fortune? And yet, despite that, she'd grown up thinking her father had been the family's breadwinner. Yes, there were times when he'd been out of the picture for months at a time. Her mother had always told them that John had gone away on business.

Surely, if her father had been a bona fide con man, *someone* would have told her. Had her ex-husband, Christopher, known? Would he, too, have kept silent to spare her? Worse, did Angelica know? She'd kept her own secrets for years. Was that a trait she'd inherited from their father?

And what about her beloved Grandmother Miles? She'd lived with the family on and off, and now that Tricia thought about it, it was during the times that her father had been absent that that wonderful woman had visited for several months at a time. Had her beloved father been in jail? Tricia now knew that her mother blamed her for the SIDS death of her twin brother. Her happiest childhood memories had been spent in the company of her father's mother. Tricia's mother had wanted a son. When he died, Sheila had pretty much maintained a hands-off policy with her youngest child. Grandma Miles had showered both Tricia and Angelica with unconditional love. She'd shared her love of mystery stories and cookery with her only grandchildren, and those tales and meals had shaped Tricia's and Angelica's lives. So much so that both had based their current livelihoods on different aspects of what their grandma had loved best.

"You're very quiet," Baker said rather kindly, rousing Tricia from her memories.

"It's a bit much to take in."

"I'll bet. But this doesn't color my opinion of you."

Was he serious? And what did that mean? She wasn't about to ask. Instead, she forced a smile. "Thank you."

"That doesn't mean I don't consider your father a probable suspect in Carol Talbot's death, either," he said, to spoil his previous statement.

"Have you spoken with everyone who was at the signing?"

"No, but only because I don't know *who* they all are. Can you give me a list?"

"Sorry, no. But perhaps if Pixie, Mr. Everett, and I put our heads together, we might come up with a comprehensive list."

"Please do."

"And what about Steven Richardson? Carol slapped him, too."

"I'm satisfied with his explanation."

"How did you track him down?"

"He called me."

Tricia felt her cheeks begin to glow in annoyance. Why hadn't the author had the decency to call *her*? She had to work to keep her tone neutral. "What did he say?"

"I'm not at liberty to share that with you."

"And why not?"

"Because it's none of your business. As you're such good friends with the man, why don't *you* ask *him*?"

"I would . . . if only he'd answer *my* calls."

"I thought you two were close."

"And why would you think that?"

"I heard about the two of you on that cruise last winter."

"Heard what?" Tricia demanded. She'd kissed the man—twice—and neither of those busses could be called *passionate*.

"That there was the start of a relationship."

"Well, whoever told you that was mistaken. The man and I had a couple of drinks together. Period—not that it's any of *your* business, either."

"You're right; it isn't." He was silent for a few moments. "I apologize."

"Apology accepted," she said, albeit rather grudgingly. "Now, is there anything else we need to go over? If not, I really need to get back to my store."

"I'd appreciate it if you'd let me know when your father resurfaces."

"After what happened last night, I'm sure somebody will gladly share the news with both of us." She hadn't meant to sound so sarcastic, but she'd spoken the truth.

Baker gave her a curt nod and did an abrupt about-face. So much for the social graces.

Feeling just a little bit depressed, Tricia headed back for Haven't Got a Clue, fearing what was left of the day would be very long indeed.

The hammering and sawing went on and on that afternoon, and, thanks to the guys' heavy work boots, it seemed like a herd of elephants traipsed overhead, but Tricia hardly noticed. She couldn't stop thinking about her conversation with Chief Baker. She needed to share what she'd learned with Angelica—not that she thought any of it would come as a surprise, but it was embarrassing to have hers and Angelica's good names sullied by their father's actions.

When a particularly long pause of quiet from above finally registered in her brain, Tricia decided to take a chance and call Angelica, but instead of her sister picking up, the call went directly to voice mail. "Hi, Ange, it's me, your sister. Just wondering if you've heard from Daddy. Chief Baker was asking about his whereabouts and . . . I'll tell you more at dinner tonight. Bye."

As Tricia put down the phone, Miss Marple, who had barely left her carrier all day, timidly emerged from her sanctuary. She looked around, as though assessing the danger level, and then looked up at her mistress.

"It's good to see you, little girl."

The cat jumped up on the sales counter, rubbed her head against Tricia's shoulder, and began to purr. "You've had a rough day," Tricia said, then looked up and was startled to find Pixie standing before her.

"Sorry. I didn't mean to scare you." She and Mr. Everett had been taking turns standing outside the shop in case customers needed assistance with the sale items. "Uh, I couldn't help overhear you mention your pop a minute ago," Pixie said. Her eavesdropping had been a bit of a problem since the day she'd first started working at Haven't Got a Clue, but one Tricia had gotten used to—or had at least become resigned to. "I think I know where your father has been staying."

Tricia perked up. "Where?"

Pixie looked sheepish. "Um . . . at Fred's apartment."

Tricia's eyes widened. "Fred—*your* Fred's place?"

Pixie nodded. "Remember I told you that Fred went after him last night? Well, apparently your father told Fred that he had nowhere to stay. Since we became engaged, Fred's spent most of his time at my place. His lease runs out at the end of the month, which is why we thought that might be a good time to get married. Well, Fred thought he was doing you—and your father—a favor by offering to let him stay there."

"Oh, Pixie—that was so very generous of Fred, but . . . you know my father's reputation."

Pixie's features seemed to sag even more. "Yeah, I do. When Fred told me, I about hit the roof. I kept remembering how upset Angelica was to find out antiques went missing from the Sheer Comfort Inn."

"Please don't tell me Daddy's walked off with any of Fred's things."

"Well, not so far. At least, not as far as I know. But I told Fred if he had anything valuable there he'd better box it up and bring it to my place PDQ. He should have already started to do that, and now he has no excuse not to."

"I'm so sorry. Please let me know if anything turns up missing. I don't want Fred to be out of pocket for anything."

"Thanks, Tricia. You're a good person."

"You *and* Fred are good people." *And way too trusting.*

An enormous, loud *bang* sounded overhead—had one of the workers dropped a five-ton safe?— sending Miss Marple back down to the floor and into her carrier once more.

"That's it," Tricia said, and bent down to secure the carrier's door. "This continual noise is pure-and-simple animal abuse. I'm taking Miss Marple back to the Brookview, and until the renovations are over, I'm not bringing her back." She grabbed her purse, sorted through her keys, and then picked up the cat carrier.

"I'm going to miss you, Miss M," Pixie said, "but I don't blame you, Tricia. Let's just hope they finish soon. I'm getting pretty sick of all this noise, too."

"You and Mr. Everett have been very good sports. Thank you."

Pixie shrugged. Honestly, what more could she say?

Tricia headed for the door. "I'll be back as soon as I can."

"Not to worry. We won't be overwhelmed with customers," Pixie called after her.

Tricia marched north up the sidewalk. She'd have to drive to the

Brookview with all the windows open, since the air-conditioning wouldn't be on long enough to cool the car, and she'd leave the AC on at the bungalow to keep Miss Marple comfortable, along with the DO NOT DISTURB sign hanging from her door to keep the maids from accidentally letting loose her precious cat.

The twinges of depression she had felt earlier had begun to grow, and Tricia wondered when she would ever feel settled again.

SIX

It was well after six when Tricia finally closed the door to her now-silent shop and abode. The construction workers had called it quits a little after four, which was a blessing to her ears, but if they worked another couple of hours every day she might get into her apartment all the sooner. Of course, what did it matter to them? Construction guys were employed only when there were projects, and when there weren't—they lay idle. Were the guys milking it to keep drawing a paycheck? Maybe—maybe not.

Tricia used her key to open the door to the Cookery, cut through the shop, and headed up the stairs to Angelica's loft apartment.

"Hello!" Tricia called as she approached the door. She heard joyful barking, and when she entered, Sarge, Angelica's Bichon Frise, jumped up and down as though he had springs for legs. "I'm glad to see you, too!" Tricia simpered in doggy-ese, patting the little guy, who wiggled and squirmed before taking off for the kitchen to announce her presence.

"Sarge! Hush!" Angelica ordered, and the barking immediately stopped, but the dog still ran around in happy circles. She turned to her sister. "You're just in time. I've just made a pitcher of martinis and was about to pour."

From past experience, Tricia knew there'd be a couple of glasses chilling in the refrigerator, and she retrieved them, setting them on the counter. Angelica poured, then added the olives on frill picks.

"What do we drink to?" Tricia asked.

"How about the upcoming wine and jazz festival?"

"Great idea."

They clinked glasses.

"What do you want me to do to help make dinner?" Tricia asked.

"You can chop the onion and garlic while I grate more zucchini."

"More?"

"Yes, I'm going to make zucchini bread later. Tommy's threatening to bring in another bushel basket before the end of the week. Apparently he planted a few too many vines. What we need for this recipe is still draining." She indicated a colander in the sink and the pool of green liquid beneath it staining the porcelain.

"Okay."

Angelica supplied a cutting board, knife, the onion, and garlic cloves for Tricia, who set down her glass, and the sisters set to work.

"So what's the news of the day?" Angelica asked, picking up a zucchini that could have doubled as a cudgel.

Tricia considered sharing what she'd learned during her conversation with Chief Baker and decided to keep it to herself—at least for the time being. Why upset Angelica? She was upset enough for both of them. And if Angelica already knew, it would only be a source of contention.

"I found out where Daddy's been staying," Tricia said, removing the onion's outer skin.

"Oh?"

"Fred Pillins's place."

"Whatever for?" Angelica asked, hacked off a large chunk of squash and began to grate vigorously.

"Oh, Fred thought he'd be doing us a favor by taking Daddy in."

"That was sweet of him. Has Daddy pawned any of his stuff yet?" Her voice positively dripped with sarcasm.

"When Pixie heard about it, she told Fred to bring anything he valued over to her place."

"Sound advice."

"I suppose we should contact him."

"I suppose," Angelica agreed, albeit not enthusiastically.

"I have Fred's number on my phone. Pixie gave it to me in case I need to contact her and didn't find her at home."

"That was nice."

Tricia took out her phone, scrolled through her contacts, and found Fred's number. It rang five times before rolling over to voice mail. She didn't bother to leave a message. "No answer." She put the phone away and started chopping the onion once again.

"How did your discussion with Russ go?"

"It didn't. He has no plans to pursue a story on Carol's death. The poor man sounded beaten, saying he couldn't take on any pursuits that might be dangerous. He seemed to lay the blame on having become a family man."

"That seems perfectly reasonable to me."

Before she'd become a stepgrandma to little Sofia, Angelica might not have been as understanding.

"Anything else interesting happen at your store today?" she asked.

"Not really. It's so loud and dirty, my customers have been few and far between. Which leads me to my next topic of conversation. I've come to a decision," Tricia said, depositing the onion pieces into a bowl and beginning to mince the garlic. "There's no way I can host Pixie's bridal shower at Haven't Got a Clue. No matter how often we dust and vacuum, we can't seem to keep it clean."

"That *is* a problem," Angelica agreed.

"I know it's presumptuous of me to ask, but is there a chance you'd let me use either the function room at the Brookview Inn or the front parlor at the Sheer Comfort Inn?"

Angelica frowned. "I'd have to check the schedules. I may own these sites, but I'm a big-picture person. I rely on my right-hand people to take care of the daily operations. If there's nothing planned, of course you can have one or the other. But you're going to have to pay for the catering."

"I figured that was a given." Tricia sipped her drink. "I know I should have done all this before now. I admit, I've grown rather used to you—and your businesses—rescuing me in these kinds of situations."

"I'm happy to do so. What did you have in mind?"

"A lovely, proper tea, reminiscent of what we had on our cruise on the *Celtic Lady*."

Angelica pursed her lips.

"What's the matter? Don't you think Pixie deserves it?"

"Pixie deserves the best of the best. Goodness knows, she hasn't had that for most of her life. But it sounds like what you have in mind is what *you* would like, more than what would make Pixie happy."

"What do you mean?"

"Pixie might consider a proper afternoon tea to be rather stodgy."

"But I want her to have a lovely time," Tricia said, and finished with the garlic. She headed for the sink to rinse her hands.

"She can—but you might want to rethink the menu, the music, and everything else."

"What are you saying?" Tricia said, heading back across the kitchen to grab her drink.

"That Pixie might enjoy a more nostalgic event."

"What's more nostalgic than an afternoon tea?"

"It depends on the era. You and I would love a tea with a string quartet, scones and clotted cream, cucumber-and-cress sandwiches, and tiny, delicate pastries. But I'm betting Pixie would be happier with a Frank Sinatra or Dean Martin soundtrack, cocktail wienies wrapped in puff pastry, Swedish meatballs, and potato salad."

Tricia nodded, feeling a bit defeated. "You're probably right."

"Of course I am," Angelica said, but her words weren't malicious. "If you don't mind, would you let me come up with the menu, decorations, and party games for the shower?"

Tricia took in her sister's hopeful expression. Angelica was right. She better understood what would make Pixie happy, and she felt more than a little down that she wasn't as tuned in to what her employee would prefer. But the whole idea of hosting the shower was to make Pixie happy, and that was Tricia's sole goal.

"Okay, but please—let me help."

"Oh, there's no question—you're invaluable," Angelica said. "You are the glue that will make this shower a tremendous success."

It sounded like Angelica was throwing her a bone, but since she trusted her sister implicitly, Tricia was willing to acquiesce.

"Okay."

Angelica wiped her hands on a dishcloth and grabbed her own drink. "Good. If it's available—and I'm pretty sure it is—I think the parlor at the Sheer Comfort Inn will suffice. I mean, this isn't a large party, is it?"

"I invited Grace and Ginny, some of my best customers, and a few of the merchants. Maybe a dozen in all."

Angelica went to the fridge, took out some eggs, and broke them into a bowl. "Then it'll be a lovely, intimate affair."

Tricia nodded. "And I thought I'd order either a cake or cupcakes from the Patisserie."

"My people could supply a gorgeous cake, but I think it would be nice to throw Nikki a little business. Why not spread the joy around the village?"

"Exactly. And let's face it, her cakes and pastries are to die for."

"Let's hope not," Angelica said. "We've had more than enough of that around here."

Tricia ignored the jibe. "What else needs to be done?"

"The sausage needs to be browned. Are you up for it?"

"Of course." She stepped over to one of Angelica's kitchen drawers and withdrew a bib apron and tied it on. She didn't want any grease splashes on her pretty peach sweater set. She grabbed one of the shiny skillets from the rack that hung over the island and set it on the stove, found the sausage wrapped in butcher paper and dumped it into the skillet, then lit the burner. She found a wooden spoon in a crock on the counter and poked at the sausage to break it up. After a few months of lessons from Angelica, Tricia felt like she was making real progress with this cooking thing. Too bad she didn't have any victims to practice on. Then again, once her new kitchen was assembled, maybe she'd invite hers and Angelica's surrogate family to dinner. And she'd make it herself. Okay, maybe she'd let Angelica supervise, but she would do the actual cooking by herself.

While she tended to the sausage, Angelica retrieved a carton of cream from the fridge, measured out a cup and poured it into the eggs, and took a whisk to the mixture.

"Once we pop this casserole into the oven, we'll have half an hour to kill. Did you still want to take Sarge for a . . ." She looked over at the doggy bed. Sarge's ears had pricked up at the mention of his name. ". . . you-know-what?"

"Yes. With my treadmill relocated to the basement and me living off-site, I'm not getting my usual amount of exercise."

"Well, you look fabulous—so it doesn't show." Angelica retrieved the bowl with the onions and garlic and handed it to Tricia. "You can add these now." She did.

Angelica rounded up the rest of the ingredients, and between the two of them, they assembled the casserole. Angelica popped it in the oven, glanced at her watch, and then polished off the last of her drink. Tricia still had half of hers. She stowed it in the fridge.

"Walkies!" Angelica called, and Sarge shot out of his bed as though from a catapult. She clipped the leash to his collar, and the three of them headed down the stairs. Once outside, Angelica locked the Cookery. "What direction do you want to go?"

"How about up Pine Avenue. I like to zigzag my way up to Oak Street."

"Okay, but we have to start back in precisely"—Angelica checked the diamond-studded watch on her wrist—"fourteen minutes, otherwise our dinner will be ruined."

"No problem."

They set off, with Angelica holding Sarge's leash. He walked at her heel, his tongue lolling a bit, his gait jaunty—happy as only a dog can be. He knew the way, of course. Tricia had taken him on this exact route a hundred or more times in the previous year after her store had burned, using their walks as her preferred mode of exercise.

Tricia only half listened as Angelica spoke about her day and the mountain of zucchini she needed to deal with at her café. Her thoughts kept going back to the body they'd found only the evening before. If she was correct, Carol had lived on Oak Street. Had her neighbors known Carol better than anyone else in the village did? From what Tricia gathered, her darts nemesis had lived in Stoneham for decades, but had pretty much kept to herself until the death of her husband.

Had the man kept her in line for some reason, or was it sheer loneliness that had forced her to seek company elsewhere?

Angelica was winding down as they turned onto Oak Street. "We're going to have to start back in just a few minutes."

"Is it that time already?" Tricia asked, looking at her own watch.

"Didn't Carol live here on Oak Street?" Angelica asked.

"Did she?" Tricia asked, playing dumb.

"Yes. That yellow house over there."

The rest of the houses on the street were either painted white or beige, or the raw shingles had been left to weather to gray. For someone who hadn't stood out in life, the color of Carol's home sure did.

As they approached the house, Tricia noticed that Carol's next-door neighbors, who must have been in their midfifties, were out watering the floral border that graced the front of their home. She didn't think she'd met either of them before, but she recognized the man as the person who had held the door for her at Booked for Lunch earlier that day. The slender, petite woman with short-cropped dark—and obviously dyed—hair noticed them, waved, and then approached.

"Is that a Bichon?" she asked, and bent down, holding out her hand to let Sarge sniff it. He did, and then he licked her fingers. The woman laughed. "What a cutie-pie."

"His name is Sarge, because he's such a brave little soldier," Angelica said. "And yes, he is a Bichon." Sarge sat down on the sidewalk, basking in the praise.

"I always heard they're like poodles—they don't smell when they get wet."

"Sarge is always as fresh as a daisy," Angelica said, rather sidestepping the question.

And now Tricia had an opening to bring up Carol. In future, she'd have to remember to take little goodwill ambassador Sarge with her on all her information-gathering forays.

"Were you thinking of getting a dog—for protection? Because Sarge is a wonderful watchdog."

The woman straightened. "I hadn't thought we needed that until last night." Her gaze traveled to Carol's house. The yard was tidy, and the curtains in the home were drawn. It looked deathly quiet.

"Wasn't your neighbor Carol Talbot?" Angelica asked.

"Yes, she was."

"So sad," Tricia said, "and unexpected."

The woman nodded. "She was a good neighbor. We have a cat, and when we went out of town, Carol would come over and feed her. She'd even spend time with her—and read to her. Not many pet sitters are willing to do that." She shook her head. "I can't understand why anyone would want to kill her. She was quiet and unassuming."

Until she had a dart in her hand, and then she was consumed with single-minded determination. But Tricia kept that opinion to herself.

"I suppose the police have spoken to you," Tricia said, noting the woman's husband kept looking up from the wand sprinkler on the end of his hose to take them in.

"Yes, and the owner of the *Stoneham Weekly News*, too. He said he was going to write a nice obituary for Carol. She deserved it."

So, not all of Russ's news-collecting skills had gone dormant.

Tricia noted the husband had turned off the faucet and was winding up the hose. "Did Carol have many friends?"

"Not that I know of. I guess she sometimes went to that bar on Main Street. My husband and I don't drink, so we've never been there, although she did ask us if we wanted to see her trounce her last opponent at darts."

Ha! Tricia had only lost to Carol on two occasions, and they'd played at least a dozen times.

"Did Carol have any relatives? What will happen to her house?"

"I don't know—to both questions."

Studying the woman's rather guilty expression, Tricia somehow doubted that.

"What were the police interested in?"

"They wanted to look around her house. We have a key and let them in."

What Tricia wouldn't give to have a chance to give the place a thorough going-over—not that that was likely to happen.

Angelica looked at her watch. "Oh, my! I've got a casserole in the oven. Trish, if we don't leave now, it'll be ruined."

Tricia would have liked to have stayed longer to pump Carol's neighbor for more information, but it sounded like Carol had been on good, but not very personal, terms with her neighbors, and since the husband had gone inside, Tricia wasn't going to get an opportunity to speak to him, either. "Yes, we'd better go. It was very nice speaking with you."

"And you. If you walk this way again, I'll look out for you. I'd love to say hello to Sarge once again."

Sarge wagged his tail enthusiastically and if she ever needed it, Tricia had an excuse to return and pump the woman for information.

The sisters waved good-bye and headed down the street. They'd spent far too long conversing and didn't retrace their steps, instead taking Poplar Avenue back to Main Street and the Cookery.

"That was rather an uninformative conversation," Angelica commented as they turned the corner.

"I agree. Not that I have a stake in finding out anything more about Carol."

"Nonsense. If you'd had more time, you would have interrogated the woman."

"What's at stake is Daddy may be considered the prime suspect in her death, as Grant told me he's ruled out Steven."

"Why's that?"

"He wouldn't tell me, but I'm still suspicious and I do intend to grill him. . . . That is, if I get the chance. I might like to speak to the husband of the woman we just spoke to," Tricia admitted.

"And how will you finagle that?" Angelica asked.

"I'll have to think about it."

"Don't you think it was a little odd that the woman didn't introduce herself?"

"We didn't introduce ourselves," Tricia pointed out.

"Just about everybody in the village knows who *I* am. I'm already a legend in my own time," Angelica quipped as they approached the Cookery.

Tricia smirked. "You mean in your own *mind.*"

Angelica ignored the jibe, unlocked the door, entered, and let Sarge off the leash. He immediately ran for the back of the shop and the stairs. Once they'd caught up, Angelica scooped him up, and the three of them headed for her apartment.

The timer on the stove went off just as they entered. Angelica hung the leash on a peg by the door. "You set the table, and I'll get the casserole out of the oven. It can sit for a few minutes while I slice the baguette I picked up earlier at the Patisserie."

"Sounds like a plan."

Tricia retrieved plates from the cupboard and cutlery from a drawer, and then snagged her drink from the fridge, topping it up and poured another for Angelica.

Angelica set the casserole on a hot pad, plunged a large serving spoon into the concoction, and set the platter of bread, as well as a stick of sweet butter, on a plate on the kitchen island, and the sisters sat down to serve themselves.

Tricia tasted the casserole and experienced a moment of bliss. "Wow—this tastes fantastic."

"Doesn't it, though?" Angelica agreed, and smiled. "And it's rather like a cross between a quiche and a soufflé." Her smile faded, however. "Do you really think Daddy's the chief suspect in Carol's death?"

Tricia reached for her glass and nodded. "I'm afraid so." For a moment, she wrestled with asking if Angelica knew about their father's past, and again decided not to mention it. It could wait.

Maybe.

SEVEN

The sky above the towering maples that surrounded the Brookview property was pale blue—a sure sign of humidity, which Tricia felt like a slap in the face as she exited the bungalow the next morning. She locked the door and had started for her car across the parking lot when she saw a familiar face. "Grace!"

Grace Harris-Everett looked around, spotted Tricia, and waved. "Hello, Tricia. Isn't it a lovely morning?"

"Humid—but I'll take this over ice and snow any day. What brings you to the Brookview so early?"

"The Stoneham Horticultural Society is having their annual luncheon today, and I'm on the decorating committee. We'll have fresh flowers on every table—all of which were grown in the Society's own gardens."

Tricia would bet that the florist who usually supplied the Brookview's arrangements wasn't too happy about that plan, but she was sure Antonio Barbero, the inn's manager and Ginny's husband, had soothed any ruffled feathers. "Sounds lovely."

"I invited Russ Smith from the *Stoneham Weekly News* to come take pictures, but he wouldn't commit."

"I'm sorry to hear that." But after her conversation with the local rag's publisher the previous day, she wasn't entirely surprised, either. "Here's hoping it's a slow news day."

It occurred to Tricia that this might be the perfect opportunity to quiz Grace on Carol, since Mr. Everett had chosen not to disclose what he knew about her.

"The news wasn't slow on Tuesday night. I mean, after what happened to Carol Talbot."

Grace's lips pursed, and she sported a guarded expression that mirrored her husband's from the day before. "Yes."

Tricia decided to push it. "Mr. Everett seems to know something about Carol, but was reluctant to say anything."

"I think you're being incorrect when you say reluctant; I think you mean he *won't* share an opinion on her."

"Exactly," Tricia agreed.

Grace nodded.

"I haven't lived in Stoneham all that long. I don't know the gossip that went on decades ago. I thought perhaps—"

"That I might be willing to tell all?" Grace asked, her expression wry.

"Oh, no—that's not what I meant." A lie if ever she'd uttered one.

"I know what you meant. And there *is* a difference between idle, malicious gossip and knowing the facts. Or at least, *thinking* one knows the facts."

"What *are* the facts concerning Carol?"

Grace seemed to weigh the merits of speaking versus keeping what she knew to herself, and Tricia wondered who else in the village might know what had gone on decades before. Stella Kraft, the retired high school teacher, might be a source of information. Then again, Tricia hadn't spoken to her for several years, and she'd heard that the poor woman had been suffering with the onset of Alzheimer's disease. And Frannie Mae Armstrong knew all the current gossip, but she hadn't resided in Stoneham decades before when Carol had arrived to live in the village.

"There's a saying I've heard since I was a young girl," Grace said, and Tricia suspected she might be on the receiving end of a lecture. "That one keeps oneself to oneself."

Was Grace talking about herself or the dead woman?

"Carol kept to herself?" Tricia guessed.

"Yes. It was only this past year or so—since her husband died—that she began to participate in village events. They kept to themselves and didn't socialize much."

"And that changed when Mr. Talbot died?" Tricia guessed.

Grace nodded. "I must say I was quite startled to see Carol begin to frequent the Dog-Eared Page on a regular basis."

"She liked playing darts," Tricia pointed out.

Again Grace nodded. "I understand she and her husband played at home. I know from experience how lonely it can be when you lose a life partner, and I suspect that was her motivation."

Though Tricia had lost someone whom she'd thought of as her life partner via divorce, she understood exactly what Grace was saying. "And his passing was the reason Carol came out of her shell?"

"Exactly. But there was another reason she kept to herself all those years. It was a bit of a scandal when she first arrived, you see."

"Scandal?"

"Yes. A number of the villagers were upset to have a murderer in their midst."

"Carol killed someone?" Tricia found it hard to wrap her mind around that announcement. Carol a murderer? Considering the number of deaths that had occurred in the village during the previous five years, Carol should have felt quite at home.

"Apparently she and her husband deliberately sought out a dying little village where they could escape her past notoriety."

It was true; before the booksellers had been invited to locate to the village in an effort to create a New England version of Hay-on-Wye in Wales, the place had seen a dwindling population and a strangled tax base. The booksellers—and the other businesses that had joined their ranks—had brought prosperity back to the village in the form of tourism.

"Who did Carol murder?"

"A schoolmate."

"How old was she?"

"I believe she was eleven at the time of the incident. Apparently the girls had been rivals. The school hosted a spelling bee, and Carol and her victim went head-to-head. Carol lost."

"So she killed the other girl?" Tricia said, aghast, and thought back to all the times she'd beaten Carol at darts.

"I don't suppose she *meant* to do it. Can a child that age understand the far-reaching implications of murder?"

"What happened?"

"This was before children could be charged as adults. As I understand it, Carol was remaindered to a juvenile detention facility back in her home state of Indiana and wasn't released until the age of twenty-one. She wasn't welcomed back to the town where the murder occurred and was forced to relocate. Apparently she met her husband-to-be soon after, and they faced unpleasantness in several communities every time her past caught up with them."

"That explains why she was so reticent, but not why someone would have wanted to kill her."

"I agree," Grace said.

"I'm sure you saw for yourself that she not only had words with and slapped my father but with Steven Richardson, too."

"Yes."

"While Steven spoke, I heard unpleasant mutterings from someone attending the event."

"It was Carol," Grace affirmed.

"Have you mentioned this to Chief Baker?"

"I have."

"Does he know about Carol's past?"

"I assume so. I didn't feel it was my place to volunteer the information. It wouldn't be hard for someone in his position to find out the woman had a criminal record."

"You don't think her record was expunged because she was a youthful offender?"

"It's possible," Grace agreed. "That would be something only Chief Baker could answer."

And Tricia intended to ask at the first possible moment. "I suppose someone from her past could have taken revenge, but why wait so long?"

"Perhaps whoever it was didn't know how to find her."

"It's not all that easy to hide these days. Thanks to the Internet, you can try to conceal information about yourself, but so much data is out there—in places that we don't even know about. Most cities have cameras on every corner, as do stores, restaurants, hospitals, and just about every public gathering place. Websites plant their cookies on your computer and can tell where you go online, to whom you communicate, and what you buy. They're collecting data twenty-four seven."

"Big Brother really *is* watching," Grace commented.

Tricia nodded ruefully.

"This whole situation with Carol is frightening," Grace said, "but it's up to the police to try to find out who killed her. I probably shouldn't say this, but, dear Tricia, you put yourself in harm's way far too often. I so worry about you."

"Thank you, Grace. But be assured, I have no intention of putting myself in danger."

"No, you never do—but you always seem to end up that way."

She said the words kindly, but it still felt like a rebuke. However, Tricia was determined not to take it personally. It felt good to know someone cared enough to worry about her—unlike her own parents.

A white van pulled into the parking lot with the Horticultural Society's logo emblazoned on the driver's side door.

"Ah, and here are the flowers."

"In case Russ doesn't show up, take some pictures with your cell phone so I can see them at our next family gathering."

"I'll do that, dear." She leaned forward to embrace Tricia. "I'll see you soon."

Tricia pulled back, and the women parted.

"See you!"

Tricia crossed the lot for her car, got in, and started the engine. Already the interior temperature had risen to an uncomfortable level. She pressed the buttons and opened all the windows. It was only a short drive to the municipal parking lot, and she could comb her hair before she left the car for her store.

As she pulled out of the lot, her thoughts returned to Carol Talbot's sordid past. A killer at eleven, and over a spelling bee. Even at an early age, Carol hadn't liked to lose in a competitive situation. Had she ever wished Tricia ill during their darts contest?

The thought was quite disquieting.

* * *

It was another morning filled with renovation noise, noise, noise—and Tricia was beginning to understand why the Grinch who stole Christmas was such an irritable guy. She also had to fight the urge to climb the stairs to check on the progress. It felt rather odd not to have free reign in her own home, but her contractor preferred to invite her up when he felt she'd be most impressed with the work they'd accomplished. She'd pushed it—the day before.

Still, it was Thursday—her favorite day of the week. Since Ginny had left her employ over two years before, she and Tricia had a standing weekly lunch date so they could catch up as friends. This was apart from the frequent family dinners Angelica hosted. Since early spring, Ginny had had to cancel on more than a few occasions because her new job as events coordinator for Nigela Ricita Associates didn't always allow her that luxury. Tricia understood. Her own life had been just as hectic when she'd worked for the nonprofit agency in New York. But she couldn't help feeling disappointed when that happened. On that morning, though, Ginny had called Haven't Got a Clue to confirm the date, so Tricia ordered two box lunches to go from Booked for Lunch.

Bev was waiting for her, and this time Tricia did pay for the meals—not that Angelica would have begrudged feeding her and Ginny. As Bev made change, Tricia noticed the man who'd held the door for her the day before—Carol Talbot's neighbor—sitting alone at the other end of the counter. He caught sight of her looking at him, and she smiled, but he looked away—turning his attention back to his sandwich. Was he employed in the village? He didn't seem dressed for work, and he was only a few blocks from home. She gave a mental shrug. Perhaps he was homebound and didn't like making his own lunch. Perhaps he'd taken early retirement and his wife still worked.

She gave herself a mental shake. What did it matter?

Bev handed Tricia a white plastic bag. "Enjoy your lunch!"

"Thanks."

Tricia turned and exited the café, nearly bumping into Ginny on the sidewalk. "You timed that right."

Ginny laughed. She looked smart in beige slacks, a white blouse, and sensible brown flats. "I was looking out my office window when I saw you cross the street to go to the café." She jerked a thumb over her shoulder toward the Dog-Eared Page. The second floor was used for office space, while the third floor had been rented as an apartment. Tricia's late ex-husband, Christopher, had lived there for a short time. Tricia and Angelica had sorted through his things, and then Antonio and Ginny had helped them empty the place. Many of the boxes still resided in Tricia's newly climate-controlled basement storeroom. Christopher's death less than a year before was still too fresh a memory. She'd set no timetable for parting with his possessions.

"We'd better get going," Tricia said, nodding toward the north and the village square. "I'm surprised, but pleased, you could make time for lunch considering your busy schedule. Angelica says you're settling in well and making great progress setting up the wine and jazz festival."

"She's being generous," Ginny said, her sunny expression turning dour.

"In what way?"

Ginny shook her head and frowned. "When it comes to management, I'm a miserable failure."

Tricia stopped. "That can't be true."

"But it is. I constantly mess up in front of my employees, and when they slack off, I can't seem to motivate them to get back to work."

"What's the problem?"

"I'm a lot younger than they are. They all started as desk clerks at the Brookview Inn. They think because Antonio is a bigwig with the company, that I got preferential treatment when this job opening came up."

Well, of course she did! She was, after all, the big boss's stepdaughter-in-law. Still, more than anyone, Tricia knew Ginny was smart and capable.

They started off again. "You've only had the job for a few months. Everybody knows that it takes a while to feel comfortable in a new work situation, and you started this division from scratch and on a very tight timeline."

"I must have been out of my mind to try to pull off this festival in such a small window of time."

"Will you make it?"

Ginny met her gaze, straightening. "If it kills me!"

Now that was the Ginny Tricia knew so well. "You excelled as my assistant, and you did even better managing the Happy Domestic. I'm betting this festival will be a huge hit and will come off seamlessly."

Ginny crossed her fingers, holding them up for Tricia to see. Then she shook her head, sobering. "I thought I'd be toiling fewer hours when I stepped into a more traditional job, but I still end up bringing work home almost every night. Once Sofia goes to bed, I've usually got an hour or more of stuff to do just to keep on top of things. I thought my weekends would be free, but I'm often juggling something during my time off then, too."

"I'm sure it will all work out," Tricia said, not knowing how else to bolster Ginny's confidence.

"I just don't want to disappoint Angelica. She could have hired someone with a lot more experience than me. And I've heard a couple members of my team talking about jumping ship because they don't see a future for themselves in the company where nepotism trumps their efforts."

Tricia could understand their point, but she also knew what a hard worker Ginny was, as well as her desire to please—not only her stepmother-in-law, but her husband, as well.

"Would you like me to speak to Angelica about them?"

"Oh, no!" Ginny said, sounding panicky. "I don't want her to think she made a bad decision by promoting me, and I certainly don't want to sound like a whiner."

"You're not a whiner," Tricia said, hoping she sounded encouraging. "You just need a sounding board."

Ginny almost laughed. "You're probably right. Thanks for listening. I haven't mentioned this to Antonio, because I don't want to disappoint him, either."

"I don't think that's possible." They'd reached their favorite bench, under the shade of a large maple. They sat down and Tricia removed the boxes from the plastic bag, handing Ginny the one marked *Egg Salad* and opening the one marked *BLT.* She withdrew the small bag of potato chips, opening it. "Now what have you got left to do to make this event a success?"

Ginny unwrapped her sandwich. "I lost one of my acts, so I've got to find time to listen to a few other bands. It's really short notice, but what I've already heard is good. I'm coordinating with Milford Nursery and Flowers to get a couple of giant bunches of grapes made with green and purple balloons. They'll look really festive, and they're not nearly as expensive as I'd feared. I've got tents ordered in case of rain, but I'm hoping the weather will hold and that we can go without them."

"What about concessions?"

"I've lined up the best—including a food truck that specializes in crepes."

Tricia couldn't help smiling. "I love crepes!"

Ginny grinned and cracked the cap on her bottle of iced tea. "I know. That's why I booked them."

"You're a doll."

Ginny's smile widened.

"How's your budget?"

"Holding steady. We may not make money this first year, but unless something unforeseen happens, we shouldn't lose any, either." She took a bite of her sandwich, chewed, and swallowed. "Okay, enough about me. We should talk about something a little more interesting . . . like Pixie's shower."

"Will you be able to make it?"

"I wouldn't miss it. Antonio has already rearranged his schedule so that he can look after Sofia. Angelica said you've changed the venue."

"There's just no way I can host it at Haven't Got a Clue. Well, I probably could—but the truth is, I don't want to. I was embarrassed the night of Steven Richardson's signing because of all the dust. No matter how many times Mr. Everett vacuums—"

"And he's never shirked his duties," Ginny put in.

"—there's always dust lurking. I noticed a couple of people at the signing the other night were sneezing. It could almost be deemed a hazardous work zone."

"Now you're joking," Ginny said.

"I wish I were."

"But your home is going to be gorgeous when it's finished."

"At least I have that to look forward to," Tricia admitted. "I'm not as good at party planning as Angelica, who volunteered to coordinate a lot of it."

"No doubt about it—no matter what she sets her mind to, it turns out well."

"I know," Tricia agreed. "It feels like I'm shirking, but in the long run, my goal is for Pixie to be happy, and if Angelica can pull it off better than me, then all is good. Still, when she volunteered, I had a feeling that she'd already been plotting something."

"What kind of something?"

"Something that she thinks is terrific and I might find embarrassing."

"In what way?"

"I don't know. But whatever it is, it will be something Pixie will enjoy."

"Why don't we look on the bright side? Whatever Angelica is plotting might also be fun for us, too. My job is so stressful, I'm looking for *any* excuse to cut loose and have a little fun."

"You're right. No wonder Antonio loves you so much."

Ginny grinned. "Well, I am incredibly cute, too."

Tricia laughed. "Yes, you are."

They ate their sandwiches and chatted about Tricia's renovation, Angelica's quest to use up Tommy's zucchini harvest, and Ginny showed off a dozen new pictures of Sofia. The one thing they didn't talk about was Carol Talbot, which was just as well. Tricia was well and truly stumped. She didn't want to believe her father or Steven Richardson could possibly be responsible.

But then who in Stoneham might have wanted the woman dead?

EIGHT

All was quiet when Tricia arrived back at Haven't Got a Clue, which seemed like a blessing until Pixie announced that all the workmen had left for the day.

"What? But it's only just after one o'clock."

Pixie shrugged. "I guess the guy who needs to do some plumbing stuff was too busy to come today, and so they're stalled on the master suite until he can find time to drop by and finish whatever it is that needs to be done."

"But my kitchen—my living room! Surely *somebody* should be working to finish those areas!"

Again, Pixie shrugged. "At least it's nice and quiet, although Mr. Everett said he'd be vacuuming and dusting again when he returns from lunch."

Tricia sighed, wondering when she'd ever get to sleep under her own roof again.

"Angelica called while you were gone."

"Did she leave a message?"

"Just for you to call her cell phone."

"Okay."

"I thought I might go down to the storeroom and sort through some of the boxes to find more Christie titles. We're running low."

"Go ahead. I can handle things up here for a while."

"I'll be back in a few minutes," Pixie said, and headed for the stairs to the basement.

Tricia retrieved her phone, then stowed her purse under the sales counter. She flipped through her contacts until she came up with her sister's number, then tapped it.

"Hello!" Angelica sang.

"It's me, your sister. Pixie said you called."

"Yes, I'm about to have a liquor emergency. I used the last of the gin on our martinis last night, and I'm up to my earlobes in work. There's no way I can go to the state liquor store. I was wondering if you'd have time to go this afternoon. They're open until seven."

Tricia was well aware of the store's hours. "It's not a problem."

"Good. Pick me up a case of the usual, and half a case of vermouth, as well."

"Anything else?"

"Well . . . I do need my dry-cleaning picked up, too, but I can handle that either tomorrow or Monday."

Tricia refrained from letting out a scream. "Good."

"You can drop the boxes off at my place, but bring over a bottle of both of them to Booked for Lunch after you close your store. We've got tons of leftovers, and I simply won't have the time or energy to cook tonight."

"All right."

"Excellent. Tootles."

"Bye."

Tricia stabbed the end call icon and looked around the empty store. Since they weren't inundated with customers, perhaps she'd go to the liquor store sooner rather than later. She was getting low on cat food, kitty treats, and litter for Miss Marple. She could stop off at the grocery store in Milford and pick up what she needed on the same trip.

With not much else to do, Tricia decided to straighten the shelves, but found everything in order. Pixie and Mr. Everett kept on top of those kinds of things. Tricia put some music on the store's stereo and returned to her station behind the register, realizing she'd forgotten to bring the paperback she'd nearly finished. There was certainly no shortage of reading material in Haven't Got a Clue, and she was about to check the nearest bookcase when Pixie appeared once more. She opened the dumbwaiter and extracted a box, then brought it over to the reading nook, settling it on the table.

"I swear these books get heavier on humid days."

"Is the dehumidifier down in the basement working?"

"It was nearly full. I emptied it. I checked the gauge, and the humidity is in the safe zone, so we're good. Did you call Angelica?"

"Yes, she wants me to run an errand for her."

"Ain't that what sisters are for?" Pixie asked, and laughed. Tricia had no idea if Pixie had any siblings. The subject had never come up.

"It seems so. I figured I'd go in a little while. Do you want me to help you shelve those books?"

"I wouldn't mind."

They each grabbed a stack of books and headed for the shelf that housed only Agatha Christie novels, sorting the titles alphabetically.

"Ya know, because of the construction, it's been really boring around here," Pixie commented.

"Sorry about that," Tricia apologized.

"It lets me catch up on my reading, but I also feel kinda guilty,"

Pixie said with an embarrassed grin. "But I've also been thinking about the dead dame."

"Carol Talbot?"

Pixie nodded. "Me and Fred seen her around town a lot these last couple of months."

"Oh?"

"Yeah. Mostly at the Bookshelf Diner. Fred likes to take me out to dinner at least once a week, and that's one of our favorite places. They make the best meatloaf and mashed potatoes around."

"I can't say I've tried them."

"Well, you don't know what you're missing."

"Did Carol ever meet someone there for dinner?"

"Nah. She usually sat in one of the back booths all alone. She always got a club sandwich, ate half, and took the rest home—probably for lunch the next day. But that wasn't the funny thing."

"Funny?" Tricia said, wedging a copy of *Taken at the Flood* between *Star Over Bethlehem* and *The A.B.C. Murders*.

"Yeah, the old gal used to sneak a little silver flash out of her purse, take a swig, and hide it again."

"Really?"

Pixie nodded. "Sometimes by the time she left the joint, she'd be three sheets to the wind. I don't think a flask holds that much, so she must have been potted before she even got to the diner."

"And this happened more than once?"

"Just about every time we went to the joint!" Pixie headed back for the box and brought the remaining books over to the shelf, letting Tricia take half of them to shelve.

"She was always sober when we played darts."

"So are you, and that's because you want to win."

That was true.

"It's never good to drink alone. Ya think she was pining for her dead husband? Lots of people become alcoholics after a tough loss like that," Pixie said.

"Yes." Tricia had imbibed wine a little too often after Christopher's death, but she didn't have a problem—although she was sure some of the villagers thought she might now that Angelica had indoctrinated her to the joys of a well-made martini, which was certainly an acquired taste.

The closest liquor store was in Milford, where Tricia just so happened to need to go. Could any of the people who worked there have known Carol?

There was only one way to find out.

Tricia steered her car into a slot in the parking lot of a little strip mall in Milford and headed for the liquor store. She was well acquainted with the shop, as she'd purchased her liquor there since moving to Stoneham more than six years before. Judging by the number of cars in the lot, the store and its neighbors saw a lot of what was known in the trade as *foot traffic*, even though everyone arrived in a vehicle.

Like in her own store, a bell jangled as she entered the store, where a number of people were milling about, checking the prices on the thousands of bottles of wine and liquor. Since she already knew what she wanted, and in what quantity, Tricia marched straight up to the sales counter.

"Hi," said a guy of about forty, wearing a blue smock over a Jimmy Buffett T-shirt. "Can I help you?"

"Yes, I'd like a case of Bombay Sapphire gin in the one point seven five liter bottle and six bottles of Carpano Bianco vermouth."

"Can do. Having a party?"

Tricia sighed. "A pity party. Or rather, a wake. Someone I know died on Tuesday night, and we're going to toast her well."

"I'm so sorry for your loss."

"It was a shock," Tricia said truthfully. "I guess she was a regular here as well. I don't suppose you knew her. Carol Talbot."

The guy held up a finger. "Great body for an older lady; but a leathery face that looked like she either smoked too much or was a heavy tanner at one time. Oh, no offense," he hurriedly added.

"None taken. So, you *knew* her."

He shrugged. "I collect odd names. Hers wasn't—but she was."

"In what way?"

Again he shrugged.

"What did she drink?" Tricia tried again.

"Whatever whiskey was on sale. Like you, she bought it by the case. She came in a lot."

"Was she ever with anyone?"

"Not that I remember." He smiled. "She was a real ball breaker."

"I beg your pardon?"

"She liked to flirt. I always played along because she'd tip me well when I carried the boxes out to her car."

Was that the truth, or was he hinting for Tricia to tip him in kind? And was it likely he knew anything else about Carol? Probably not.

"I'll go get the stuff you want." He moved from behind the counter.

"Thank you."

So, Carol *was* a lush. Tricia had suspected that after her conversation with Pixie; the counterman had only substantiated it. Still, it was one more piece to the puzzle that was Carol Talbot.

Was Pixie right? Did Carol turn to alcohol after the death of her husband, or was there another reason she'd recently taken up drinking? Was she haunted by her past, the present, or her future?

And . . . was there a way Tricia could find the answers to those questions?

NINE

Tricia dropped off Angelica's liquor at the Cookery. She sent the boxes up to the third floor via the dumbwaiter, then headed upstairs. As usual, Sarge was ecstatic to see her, and she had to make a big fuss over him before she could unload the boxes and leave the contents on the kitchen island. After procuring a bottle of each, she found a paper grocery bag to put them in and then grabbed the dog's leash.

"Sorry, buddy; I can't take you for a walk, but I can take you outside for a quick comfort stop."

Sarge wasn't hard to please, happily wagging his tail.

Ten minutes later, Tricia strode into Haven't Got a Clue.

Pixie stood behind the cash desk, carefully holding a paperback so that she didn't crack the spine. "You're back." She glanced at the clock on the wall. "Just in time for closing."

"I didn't realize it was so late."

"Since it was so dead—we only made about thirty bucks all day—Mr. E felt guilty and left an hour early."

"I'd feel bad if he needed the money—which he doesn't—but I'm sure Grace has a lot to tell him about the Stoneham Horticultural Society's annual luncheon at the Brookview Inn."

"Oh, yeah. I'll bet that'll be *real* interesting," Pixie said and rolled her eyes.

"Now, now."

"Yeah, yeah. Different strokes for different folks." Pixie picked up a bookmark and inserted it between the pages of her book before closing the cover and stowing it under the counter. "Want me to hang around until the hour strikes six?"

"That won't be necessary. As it's been so slow, I may as well close for the day anyway. Have you got any plans for the evening?"

"Not much. We decided to head to Portland for our honeymoon. We're gonna feast on lobster at least once every day. I got me a kind of a sailor dress off eBay that's god-awful cute, and it only needs to be hemmed. I figured I'd get that out of the way. How about you?"

"Just dinner with Angelica."

"Same old, same old," Pixie said, nodding.

What was that supposed to mean? "She's good company."

"Not as good as having a man around the house," Pixie said rather pointedly.

"I guess that depends on the man."

"Yeah. You're probably right. Have you heard back from that author guy yet?" She waggled her eyebrows suggestively.

"No." And Tricia was beginning to think she never would.

"Damn him."

"My sentiments exactly." Only Tricia wasn't thinking of the guy in a romantic sense. Obviously Richardson knew about Carol's past. Had he tried to blackmail her about her past indiscretion—if one could trivialize murder in such a way? What did he have to gain? Tricia had a pretty good idea of what Carol had to lose.

Pixie grabbed her purse from under the counter. "I'm off."

"Happy hemming," Tricia called as Pixie exited the shop with a wave over her shoulder.

After she'd gone, the silence was unnerving. Tricia pulled down the blinds on the front display window, checked the cash drawer and found exactly thirty-two dollars in it, and decided to leave it there for the next day. If she got robbed overnight, she wasn't going to shed tears over the loss.

Grabbing the bag of gin and vermouth, Tricia paused at the door long enough to turn the sign on it to CLOSED, turned off the lights, and locked the door behind her.

Traffic was sparse as she jaywalked across Main Street, heading for Booked for Lunch. As expected, the sign said CLOSED, but the lights inside were on and the door was unlocked—yet Angelica was nowhere in sight.

"Ange?" Tricia called.

"In the kitchen!"

Tricia set the bag down on the lunch counter and headed toward the back of the restaurant. Pushing through the swinging double doors, she found her sister standing in front of the huge stainless steel refrigerator—its doors thrown open—perusing its contents.

"What are you in the mood for, love?"

"Ha-ha," Tricia quipped. "What have you got?"

"Just about everything on the regular menu—but if you want something different, I can whip something up fast; say, an omelet."

"You said you were too tired to cook. I'm not going to make you do that."

"And you're a saint." She shut the doors to the fridge. "Did you bring the booze? Let's have a drink."

"You don't have a shaker."

"No, but I do have a milk shake machine. I can use the canisters for that and top it with a glass. Voila! Instant shaker."

"You amaze me."

"Give me a pig's ear, and I'll make you a silk purse," Angelica said, swished past her sister and entered the dining room.

Tricia followed her. Angelica went behind the lunch counter, and Tricia settled on one of the stools. Angelica already had the olive garnishes ready and quite expertly made their martinis in a water pitcher, then doled them out.

"You make it look easy."

"If pushed, I'm sure I could work a shift at the Dog-Eared Page, but then that would probably give away my secret identity as Nigela Ricita."

"We can't have that," Tricia agreed as Angelica presented her with her drink in a juice glass. "Cheers."

Tricia raised her glass in salute. But before she took a sip, she needed to get something off her chest. "We need to talk."

"This sounds serious. What's the subject?"

"Daddy."

"Oh, dear," Angelica said, and then downed a mighty gulp of her drink. "Okay, I'm fortified. Spill it."

Tricia also raised her glass, but took a much smaller sip. "I spoke with Grant yesterday."

"Concerning Daddy?"

Tricia nodded.

"And?"

"It may be hard for you to hear this—or not at all. But it turns out our father—"

"Is a rat with a past," Angelica supplied, sounding none too happy.

"So, how long have you known?" Tricia asked, not sure she really wanted to know the answer.

"Since February."

"Oh!"

"What do you mean?"

"I thought you were going to say for years."

"No. After he left here in January, I was so angry, I hired a private detective in Boston to do a background check. I've used the guy before to report on potential employees. He's very good."

"And?" Tricia prompted.

"Our father turns out to be a very big disappointment."

"Why didn't you tell me this?"

Angelica took another mighty big slug of her drink. "I was angry. *Very* angry. I knew you were just as disappointed in him as I was, but I wanted to spare you—at least until he turned up to screw us once again."

Tricia toyed with the olive-studded frill pick poking out of her glass. "You shouldn't have had to carry that kind of burden alone."

"Well, I'm your big sister. It's my job to protect you—although I wish I'd done a much better job in years past."

"I'm a big girl. I put my big-girl panties on every day and face the world head-on."

"Yes, you do. And you're right. I should have told you. Only . . . I'm mortified not only for the two of us, but for Daddy, too. Except, his past doesn't seem to embarrass him in the least. Have you tried calling Fred's place today?"

Tricia took a sip of her drink before answering. "No. My day was pretty full."

"Frannie called me with her end-of-day report and told me you'd let Sarge out a while ago. Thanks for that."

"You're welcome." Tricia changed the subject. "Pixie told me she thought Carol might be a lush. I dropped her name when I was at the state liquor store, and the guy behind the counter confirmed it. She drank cheap whiskey, and Pixie intimated she drank a lot of it, and it turns out with reason."

"What do you mean?"

Tricia spent the next five minutes telling her sister about her conversation with Grace.

"Good grief. A child murderer." Angelica shook her head and topped up both of their glasses. But before they could drink, a knock sounded at the door. They turned to look and saw none other than their father standing before the café's door.

"Oh, God," Angelica groused, but raised a hand to beckon him in. "Pardon my French, but I believe the you-know-what is about to hit the fan."

"Hello, my darling girls," John called as he entered and closed the door behind him. He paused to sniff the air. "Is that the seductive aroma of gin and vermouth I smell?"

"Sit down and I'll pour you one," Angelica said, already reaching for another glass. She'd made a very big pitcher of hooch.

John bestowed a kiss on each of their cheeks before he took a seat next to Tricia at the counter.

"Daddy, where have you been?" Angelica admonished.

"Around," he answered evasively, then raised his glass in salute and took a mighty tug on his drink before answering. "Damn good stuff." He shook himself. "Since my darling girls had no room for me, I've been staying at a friend's place."

"Pixie told me you'd been staying at Fred Pillins's apartment," Tricia said.

"I am."

"Then why haven't you answered the phone? I've called a number of times," Tricia said.

"Well, I figured any calls that came in would be for Fred, not me."

Tricia resisted the urge to roll her eyes.

"But where have you been all day?" Angelica asked.

"Here and there."

"Did you know the police are looking for you?"

"Whatever for?"

"Oh, I don't know," Angelica said rather flippantly. "Just a possible murder charge."

"Murder? Who am I supposed to have killed?"

"Carol Talbot."

"*Cara mia* mine is dead?" he repeated, sounding genuinely shocked.

"Yes, and not half an hour after she slapped you. Would you like to tell us why that happened?—and then I suggest you tell it to Chief Baker, as well," Tricia asserted.

John held his head high. "It may surprise you to learn that Carol and I were lovers."

Tricia's mouth dropped, while Angelica's eyebrows rose to what had to be a painful height.

"Daddy!"

"I may be in my seventies, but I'm not dead!" John said without shame.

"But—what about Mother?" Angelica asked.

"As you know, we're separated."

"Yes, but—"

"She threw me out, telling me to never darken her door again. Well, a man needs a little companionship. Some tender loving care."

"And you got that from Carol?" Angelica asked, skeptical.

"She had her moments."

And Tricia would bet they were few and far between.

"Did you know she was a murderess?" Angelica asked.

"Carol?" John asked, shocked.

Tricia nodded.

"I can't say that ever came up in conversation," he said, not sounding at all pleased.

"So why did she slap you the other night?" Angelica asked.

"Er, she was a little upset with me."

"And why was that?" Tricia asked.

"It seems she was a bit perturbed when I left town back in January without mentioning it to her first."

"Yes, I can see where that might have been a bit upsetting," Tricia said.

"Yes, and it was to us, too. It's a subject we need to talk about," Angelica said in a tone that meant business.

"Talk about what?" John asked, sounding clueless.

"For one, why you're back here."

"I told you; I'm here to see my two best girls." Considering he'd pulled a disappearing act for two days, it hardly seemed a truthful statement.

"And what else?" Angelica pressed.

"Well, I *could* use a little influx of cash," he admitted sheepishly.

"What for?"

"Expenses. It takes money to navigate these troubled times. There's really nothing much to eat at Fred's house. And several times a day he shows up and takes away more and more of my creature comforts."

"*His* creature comforts. He did mention he's moving at the end of the month, didn't he?" Tricia said.

"I think he said something to that effect."

"Do you have plans to move on, and if so—when?" Angelica said.

"You should have your couch back from the upholsterers by the end of the month, right?"

"There's been a delay in obtaining the fabric I ordered," Angelica said evasively. "It may not be returned until October."

"That's not very convenient," John said.

"No, it isn't," Angelica agreed.

"Will your apartment be finished by the end of the month?" he asked Tricia.

"I'm beginning to wonder if they'll *ever* complete the work." She could be just as evasive as her sister.

"Have you thought about reconciling with Mother?" Angelica asked hopefully.

John frowned. "That wouldn't be my first choice. Your mother is a very difficult person to live with. I'm surprised we managed to last fifty years together."

Fifty years? But Angelica was fifty-one. Surely he'd made a mistake with the math—or was he just being flippant?

"Have you at least spoken to her?" Tricia asked.

"Yes. I was hoping to convince her to send me some cash—just to keep body and soul together—but she's as hard-hearted as ever."

He'd never seemed hard up for cash in the past.

"What did you fight about?" Tricia asked, already anticipating his answer.

"Our trip to Bermuda, of course. She felt as though she'd been ambushed by your sister and me."

"I can see her point," Tricia said charitably. "But what's done is done. It's time for you two to kiss and make up."

"Ah, but Princess—neither of us wants that. I'd just as soon file for divorce and get a nice, fat, juicy settlement. After all, I've given her the best years of my life."

Isn't that what divorce lawyers usually told women?

John polished off his drink. "I could go for another, but I really could do with some sustenance. Any chance you could rustle up a little something for your old dad, Angelica?"

"Of course. What would you like?"

"Tommy gave me the grand tour of your kitchen last winter. Could I rummage through the fridge? I'm sure I can find something."

Angelica shrugged. "I guess."

"Pour me another drink, and I'll be back in a jiffy."

The sisters watched their father get up and pass through the double doors into the café's kitchen.

"Well?" Tricia whispered. "Do you think he's telling the truth?"

Angelica shrugged wearily. "I don't know. He could be telling us exactly what we want to hear."

"About him and Carol being lovers?"

"That does seem a bit far-fetched. She was no beauty, but she did have a nice figure. But I guess if it was dark, a man *could* pretend she was an Aphrodite."

They could hear the distinct sound of rummaging in the kitchen, the *thunk* of something heavy hitting the counter, the *chink* of heavy restaurant china, and the clatter of cutlery.

Angelica shook her head and again refilled their glasses. "We're going to be alcoholics before Daddy's visit is over."

"I hear you," Tricia agreed.

While they sipped their drinks, Angelica lamented the overabundance of zucchini and the ideas she had for using it up. It must have been five or ten minutes later when they realized it had gotten awfully quiet in the kitchen.

"What is he doing? Standing over the sink eating a sandwich?" Angelica asked.

"I'll go see," Tricia said, leaving her perch. But when she entered the kitchen, she found the industrial-sized fridge wide open with a number of empty shelves, an untidy mess on the counters, and the back door propped open.

"He's done it again!" Tricia hollered.

Angelica suddenly appeared behind her. "This kitchen was immaculate not fifteen minutes ago!" She took in the fridge and two of the shelves, which had held the cold cuts for the rest of the week and were now totally empty. "Daddy!" she hollered, loud enough to make Tricia wince. "Now what will we do for our dinner?"

Tricia shrugged, feeling weary. "I guess we can always call for a pizza."

TEN

Despite Tricia calling and leaving a number of messages on Fred's answering machine, John never picked up the phone. Tricia called Pixie's number several times and got no answer there, either. So she did the next best thing: she consulted Google, found a website that would do a reverse phone number search, and—voila!—found Fred's address in Milford. Okay, that told her where her father was staying, but he couldn't have gotten away on foot when leaving Booked for Lunch. Not when he was toting ten or twelve pounds of cold cuts and cheese. And what was he going to do with the stuff, anyway?

Since it was quite late, Tricia decided confronting John could wait until the next day. She tried calling several times the next morning, but still got no answer.

Pixie was about to unlock the door to Haven't Got a Clue when Tricia showed up. "Hi, Pixie. Did you get my phone message last night?"

Pixie stood there, key only partially inserted into the lock, looking guilty. "Uh, no. Is there a problem?"

"I wanted to get Fred's address. I've been trying to get in contact with my father, but he won't answer the phone."

"Sorry. Was it an emergency?"

Not hardly. "No. I managed to find it online. But I may have to bow out to go over there this morning." She didn't want to mention her father's latest larceny.

The construction workers were still among the missing, and, deciding to let Pixie get the shop ready for the day, Tricia called Jim Stark. Unfortunately, the call immediately rolled over to voice mail. Didn't anybody ever answer their phones?

And no sooner had she put the receiver down when the shop phone rang. Tricia picked it up, thankful for the quiet interlude. "Haven't Got a Clue; this is Tricia. How may I help you?"

"Is there a chance you'll forgive me for standing you up for lunch the other day?"

"Hello, Steven." Tricia took a breath, considering what else she *wanted* to say, and what she probably *would* say to Richardson. As usual, Pixie, who stood nearby, cocked her head to listen.

"Well?" he asked, sounding hopeful.

"Maybe."

"I'd like to make it up to you."

"Oh?"

"We could try again. I mean, it *is* nearly that time of day."

Tricia glanced up at the clock on the wall. "It's barely ten."

"How about I pick you up at your store at twelve?"

Mr. Everett arrived, waving to Tricia as he entered the store. She waved back and addressed Richardson. "I can't just take off. I have employees who have a regularly scheduled lunch break."

"Can't they cut you some slack?"

Pixie was practically hopping up and down. "Go to lunch—go to lunch," she whispered, but her voice was probably loud enough for Richardson. "We'll wait."

Tricia looked toward Mr. Everett, who also nodded.

"It seems I can change my plans after all."

"Great. See you at twelve."

He broke the connection, and Tricia replaced the receiver.

"So, lunch," Pixie said enthusiastically, virtually hovering.

"Yes, lunch," Tricia repeated, resigned.

"That's a hopeful sign."

"Why's that?"

"Because it means he's still interested in you."

Tricia wasn't sure she liked that analogy. She decided not to comment. She busied herself by tidying up the cash desk, while Mr. Everett wandered toward the back of the shop, no doubt to get his lamb's wool duster.

Pixie moved closer to the sales counter. "Well, aren't you going to *do* something?"

"Like what?"

"I don't know. Get ready."

"I'm ready," she said flatly, and straightened up a pile of bookmarks.

"Are you sure?"

"Yes, I'm sure!"

Startled by her tone, Pixie practically jumped. "Okay—okay!"

Mr. Everett continued dusting, studiously ignoring them.

The UPS man chose that moment to deliver a couple of boxes. Pixie found a box cutter and emptied them, then began pricing the new inventory.

Tricia had planned to go to the basement to work on the computer for a while, but it was such a pretty day, and she had nearly two hours to kill before her so-called date, that she felt restless. What she needed to do was go check Fred's apartment in hopes of catching her father there and giving him a stern talking-to—not that she thought it would help. Angelica had been so upset to find that John had stolen from her once again. And where could someone fence cold cuts anyway?

Grabbing her purse, Tricia headed for the door. "I'll be back in a while."

Again, Mr. Everett waved, but Pixie barely looked up from her work, making Tricia feel like a heel. She'd somehow make it up to her assistant later that day.

Fred lived on the second floor of a small, rather seedy brick apartment building not far from the highway, and Tricia made it there in less than five minutes.

She exited her car and pressed the fob on her key ring to lock it. The metal security door looked like it might have been kicked in at one point, and Tricia felt sorry for Fred having to live in such an unwelcoming place. That he'd entertained Pixie there was even more appalling. And what a comedown the place had to be for her father, who, in comparison, had for decades lived in the lap of luxury. Tricia's mother would have never settled for less.

The building housed six units, each with a buzzer. Tricia pressed the one marked five several times, and though she could hear it ring, no one let her in. On impulse, she pressed the first button. Again, no answer. Besides her own, there were three cars parked out front. Surely somebody was home—if that's what you could call the shabby building.

A window to her left opened and out popped the head of an elderly woman whose face seemed to have collapsed thanks to her lack of teeth. "Ain't nobody gonna answer the door."

"Why not?"

"'Cause they scared of the repo man or the summons server."

"Do I look like either?"

The woman sized her up. "No, but you sure don't look like you know the likes of anybody lives here."

"As a matter of fact, I do. Fred in number five."

She nodded. "He's a nice guy, but he's hardly ever home since he got engaged. Too bad. He's been real nice to me. Brings me ground turkey and hamburger on a regular basis."

Fred was a deliveryman for a local meat distributor. He delivered cold cuts and meat to Booked for Lunch, the Brookview Inn, and other local eateries.

The fact that her father had stolen the café's meat and absconded had to mean something. Tricia didn't want to think that Fred might not be on the up-and-up. Pixie had only recently been discharged from the state's parole system. Was Fred just another lowlife? Because of her past, was Pixie attracted to that kind of man?

Tricia didn't want to think about it. Despite her past failings, Pixie was a tremendous asset to Haven't Got a Clue. Much as Tricia loved Ginny, she hadn't had a real love for vintage mysteries like Pixie did. She was too young. Pixie spoke the mystery language to the mostly older readers who appreciated the vintage tomes Tricia also treasured. She was good with customers. Her flamboyant, vintage style helped to sell the work of authors who long ago had been reduced to dust.

"So what you gonna do?" the old woman asked.

Tricia dug into her purse for one of her business cards. "My father is staying in Fred's place."

The old woman's eyes seemed to sparkle. "That guy's a stud."

Tricia was taken aback. Her father . . . a stud?

"I've been trying to track him down, but he seems to be avoiding me and my sister. We're very worried about him. You see, he and our mother have separated—"

The woman's eyes widened with what seemed like pleasure, and she actually giggled. "You mean he's eligible?"

"Like any child, I want my parents to get back together. They've been married for over"—or at least—"fifty years."

"Oh." The woman looked crestfallen. Carol hadn't been anywhere near pretty, but she had been a lot more attractive than the poor lady in the faded green housedress before her.

Tricia handed her the card. "If he comes around, would you please call me? I worry about him."

"You're a good daughter—not like the piece of crap kid who dumped me here in this flea trap and only comes around when she thinks she can get my social security."

"I'm so sorry," Tricia said sincerely. She thought of Grace and Mr. Everett, neither of whom had a child to care for them in their dotage, but she knew she—and Angelica—were willing to step up and help them in any way they could should the future darken for either or both of them.

"Take care," Tricia said, with the sinking feeling that this poor woman had no one to look out for her welfare.

"You, too, honey."

The woman pulled her head back inside the apartment and shut the window.

Tricia turned, noticing a Dumpster by the side of the building, and took a detour to look inside. The sun was already beating down, and the smell of rotting garbage emanating from it was rather pungent. Still, she took a deep breath before opening the side gate and peered inside. As she had feared, she saw unopened packages of ham, roast beef, several salamis, processed chicken rolls, and big slabs of various cheeses, still in their original packaging—obviously what had been stolen from Booked for Lunch's refrigerator the previous evening.

Why? Why on earth would her father steal food from his own daughter and then throw it away?

But Tricia also wondered about the connection between Fred and her father. Had John concocted some kind of scheme to steal the meat from the café and have Fred resell it right back to Angelica, cutting himself in on the deal? But that couldn't be. Fred had always seemed like a quiet, decent man. Could her father have stolen the meat and cheese without consulting Fred first, only to find Pixie's fiancé had no interest in risking his job and a possible jail sentence for such larceny? No doubt Pixie had filled Fred in on just how terrible being incarcerated could be.

Tricia walked back to her car, that feeling of depression settling around her shoulders once more. Who was the man who had masqueraded as her father for so many years? Had his quip about being married to her mother for a year less than her sister's age been a slip of the tongue—or were she and Angelica actually only half sisters? After only recently learning of other long-held family secrets, nothing else would surprise her.

Half sisters/whole sisters, what did it matter? She and Angelica were sisters of the *heart*, and after too many years of estrangement were now effectively joined at the hip. If Tricia had learned anything in the past turbulent year, it was that family wasn't necessarily defined by a shared genetic code. She considered Grace and Mr. Everett as her loving pseudoparents. She loved Ginny like a sister. She adored Sofia as her great-niece, even if they had no shared heritage. And above all, Tricia loved Angelica—as a friend, as a mentor, and as her own personal guardian angel—and she believed her sister felt the same way about her.

But the problem of what they should do about John Miles still hung over them like a five-thousand-pound weight on a rapidly fraying rope.

Tricia started her car, shifted into reverse, and pulled out of the scantly graveled parking lot, hoping she would never have to return to this terrible, dingy dwelling. Fred would be much better off leaving this place and establishing a home with Pixie.

As she drove back toward Stoneham, Tricia wondered how she was going to break the news of what she'd learned to Angelica.

ELEVEN

Strains of Frank Sinatra crooning "I Could Write a Book" filled Haven't Got a Clue as Tricia entered—one of Pixie's contributions to the store's musical library. Four customers perused the shelves . . . a hopeful sign that they might just make enough sales to be in the black for the day.

"Everything go all right?" Pixie asked, as though their little altercation an hour earlier hadn't occurred.

Tricia forced a smile. "I was hoping to find my father at Fred's apartment, but no one answered the bell."

"You should have told me you were going there. I could have given you the key to get inside the security door."

"Thanks. I might try again later."

Pixie scrutinized her face. "Are you okay? Your eyes look funny. Like you might want to cry or something."

"It must be pollen. There are lots of flowers in bloom."

"Uh-huh." But luckily, further discussion was thwarted, as one of the customers approached the sales counter, her arms filled with books.

For the first time since the construction crew had arrived weeks before, Haven't Got a Clue had a steady stream of customers, which kept Tricia and her employees busy while Benny Goodman's and Tommy Dorsey's orchestras kept the customers entertained.

At exactly twelve o'clock, a black Mustang convertible showed up outside the shop's door. Steven wore a Red Sox baseball cap and aviator sunglasses. He tooted the horn.

Tricia retrieved her purse from under the cash desk. "I'll try to be back by one."

"Take your time—we're in no hurry, are we, Mr. Everett?"

"Not a bit."

"Very well. And thank you." Tricia strode out of the shop, walked six or seven feet, and stood before the car. Obviously Richardson wasn't going to leap out and open the door for her, so she did it herself and got in, reaching for the seat belt.

"You look great."

"Thank you."

"Where shall we go?"

The most expensive place to dine for lunch in the area was the Brookview Inn. It would serve him right for standing her up two days before. "The Brookview. They may be full, but I know the manager, so we can probably still get a table."

"Just give me the directions."

She did.

Less than five minutes later, Richardson pulled up to the Brookside Inn. As Tricia had suspected, the parking lot was nearly full. She strode up the front steps of the beautiful old inn and waited for Richardson to open the door for her, then she headed for the hostess station.

"What can I do for you?" asked the perky blonde. Her name tag said *Cindy*.

"Lunch for two, please."

"I'm sorry. We're fully booked. But if you'd like to wait."

"How long would that be?"

The woman frowned. "At least an hour, I'm afraid."

"We can go somewhere else," Richardson said.

"Is the private dining room available?" Tricia asked.

"Well, yes. But—"

"We'll take it," Tricia said, keeping her expression bland.

Cindy did nothing to accommodate them, just stared at Tricia.

"Is there a problem?"

"Well, it's just—"

"Is Mr. Barbero in?"

"Well, yes, but—"

"May I speak with him, please? Tell him it's Tricia."

Cindy forced a smile, picked up the telephone on the desk, and pressed a button. "Um, there's a Tricia at the front of the restaurant who'd like to speak to you." She listened for a moment, and then hung up the phone. "He'll be right out."

Richardson eyed the elegant surroundings.

Tricia smiled.

From an office just off the lobby, a door opened, and Antonio stepped out. "Tricia!" He held out his hands to take hers, and then leaned in to kiss her cheek. "To what do I owe the pleasure?"

Tricia never tired of hearing Antonio's delightful Italian accent. "I understand the dining room is fully booked, and my friend and I would like to have lunch. Is the private dining room available?"

"For you, always. And I would be happy to seat you myself."

"Thank you."

Antonio gestured for Tricia to lead the way down the short corridor to the pretty room Tricia had been in so many times before. A table set for two sat before the fireplace, which in summer boasted a fern in the firebox. Antonio seated Tricia and bent down to whisper in her ear. "I will of course comp your lunch."

"You'll do no such thing," she muttered.

Antonio straightened, looked her in the eye, then glanced over at Richardson, who had seated himself. He nodded. "Andre will be your server, but may I take your drink order?"

"That's so sweet of you, yes. I'll have my usual."

"And you, sir?"

"Uh. A beer. Whatever you've got on tap."

Antonio nodded. "Please let me know if there's anything I can do to make your visit more pleasant."

Tricia smiled and watched Antonio leave the room, closing the door behind him.

"Wow. Swank place," Richardson commented.

"Nothing's too good for a *New York Times* bestselling author. I see *A Killing in Mad Gate* is still on the list for the third week."

"Yes. I'm very pleased."

Tricia smiled again. Was it mean of her to make Richardson pay for what would be an outrageously expensive lunch?

Maybe.

"You still haven't told me why you stood me up the other day?"

"I do apologize. As I told you, I had a meeting that morning. It ran late."

"You also told me you needed a copy of your book to give to a local reporter—except our news guy says he never spoke to you on Wednesday or since."

Richardson said nothing.

"You also told me that you were staying at the Sheer Comfort Inn, and you weren't. And aren't."

"There was a mix-up."

Tricia kept her tone light. "Did I mention that my sister owns a share of that lovely establishment? She knows everything that goes on there. I enjoy hearing her talk about her businesses."

Richardson had the decency to look embarrassed at being caught in a lie. "Well, you see . . ." He seemed to run out of an explanation.

A knock at the door captured their attention. A waiter in dark slacks, white shirt, and black bow tie entered the room carrying their drinks on a tray. He set a cocktail napkin embossed with an image of the inn in gold before Tricia and set down her martini, then did the same for Richardson. He poured half the beer into the glass.

"I'm Andre. I'll be taking care of you this afternoon." He turned and procured two menus from a bracket attached to the wall. He opened them both, placing them before his charges. "I'll give you a few minutes."

"Thank you," Tricia said, her gaze zeroing in on the most expensive item on the menu. She set it aside as Andre left the room.

Tricia picked up her glass and took a sip of that damn fine cocktail before setting it down once again. "The talk all around town is about Carol Talbot's murder."

"Is it?" Richardson took a sip of his beer.

"How well did you know Carol?"

"Why do you ask?"

"You spoke to her not thirty minutes before her death. She slapped you. That tells me you two had more than a nodding acquaintance."

"I asked a question she thought impertinent." He took another sip of his drink, apparently unwilling to explain further. "How well did *you* know Mrs. Talbot?"

Tricia sighed and took another sip of her drink. "Not well. She and I were rivals at the Dog-Eared Page's darts tournament nights."

"Yes, I remember back on the ship your sister mentioning something about your prowess at the game."

"She exaggerates," Tricia said, but it wasn't exactly the truth. It still seemed a little strange to her that not only had she developed a liking for the game but that she had gotten so good at it.

"Would you like to play a game sometime?"

"Are you staying in Stoneham for a few more days?"

"It's a good possibility." Richardson sipped his beer. "I understand you've done your fair share of sleuthing."

"I've been known to ask a question or two."

"Like interviewing Mrs. Talbot's neighbors?" he probed.

Word did get around.

"I didn't interview them. I took my sister's dog for a walk and just happened to meet them when they were watering the flowers in their front garden."

"And did you find them as useless as witnesses as I did?"

"I wouldn't say *useless*; perhaps *clueless*. I mean about Carol's life prior to her being their neighbor."

"Don't be so sure."

Was that a challenge?

"And what do *you* know about Carol's life before she came to live here?" he asked.

"I assume you're referring to her murder conviction."

Richardson raised an eyebrow. "So you *have* been doing a little sleuthing."

Tricia merely shrugged. "What's your interest?"

"I want to write a fictionalized account of the case. Mrs. Talbot didn't want to rake up the past."

"Can you blame her?"

Richardson didn't comment, taking another sip of his beer.

"Will you have to go to Indiana to investigate the crime firsthand?"

"I've already been there. I've read the police reports, the newspaper accounts, talked with anybody who would respond, and came up with a whole lot of nothing new."

"Perhaps it was an open-and-shut case."

He shook his head and frowned. "Why would a child kill?"

"According to what I heard—and fourth- or fifth-hand, I might add—it was childish jealousy."

He shook his head. "That's too pat an explanation. I want to dig deeper."

"Now that Carol's dead, can you?"

He shrugged.

"Chief Baker said he was satisfied that you weren't a suspect in Carol's death."

"Am I to assume you don't feel the same way?"

It was Tricia's turn to shrug. "Well, you lied to me when you said you were staying at the Sheer Comfort Inn. You lied about to whom you were giving the book you bummed off me. Why should I believe you now?"

Richardson managed a wan smile. "A lie of omission."

"A lie nonetheless."

He let out a breath. "The Sheer Comfort Inn cost more than I wanted to pay."

Tricia eyed him skeptically.

"You know how it goes; publishers pay twice a year. I've overextended myself, and it's a long way until October and my next check. I'm on a strict budget, which it looks like this lunch is about to blow sky-high."

"*You* asked *me* out on Tuesday night, and again today," Tricia reminded him.

"So I did."

"And why was that?"

"I thought maybe you could help me convince Mrs. Talbot to open up to me."

"And what made you change your mind and stand me up? The fact that once she was dead, I couldn't help you in that regard?"

Richardson offered a weak smile. "I told you, my meeting ran over."

"But you didn't call. Not for two days."

"I did apologize."

Big deal.

He leaned closer. "We could still work together on this, you know."

He *was* challenging her. *Hell hath no fury like a woman scorned.* Tricia wasn't exactly *scorned*, but *annoyed* pretty much covered it. And she was determined not to feel guilty. If nothing else, she knew Richardson would no doubt have a good line of credit and could deduct the cost of the lunch as a business expense. And what was she likely to get out of his proposed alliance? A sentence in the acknowledgments of his next book? That was hardly an inducement.

"I'll have to think about it."

Yes, she needed to think about Carol's death, the questions she needed to ask—and at whom to direct them—to figure out who'd killed the woman and why. Sharing that information with Richardson? She wasn't so sure about that. "I'll think about it."

"And when are you likely to give me an answer?"

"In a few days."

He nodded, almost smirking. "You're going to punish me, right?"

"Maybe just a little," she admitted.

His smug expression deepened.

Play cat and mouse with me and you might get badly scratched, Tricia thought.

"Why don't we talk about it in a day or two? And in the meantime, why don't we have a lovely lunch and converse about other subjects?"

"As you wish."

A knock on the door preceded Andre's return. "Ready to order?"

"Ah, just in time. I'll have the truffled lobster risotto." The richest, most expensive item on the lunch menu.

"With a side salad?" Andre asked hopefully.

"Of course. House dressing will be fine."

Richardson scowled. "I'll have the French dip."

Not nearly as exciting—or as pricey—as the lobster.

"And another round?" Andre asked.

"That would be lovely," Tricia said, and smiled sweetly at her companion.

Maybe she was just a *little* bit scorned after all.

TWELVE

On the drive back to Haven't Got a Clue, Tricia decided she would indeed accept Richardson's proposal—but she was determined to do it on her own terms. And that meant she might not share everything she learned. At least not immediately.

He was a stranger in the village, and while she wasn't a native of Stoneham, she certainly had more contacts than Richardson—one of whom worked in her store. Mr. Everett would never speak ill of anyone, but he was still a potential font of information. If she asked just the right questions, and in a nonchalant way, it was likely he'd answer them. And if not, she could always go back to Grace.

Richardson dropped her off in front of Haven't Got a Clue, but instead of entering her store, Tricia remembered she needed to stop at the Patisserie. Not only did she need to check on the cake order for Pixie's wedding shower but she wanted to buy a dozen raspberry thumbprint cookies—Mr. Everett's favorites—to help grease the informational wheels. Luckily, Nikki Brimfield-Smith was ringing up a sale for the only other customer in the shop. "Be right with you, Tricia." She turned back to the guy with a white bakery box before him on the counter. "Here's your change. Enjoy!"

"Thanks."

They watched him leave.

"Long time no talk to," Nikki said.

"It's been hectic since the renovation on my loft began. I'll be glad when it's over."

"I'd love to see the final results."

"I'll finally have enough space to entertain—and it'll be fun to show it off, so I think a party will definitely be in order." She changed the subject. "I understand little Russell is now in day care."

Nikki nodded sadly. She had wanted to be a stay-at-home mom, but it hadn't made economic sense. "I was hoping we wouldn't have to go that route, but he was getting too big to have here in the shop—it's just too dangerous for a small child. And I got a great deal for signing him up at Stoneham Day Care." Another enterprise of Nigela Ricita Associates.

"Really?"

"It was the darndest thing. They told me I was the hundredth person to walk through the door and gave me an astounding discount. And it's good for five years. That'll take Russell Junior right up to kindergarten."

"Wow, that *is* amazing." Tricia made a mental note to quiz Angelica on that later.

"I spoke to Russ yesterday. I was surprised he isn't looking into Carol Talbot's murder."

Nikki's expression soured. "No, and he won't be doing any of that crusading reporting in the future, either. He's got a family now," she said firmly.

"But being a reporter is his life."

"He can report on all the other—much more pleasant—things that happen around Stoneham. Like the Girl Scouts planting that tree in the village square; the recipe of the month—I'm helping him with that; and other cheerful or inspirational things."

In other words, soft—very soft—news.

"He sounded a little down," Tricia observed.

"He'll get over it," Nikki said rather flippantly. Didn't she see that taking away the thing he loved most might be detrimental to their long-term relationship? That it might just drive a wedge between them? Nikki had been jealous of Tricia's past relationship with her husband, so Tricia wasn't about to voice her opinion on the subject.

"Now, what can I do for you today, Tricia?" Nikki was back to being her usual cheerful self.

"I came by to make sure the cake for Pixie's bridal shower will be ready to pick up tomorrow morning."

"No need. I'll be delivering and setting it up myself."

Tricia blinked. She wouldn't have thought half a white sheet cake with pink flowers would be worth the trouble. But then she knew Nikki considered herself to be an artist when it came to cakes and pastries. She probably would have preferred to make something much more elaborate, but this was to be a small party. Besides, Tricia knew Pixie was already thrilled at just the prospect of a shower thrown in her honor.

"Anything else?"

"Just some—"

"Thumbprint cookies," Nikki said, anticipating the answer.

"Yes. They're Mr. Everett's favorites." And obviously Tricia had ordered them far too many times.

Nikki scooped up the cookies, depositing them in a white pastry bag, and Tricia paid for her purchase. "I'll see you tomorrow."

"Bye!"

Tricia left the shop and headed down the sidewalk for her own store. But before she even entered, the sound of clanging—like someone playing the "Anvil Chorus"—permeated Haven't Got a Clue, making her wince with each tooth-rattling bang. She could see by the tufts of orange sticking out of Pixie's and Mr. Everett's ears that they were back to wearing earplugs and that, thanks to the noise, the shop was once again devoid of customers.

Tricia set the white bakery bag on the counter and reached for a pair of the onetime-use plugs when, suddenly, the noise stopped.

"Thank goodness," Pixie said, and yanked out one of her plugs.

"What's going on?" Tricia asked.

"They're replacing the sewage pipe."

Tricia wrinkled her nose. There were some aspects of the renovation for which she just didn't need the details.

"How long do you think we have before it starts up again?"

"Maybe a minute."

"How was your lunch, Ms. Miles?" Mr. Everett asked.

"Delicious. I had the truffled lobster risotto."

"Whoo-hoo!" Pixie whooped.

"I was tempted by dessert, but decided I would rather share something with the two of you, so I stopped at the Patisserie and bought some cookies. Thanks to all the dust, we haven't had them in a couple of weeks."

"Aw, you're the best," Pixie said, picking up the bag and taking a peek. "Ohh, your favorite, Mr. E."

Mr. Everett immediately brightened.

Pixie took a cookie and passed the bag to her coworker, who did likewise. Stuffed with lobster, Tricia passed.

"So, what did you and the big-time author talk about?" Pixie asked.

Tricia could have fibbed, but chose to tell the truth. "Poor Carol. Apparently he's been asking questions about her around the village. He thinks she'd be a great subject for his next book."

"Really?" Pixie asked, skeptically.

"Really?" Mr. Everett repeated, sounding aggrieved. Of course, he knew about Carol's past and Pixie didn't. Yet. Tricia wasn't going to go around gossiping about it, but it was sure to be brought out in the open once again for a new generation to learn—or wouldn't Nikki allow Russ to report that, either?

"I must admit, despite our many darts games, I really didn't know much about Carol. Like—did she work? What were her other hobbies? Did she have friends and family who will mourn her loss?"

"Gee, I dunno," Pixie said, sounding clueless.

"Life is so fragile," Tricia went on. "I wish I'd taken the time to get to know her better."

Mr. Everett let out a breath. "Although I wasn't friendly with her, I know that she worked at the library."

"Oh? I guess I don't remember seeing her on my visits to see Lois Kerr."

"She didn't work at the checkout desk, but I used to see her shelving books and performing other duties."

The cookies had worked, and now Tricia had a starting point for her own investigation into Carol's death.

The construction guys must have taken only a five-minute break, for suddenly the banging two floors up started in again. Tricia, Pixie, and Mr. Everett immediately stuffed the plugs back in their ears. Tricia grabbed the pad of paper and a pen that sat next to the phone and scribbled down a note, reading it over before handing it to her employees.

Going to run an errand for Pixie's shower. Should be back in an hour or so.

Pixie grinned, her gold canine tooth flashing. "You're the best," she mouthed.

Mr. Everett merely nodded.

Grabbing her purse, Tricia made a break for the exit, feeling guilty to be leaving her staff to face the noise and dust without her, but, she told herself, it was for a good cause. She was determined to find out who killed Carol Talbot before Steven Richardson could.

Tricia was ashamed to admit that it had been more than a year since she'd visited the Stoneham Public Library. But, really, if she wanted a book, she could afford to buy it—and buy them she did, in droves. While the many used bookstores in Stoneham brought prosperity to the village—and to most of the booksellers—it didn't help the average citizen. Lots of people without discretionary cash depended on the local library to fulfill their yearning for new, bold, adventurous entertainment. Tricia had contributed to the library—with both books and checks—but sometimes it was just nice to pay a visit and soak in the wonderful aura that the library exuded.

And while it had been quite some time since she'd visited, it had been even longer since she'd spoken to the library's director, Lois Kerr.

Tricia bypassed the reception desk and headed straight for Lois's office. She found the director's door open and Lois hunched over her computer, furiously hacking at the keys. The years had not been kind to the director, who looked like she'd aged a decade since Tricia had last spoken with her. She knocked on the doorjamb. "Hi, Lois. Have you got a minute?"

Lois momentarily held up a hand, pounded out a few more words, and then stabbed the enter key with such force, it could have broken something. She looked up. "Gosh, that felt good."

"What on earth were you typing?"

Lois shook herself. "A note with the intent to reason with an idiot. A member of the Board of Selectmen wants to cut our budget by fifty percent because he feels that, thanks to the Internet, libraries are obsolete. What an—" She stopped herself, but Tricia had a feeling she knew the particular noun the librarian would have liked to have said, and she smiled despite herself.

Lois stood and gestured toward the guest chair before her desk. "Sit down and tell me what's up, although I have a feeling I know why you're here."

Tricia stepped forward, took the seat, and succinctly said, "Carol Talbot."

"I'm not surprised." Lois moved to close her office door before she resumed her seat. "All of us here at the library were sad to learn of her death."

The words were right, but Lois's expression seemed to say another thing entirely.

"Did you know her well?"

Lois seemed to squirm. "Well enough."

And what did that mean?

Tricia chose her words carefully. "Did you know about Carol's past?"

"It seems you did," Lois said, without admitting anything.

"I've heard secondhand. Did you hear firsthand?"

Lois nodded. "Yes. When you work with someone for almost thirty years, the dirty laundry is sometimes aired. I know all about Carol's murder conviction. Truth be told, I Googled it only a couple of years ago out of morbid curiosity. But, actually, Carol was pretty up front about it."

"And how did you react?"

Lois offered a weak laugh. "I didn't. Because it seemed to me that when Carol spoke of her past it wasn't with remorse—more like annoyance. Being incarcerated interrupted her life and changed its course. It was then I decided I didn't want her as a friend."

"How sad; for both of you."

Lois nodded. "Like you, I read murder mysteries for entertainment, but actually knowing a murderer—murderess—changed the way I feel about such books."

Sadly, Tricia had been acquainted with far too many murderers, the worst of which was the man who'd killed her ex-husband. Somehow, she'd managed to hang on to her love of mystery fiction, because it was the one place where justice always seemed to prevail. Was there a chance Bob Kelly would get away with murdering her ex-husband—despite the stacks of evidence against him? If there was one person on earth who could weasel out of trouble, it would be Bob. Though she might be in denial, Tricia refused to accept that scenario.

For the most part.

Damn, but she hated that debilitating feeling of uncertainty. Bob's attorneys had succeeded in having his trial postponed time after time. It was now scheduled for the fall, and Tricia felt conflicted. The idea of having to go over that horrible day in front of a courtroom of people filled her with dread, but the prosecution needed her testimony to convict him. She would do whatever was necessary to assure that outcome.

She put it out of her mind.

"I'm assuming Carol was at least an acceptable employee," Tricia said.

"For the most part. She performed her duties in a reasonable fashion."

"And what is it you're not saying?"

Lois shrugged. "I guess because of her past, it shouldn't be surprising that she wasn't good at relating to people—our patrons. As long as she worked behind the scenes, she was an exemplary employee. But put her in front of the public and there was a real disconnect. She didn't seem to have a sympathy chip. If someone came in and said they'd lost a loved one, Carol missed the opportunity to empathize."

How sad.

"Of late, there were other problems, but Carol was addressing them."

Lois didn't elaborate, and Tricia got the feeling that asking what she meant wouldn't get her any answers. She changed tacks. "Did Carol have many friends?"

"She only ever spoke about her neighbors—and even that wasn't often. She did seem a little bit more outgoing after she lost her husband."

"She was lonely?"

"I think so."

"Did you know her husband?"

"Not really. He came to some of our celebrations, but he didn't speak much or mix—not even with Carol. I got the impression they weren't particularly devoted."

"Why was that?"

"Even when they were together—they weren't. Their body language, maybe." Lois shrugged and then looked Tricia in the eye.

"Did she have any hobbies—besides playing darts, I mean?"

"Yes, she mentioned that she'd been playing regularly at the Dog-Eared Page. I gather you two went head-to-head on a regular basis."

"We did play often—and usually not on the same team. But other than that, what did she do in her leisure time?"

"You mean like gardening or something?"

Tricia nodded.

Lois frowned. "She often mentioned her husband's collection."

"What did he collect?"

"I'm not sure. She never really specified. She mentioned artwork and playing cards. For all I know, he could have collected football or baseball posters and trading cards. I gather some of the old cards are very valuable."

"I've heard that, too."

Lois leaned forward. "Bright and early Wednesday morning, I had a visit from thriller author Steven Richardson asking the very same questions as you."

"Oh?" Tricia asked with faux sincerity.

"Yes. He told me he wanted to write about Carol's unfortunate past."

"And what did you tell him?"

Lois's smile was ironic. "A lot less than I've told you."

That the librarian held her in such esteem meant a lot to Tricia, and yet it didn't seem appropriate to say anything in reply.

"He came bearing a gift—his latest book."

So that's where it went. Had it been the reason Baker had eliminated Richardson as a suspect so quickly? But how could the author have proved that that particular copy of the book was the same tome he'd taken from Haven't Got a Clue?

"I suppose you've spoken with Chief Baker as well," Tricia said.

Lois nodded. "Not ten minutes after Richardson left my office."

"Did he know about Carol's past?"

"Yes. I don't think he learned anything new during our conversation." She eyed Tricia. "I'm rather surprised you didn't come to see me sooner than this."

"There have been many distractions," Tricia said truthfully.

Lois nodded, but didn't inquire further.

Tricia stood. "Thank you for speaking with me. I appreciate your candor."

"I know you have Carol's best interests at heart. Not many people would."

A pang of guilt cascaded through Tricia. Carol's best interests? Hardly. She wanted to prove her father was innocent of the crime, if only to stave off even more embarrassment from his antics. And she still had to report his latest indiscretion to Angelica, which was going to be painful for both of them—the telling and the listening.

Tricia turned and opened the office door, but paused. "I hope it won't be so long before we have an opportunity to speak again, and under much better circumstances."

"As do I."

Tricia had hoped she'd feel better after speaking with the library's director, but as she walked back to her car she realized she had a lot of catching up to do if she was going to figure out who killed Carol Talbot before Steven Richardson did.

She was already more than two steps behind him.

THIRTEEN

"And how was your day?" Angelica asked as she poured their first martinis of the evening. It was going to take that kind of rocket fuel to get through the ensuing conversation. Tricia was glad Angelica had stopped somewhere and picked up a cheerful bouquet of mixed flowers. The pink and red roses, lilies, and greenery not only looked beautiful and brightened Angelica's kitchen, but their heavenly scent permeated the kitchen as well.

"After a morning of doing nothing, the construction crew showed up and attacked the main waste stack, which meant we had no bathroom for several hours. But now I guess the upstairs bathroom is set to go as far as plumbing is concerned."

"That's good."

"Good, yes. But not everything about today was good. In fact, I have some very unhappy news for you."

"I don't know what could be worse after what happened last evening."

"Then take a good, stiff swig of your drink, because what I have to tell you will be hard to hear."

Angelica did as she was told and then plunked her glass back onto the counter with a noticeable *thud*. "Okay. Give it to me straight."

Tricia let out a long and heavy breath. This was not going to be an easy conversation. "I went to Fred Pillins's apartment this morning. If Daddy was there, he wouldn't open the door to see me."

"Which isn't surprising."

"But since I was there, I went to have a look at the Dumpster in the parking lot."

No sooner had she said those words than tears began to form in her sister's eyes. "Please don't tell me—"

Tricia nodded. "I'm afraid so. Everything Daddy stole from you last night was in there—rotting."

"What on earth was he thinking?" Angelica cried, her anguish quite palpable.

"My guess is he thought he could rope poor Fred into trying to flog the stuff to his regular customers, but no way was Fred going to be open to that kind of deceit."

Tears leaked from Angelica's eyes. "That Daddy could steal from me is one humiliating thing. That he would try to rope a law-abiding citizen into aiding and abetting his despicable actions . . ."

She didn't have to say more. Tricia knew exactly how she felt.

"Have you reported the theft to the police or your insurance company?"

"No. Much as I would like to see Daddy pay for his abhorrent behavior, I'm still his daughter."

Was she?

"What are we going to do about him?"

Angelica sighed. "Perhaps the only thing we *can* do is just give him what he wants—money—and tell him to go away."

"So that he can wreak havoc on some other community?"

"It's not a perfect solution, but the only viable thing I can think of to do." Angelica picked up her drink once more. "Please, can't we talk about something—*anything*—other than Daddy?"

Tricia thought about telling her sister about her visit to the library, but that might bring up the subject of their father once again. Was her lunch with Richardson a safer subject, or just as potentially volatile?

She decided to risk it.

"I finally had lunch with Steven."

"And?" Angelica prompted.

"In the Brookview's private dining room. Antonio offered to comp it, but I told him no. I was determined to make Steven pay for his lies and for the way he treated me."

"You little bitch, you."

Tricia smiled. "The truffled lobster risotto was excellent."

"Just another recipe I picked up on my travels," Angelica boasted, but then frowned. "I suppose you only spoke about Carol's murder."

"It was the main topic of discussion. He already knew all about her past, and apparently her present. He's way ahead of me."

"And why do *you* care?"

"I think we both know the answer to that."

Angelica sighed, nodding. "Let's talk about something completely different."

"Such as?"

"Pixie's shower. I've spoken with catering at the Brookview, and we're set to go for the food tomorrow, and I contacted everyone on your list to tell them about the change of venue."

"Great. I've already ordered half a white sheet cake from the Patisserie."

"Um, yes, I know," Angelica said, her voice just a tad higher—meaning something was up.

"And?" Tricia asked.

"I think it's a great idea to have a white cake. But I spoke to Nikki about the presentation."

"Presentation? It's a sheet cake."

"But that's so pedestrian. Honestly, it needs to go with the theme of the party."

"It's only going to be eaten."

"Yes, but don't you want Pixie to remember this party for the rest of her life?"

"She'll have her wedding cake to remember for the rest of her life. Tomorrow we'll take pictures of the cake before it's cut and they will refresh her memory in years to come."

Angelica scowled.

"I'm not going to win this one, am I?"

"I'm afraid not," Angelica said contritely. "Nikki thought my idea was perfect and made a sketch right on the spot."

"A sketch?" Tricia could see the dollar signs mounting. Not that she couldn't afford to make a grand gesture, but a simple shower for less than a dozen seemed to be turning into an extravaganza.

"You know that Pixie is all about vintage clothes. What better cake than a doll in a big nineteen-fifties dress. Think Lucille Ball; she was the quintessential woman of that era."

Tricia frowned. "Like a Barbie doll?"

"No, no, no. That's too childish. Perhaps a mannequin. That's what Nikki sketched." She turned and retrieved a piece of paper from the counter behind her.

Tricia studied the drawing. The mannequin did indeed wear a shirtwaist dress, with a wide belt at the middle and pearls around the neck. It kind of did remind her of the costumes Lucille Ball wore on *I Love Lucy*, which she'd seen in reruns since she was a child.

"Mind you, this was just the *first* sketch. We discussed it in more detail, and we'll see the final result tomorrow."

"Well, I have to admit, I do think Pixie would enjoy it. But how do you cut such a cake?"

"That's not your concern. You just have to pay the extra it will cost. In fact, since we're hosting this little soiree, I decided to hire one of the waitresses from the Brookview Inn to act as our server. Nikki will give her instructions on how to cut the cake, and we can feel free to mingle with our guests."

The costs for this little shindig were beginning to spiral out of control.

Angelica leaned forward. "Are you okay? You look a bit dazed."

"I'm a little overwhelmed," Tricia admitted.

"You *do* want Pixie to be happy, don't you?" Angelica pressed.

And now she was pulling a guilt trip?

"Yes, I do."

"And it'll be *fun*. Just wait until you see your costume."

"Costume? This isn't Halloween."

"Oh, but it's a theme party. I've asked everybody to come in an outfit from the era. And for those who don't, I'll have a dress-up box."

"Like we had when we were kids?"

"Oh, I'd outgrown all that by the time you were ready to use it."

"Uh-huh?" Tricia seemed to recall a few times when Angelica had condescended to play with her younger sibling—but only because a blizzard howled outside and she was bored.

"Ginny thinks it's a great idea," Angelica added.

"You spoke about this to Ginny before you spoke to me?"

"Well, I wasn't sure how you'd react."

"Oh, yes, you did."

"I hoped you'd be open to the concept. And it would—"

"Make Pixie happy—I know." Tricia let out a breath. She hadn't dressed up in costume in ages. Not since she'd hosted a Halloween fund-raising party for the nonprofit she'd worked for in New York. Those attending had really gotten in the spirit of things—pun intended—and it had been a rollicking success.

"Okay, so what *is* my costume? A poodle skirt?"

"Oh, no—that's mine."

"Why do you get to wear a poodle skirt?"

"Because Sarge will be my accessory."

"He's not a poodle."

"He doesn't know that."

Tricia had no answer for that leap in logic.

"I thought you'd look terrific as Sandy from *Grease*. You know, an off-the-shoulder tight black blouse, tight black Capri pants, and red heels. You've got the body for it and already have the shoes. Curl and tease your hair, and you'll look perfect!"

Perfect? Tricia doubted that. But it might be fun. Still, she wasn't about to let her sister know that.

"I guess I could," Tricia said, sounding just a little bored.

"Excellent."

"What's Ginny dressing up as?"

"I thought she'd make an adorable Holly Golightly."

"A redheaded Audrey Hepburn?"

"All she needs is a little black dress, some rhinestones, and a cigarette holder."

Tricia shrugged. "If she's game, I don't see the problem. What about Grace?"

"Uh, she may not want to appear in costume—that's what the dress-up box is for."

"Okay," Tricia said, feeling just a little beaten.

"Great."

Angelica's mood had done a one-eighty since they'd changed topics. And if Tricia was truthful, her own spirits had risen, too.

The next day's forecast was for sunny skies; the location was wonderful. The food and cake would be divine. Pixie's shower would be perfect, filled with happy memories, and a good time would be had by all.

Of that, Tricia had no doubt.

FOURTEEN

As predicted, the skies dawned clear, and the weatherman assured his audience that the temperature wouldn't go higher than seventy-six.

Tricia showed up at her store just before opening. She'd given Pixie the day off, and Mr. Everett arrived looking dapper in a crisp white shirt and blue-and-white polka dot bow tie, which had been a birthday gift from Pixie. He looked very pleased indeed. It wasn't often that Tricia left the store in his charge. Not because she didn't trust him—because she did; with her life. But he worried so about making a mistake or charging a customer too much. But this was to be a very special day, and Mr. Everett had been adamant about not closing the store during Pixie's bridal shower.

"That woman stuff is just that—for ladies. I wouldn't be comfortable in that kind of situation, and this way I can not only give you a break, but assure that dear Pixie will have a wonderful day."

"You are so sweet," Tricia said, and gave him a peck on the cheek, which made his cheeks glow a rosy pink.

Angelica's car pulled up outside Haven't Got a Clue, and she honked the horn.

"You'd better get going," Mr. Everett advised, and Tricia grabbed her shoes—the only part of her costume Angelica would let her provide—and headed out the door. "I've got my cell phone. Call me if you have any problems."

"I will," he promised, and waved a cheery good-bye.

Ginny was already in the car, riding shotgun, and both she and Angelica were wearing matching (and probably brand-new) Ray-Bans.

"Do we look cool or what?" Ginny called as Tricia hopped into the backseat.

"Very cool," Tricia agreed as Ginny handed her a pair of the same glasses, which she donned before buckling up.

Angelica checked her side mirror and then took off with a girlish squeal.

"I've only been gone from home for ten minutes, and already I'm loving girls' day out!" Ginny called as the wind rushed through their hair from all four open windows.

"We are in for some serious pampering today, girls. Hair, makeup, nails, lunch—the works!" Angelica promised.

"Shouldn't we have invited Pixie to join us? I mean, it *is* her day."

"I *did* invite her," Angelica said, "but she said she had some last-minute details to take care of. She bought a new dress—"

"New?" Ginny demanded, laughing.

"New for *her*," Angelica clarified, "and it needed some alterations."

"I sometimes think Pixie would be better off working as a tailor," Ginny said. "She does beautiful work."

"Hey, I need her. It took pretty big feet to fill your shoes. The third time might *not* be the charm," Tricia said, and Ginny laughed.

The Stoneham Salon and Day Spa wasn't far from the heart of the village, and Angelica pulled into their crowded parking lot. "I dropped off our frocks—and your pants, Tricia—earlier. After lunch, we can dress right here and go straight to the party."

"Sounds like another one of your great plans," Ginny said with enthusiasm.

They got out of the car, each of them bringing their purses and extra shoes, and entered the day spa.

Tricia hadn't yet had an opportunity to check out Angelica's latest business venture under her Nigela Ricita umbrella, but it was undoubtedly classic Angelica. In other words: gorgeous. And, Tricia was pleased to note, every hair and nail station was occupied. And it wasn't just tourists who were partaking of the services on offer. Tricia recognized a few familiar faces, including Carol Talbot's neighbor, who was having her roots touched up. She gave Tricia a vague kind of wave as she, Ginny, and Angelica were escorted to their private room.

Private room! It reminded Tricia of the spa on board the *Celtic Lady* cruise ship, where she and Angelica had had their nails done. And like at that spa, the three women were given pretty pink smocks and led to the pedicure baths.

"Oh, I could get used to this," Ginny said as they took their seats at the three pedi stations. And soon their toes were surrounded by warm, swirling water. "*This* is the life," she said, then leaned back in her padded chair and sighed. "I feel like I haven't got a care in the world. Until I start thinking about Monday, that is."

"Oh, don't do that," Angelica admonished.

"But I *need* to. I have so many things on my plate if I'm going to get this wine and jazz festival finalized before Wednesday. I feel terribly guilty for taking a day off right before the final push."

"But that's *exactly* when you need to be your freshest. And you can't do your best work if your muscles are tied up in knots and your nail polish is chipped," Angelica said. To Tricia's knowledge, her sister had *never* had a chipped nail in her entire life.

"I have learned so much in the past few months, sometimes I think my head will explode," Ginny said as one of the spa's workers entered the room, offering a refreshing cucumber-and-lime-infused mineral water to each of them.

"No, thanks," Angelica said. "We're fine."

Ginny looked a little confused, and Tricia surmised that she would have liked to try the concoction. But then Angelica reached for her enormous purse and pulled out a thermos and, from a plastic bag, three plastic cups. "I thought it might be nicer to share a few mimosas."

Ginny perked right up. "I'm game."

And so the women sipped their drinks while their tootsies soaked.

"So what's the latest gossip around the village?" Ginny asked.

"Not much," Angelica said, giving Tricia a knowing look. There was no way either of them was going to mention their father—and they hoped no one else would, either.

"Next to the wine and jazz festival, Carol Talbot's murder pales," Tricia said, noting how the color of her drink went so well with the decor.

"Everybody in my office—except me, that is—knew her," Ginny said. "They all had stories to tell, too."

"Oh?" Tricia asked.

"That she was a bit of a lush."

Knew that. Move on, Tricia thought.

"That she used to take very long walks around the village, sometimes walking to Milford or Wilton and back."

Did Carol do a lot of thinking—contemplating—on those walks?

"And one of the girls said she saw the old bat at the professional building up by the highway."

That was where several doctors and dentists who served the village worked.

"Any office in particular?" Angelica asked.

"Yeah, Dr. Kennedy—the shrink."

"Really?" Angelica said, sounding halfway interested.

Ginny nodded. "The girls, and I don't know why I call them that, since all of them are at least ten years older than me, had a field day speculating about Carol's problem."

Her problem was that she was a child murderer and may have never gotten beyond that terrible crime. Or maybe—as Lois Kerr had pointed out—she hadn't ever come to terms with that fact and hadn't appeared to feel any remorse. Ginny didn't mention Carol's sordid past, so maybe none of the women in her office was old enough to remember. Or was it that people in New England just didn't talk about those things? Although Tricia had never had much trouble getting some of the citizens of Stoneham to open up to her. Perhaps it was because she had an honest face. She'd inherited it from her Grandma Miles, who apparently hadn't passed that trait along to her ne'er-do-well son.

"This latest murder has once again put us at the bottom of the list for safest village in New Hampshire," Angelica groused. "Why couldn't we be just some lovely, sleepy village? No, instead there seems to be an undercurrent of passion that boils twenty-four/seven beneath the soil—or is it something in the water?"

"Maybe," Ginny agreed, "but I'm guessing there's no water in these drinks, so I think we're safe."

Tricia couldn't help herself, and she grinned.

The conversation turned back to the upcoming festival, and Angelica listened, enraptured, as Ginny went through the tasks she was doing and overseeing to make this first incarnation of the festival a success. But Tricia's thoughts circled back to Ginny's mention of Carol consulting a psychologist—or was the doctor a psychiatrist? Because of doctor-patient confidentiality—and HIPAA laws—Tricia was never likely destined to find out.

* * *

After a light lunch catered by the Brookview Inn—which consisted of field greens with a vinaigrette dressing—that Angelica said was more than enough, as there was to be an ungodly amount of appetizers, sugar, and fatty retro foods sure to clog everyone's arteries at the party, they donned their costumes and Angelica drove them to the Sheer Comfort Inn, parking in the reserved spot that was always open just for her.

Pale pink roses spilled over the picket fence out front, while white wicker chairs, love seat, and tables with matching blue-and-white striped pillows decorated the porch. The weather cooperated, delivering a sunny day that wasn't too hot—and with low humidity.

They entered through the kitchen and met Sarah Morgan, the current innkeeper, who assured Angelica that everything was indeed ready for the party.

They walked through the dining room and into the living room, both of which had gone through an astounding transformation. Gone—or at least disguised—were the antiques and quaint furnishings that fitted the Victorian-era home. The place now looked like it had been primped by a set designer.

Sarah had performed the sleight of hand, covering the furnishings with white sheets and adding black-and-white-checked throw pillows. Posters of movie stars and singers adorned the walls. An old record player sat on a table in the corner with a stack of forty-five RPM records on the spindle: Patti Page, Buddy Holly, Connie Francis, Elvis, and more. In the dining room, the sideboard was covered in the same checkered fabric, with a matching throw rug to complete the transformation. Pink fuzzy dice hung from the chandelier. Where had they gotten all the memorabilia?

Grace was the first of the guests to arrive, and she gushed over the party's nineteen-fifties theme. She was soon followed by Mary Fairchild and a couple of members from Haven't Got a Clue's Tuesday night book club.

Grace had donned a blue pillbox hat with a short veil that perfectly set off the pearls that hung from her neck. The other guests raided the dress-up box and were busy taking selfies when at precisely two o'clock, Grace said, "Everyone's here but Pixie."

"She's probably going to make an entrance," Ginny guessed, and struck a pose with her cigarette-holder prop. She looked adorable dressed as Audrey Hepburn.

The roar of a big engine caused the women to move en masse to the parlor's front windows. Pixie had indeed arrived in style. In fact, in a big classic convertible. It pulled up to the front of the Sheer Comfort Inn with Fred behind the wheel. He parked, got out of the driver's side, and ran to the passenger side to open the door and help his white-gloved lady disembark. Pixie was dressed to the hilt in a firecracker-red polka dot dress that perfectly matched the car's paint job, sunglasses, and a white scarf draped around her head to preserve her do from the wind.

Everyone ran onto the porch to laugh and applaud as a red-faced Fred escorted Pixie up the walk. Pixie looked like a movie star from the golden age of Hollywood—looking joyful—as though she were greeting her fans on a red carpet.

"Welcome!" Tricia called and laughed. For some odd reason, she felt as though she ought to be throwing confetti.

"Oh, you look divine!" Angelica called.

"Thank you, thank you," Pixie said as she mounted the stairs, blowing kisses to her waiting public. "Thank you all for coming."

"Let's get this party started," Ginny called, and opened the porch door to allow first Pixie to enter, and then the rest of the ladies.

"Great car, Fred. Is it yours? What make is it?" Tricia asked.

Fred fumbled with the set of keys in his hand, not meeting her gaze. "A nineteen fifty-nine Cadillac Eldorado. It's not mine. I borrowed it from a buddy of mine. He takes it to all the car shows around the state. I thought Pixie might like to arrive in style."

"Would you like to stay for the festivities?" Angelica said.

"Uh, no, thanks. All this girl stuff makes me crazy. Besides, I don't want to leave the car alone for a second. My buddy will kill me if I return it with a scratch on it."

"We'll save you some goodies. I assume you'll be back to pick Pixie up."

"Sure thing."

He gave a good-bye wave and headed back for the car. Angelica went back inside the inn, but Tricia hung back. "Fred!"

Fred turned.

Tricia hurried over to the car. "Is something wrong?"

"Uh. Well." He seemed to find the front seat of the vintage car to be of infinite interest. "I, uh . . ."

"What is it you're trying not to tell me?"

"Well . . . I sort of had to ask your father to leave my apartment."

Of course.

"Can I ask why?"

"It just wasn't working out."

"Did it have anything to do with the stolen cold cuts from Booked for Lunch?"

Fred looked panicked. "I didn't know where they came from. Thursday night he called me with some screwy plan," Fred babbled. "I didn't want anything to do with it. I told him—"

"It's okay. Don't worry about it." Then Tricia forced herself to ask the next dreaded question. "Has he stolen from you?"

"No! Well. Not stolen. Borrowed and . . . hasn't returned it."

Oh dear. And after Pixie had warned him to take all his valuables out of the apartment.

"Can it be replaced?"

"Not really. It was my father's watch. It wasn't worth much, just sentimental value."

"I see." She forced a smile. "I'll do my best to see that it's returned to you."

"I'd appreciate that, Tricia."

"And I appreciate your kindness to my father and am so sorry he repaid you in this manner."

Fred just shrugged and again didn't seem able to look her in the eye.

Peals of laughter came through the screened windows overlooking the porch, reminding Tricia she had a party to attend.

"Thank you for all you've done for Pixie. You've changed her life," Fred said.

"And so have you."

A blush inched up Fred's neck to color his cheeks. "I'd better get this car back to my friend."

He climbed behind the wheel and started the engine, while Tricia returned to the porch, standing there long enough to wave good-bye before she joined the rest of the ladies in the parlor.

Pixie had removed her scarf, glasses, and gloves and stood in the center of the room. "I can't believe it. This is the first party that anyone's ever thrown for me!" she squealed with delight.

"Wait'll you see the cake and the stack of presents," Ginny sang.

"I get presents?" Pixie gushed.

"Of course. This is a bridal shower," Angelica said, and laughed.

"Will there be games, too?" Pixie asked.

"What's a shower without games?" Grace called.

Debra, a server from the Brookview Inn, was decked out in a black vintage waitress dress with a crisp white apron. "Would anyone like some punch?"

"I would," Ginny called as everyone was seated.

Pixie pulled Tricia and Angelica aside. "I don't know how to thank you guys."

"We're happy to do it," Tricia said.

Pixie took in the decorations and peeked around Angelica to see the cake standing in the place of honor on the dining room's sideboard. "And that cake!"

"Nikki made it."

It was a cake to behold. In honor of Pixie's vintage wardrobe, Nikki had fashioned a two-foot-high confection in the shape of a dressmaker's mannequin, but she'd changed the design to a stylized wedding gown with a sweetheart neckline, a skirt with oodles of fondant ruffles, and a string of pearls.

"Oh, it's gorgeous." Tears filled Pixie's eyes. "You know, I've always been afraid to let myself be truly happy, because something always happens to spoil it. But right now—this is the best day of my entire life."

"Well, you have many happy days in front of you, too. You *and* Fred," Tricia added.

"Beside you guys, he's the best thing that ever happened to me."

Tricia beamed.

"Would someone take my picture with the cake?" Pixie asked.

Calls of "I will—I will!" flooded the room, and most of the guests pulled out their phones once again, hurrying to join the bride-to-be.

Mary Fairchild, owner of the By Hook or By Book craft shop, hung back, looking wistful. She'd recently become engaged to Chauncey Porter, owner of the Armchair Traveler. The ring on her left hand was no bigger than Pixie's, but unlike Tricia's assistant, Mary seemed embarrassed by its size.

"It's always a thrill the first time," she lamented.

Tricia's wedding to Christopher sure was. If she ever decided to tie the knot again, she vowed to skip the pageantry and elope.

"Have you set a date?" Tricia asked.

Mary shook her head. "Chauncey wants to get married by a justice of the peace, with no fanfare. He doesn't see the point of spending a lot of money on frivolity." She didn't look happy about the situation. "He said that because this is my second marriage, we shouldn't make a fuss."

"Everybody deserves at least a *little* fuss on their wedding day," Angelica said kindly.

Mary shrugged.

"Men!" Tricia said in exasperation, because Mary wasn't looking for advice—just commiseration.

"I guess," Mary said.

A gushing Pixie and her entourage returned to the parlor. "Everything's just so beautiful. Party favors and everything!"

"Why don't you sit down and have some punch and we can get started with the rest of the party?" Angelica suggested. "You sit there—in the chair of honor."

Pixie actually giggled. "Okay."

She sat down, and Debra stepped forward once again to offer her a glass of punch from the silver tray in her hand.

Angelica made to step forward, but Tricia grabbed her arm and turned her aside.

"What's up?"

"I spoke with Fred before he left," Tricia said, keeping her voice low.

Angelica inspected her sister's face. "Why do I get the feeling I'm not going to like what you have to tell me?"

"Because I wasn't happy to hear the news, either. Fred had to ask Daddy to leave his apartment."

"Oh, no!"

"Oh, yes. What are we going to do about him now?"

Angelica took in the guests filling the parlor. "We'll get through the party and then we'll think about it. I'm sure Daddy will show up sooner or later. And when he does, I'm going to give him what for!" She eyed the glasses of punch being handed out. "I know where the liquor is kept. I may go spike my drink."

"And I may join you."

But before Tricia and Angelica could grab glasses, a familiar figure opened the swinging door from the kitchen to the dining room, beckoning them forward.

"Oh, no," Angelica groused. "What on earth is Daddy doing here?"

"We'd better find out—and fast," Tricia said.

Angelica charged forward like an angry bull, and Tricia turned to her guests. "We'll be right back," she said, and smiled, but since everyone was conversing, she doubted anyone really noticed.

She pushed through the swinging door.

"Oh, there you are, Princess."

"Daddy, what are you doing here?" Tricia asked, noting that though it wasn't hot, her father's upper lip was beaded with sweat.

"I came to say good-bye. I know my being here in the village has just upset you girls, and it's time for me to say *au revoir*."

"And not a moment too soon," Angelica interrupted.

"That is, if you can spot me a few hundred," John amended.

"Are you okay?" Tricia asked her father.

Angelica barreled on. "You have the nerve to ask for money after clearing my café of cold cuts and then trashing them!"

"Just as a loan. I'll pay you back—I promise!"

"Are you feeling all right? You don't look well," Tricia said.

Angelica paused in her hissy fit to take in John's face, and her strong streak of compassion overwhelmed her anger. "No, you don't look well."

"I'm fine. And I know it's an imposition, but you see, I've got this business opportunity, and"—he took a deep breath and waved a searching hand behind him—"I think I might like to sit."

The kitchen was used as a work area only, and the only seat was a utilitarian stool. Still, Tricia grabbed it and shoved it under her father's posterior before he could fall.

"Daddy, you look positively green. I think we'd better call the paramedics."

"Nonsense. It's just the heat of the day."

"The weather is perfect—unless you're wearing a pink wool poodle skirt, and then it's a little toasty," Angelica groused.

"I'm perfectly fine. But I could use a lift to the bus station in Nashua. There's a Greyhound to Boston at six o'clock. I've got plenty of time, so maybe one of you girls could take me after your little party."

"You're not going anywhere," Angelica said, and turned for the phone on the wall.

"Who are you calling?"

"As Tricia suggested, the paramedics."

"No!" John said, struggling to his feet, but the effort seemed to tax him. Clutching his chest, he sank to the floor.

FIFTEEN

Tricia paced the confines of St. Joseph Hospital in Milford. The fact that the ambulance crew had brought her father there instead of heading for its big brother in Nashua probably meant that his life wasn't in danger.

She hoped.

Still, she felt more than a little foolish to be seen in her trashy-looking Sandy Olsson *Grease* costume. Angelica managed to look dignified no matter what the situation. No one had asked about their choice of attire, for which she was extremely grateful.

Tricia gazed through the window to the parking lot outside the ER's waiting room. "Poor Pixie. She said she was afraid to be happy because something always comes along and spoils it. And then Daddy had to show up and ruin her shower."

"He didn't ruin it," Angelica said, sounding weary. "Ginny stepped right in with all the poise of Audrey Hepburn and took over. I'm sure she made sure all of the guests had a wonderful time."

"I so wanted to see how that cake was going to be cut," Tricia lamented.

"I'm sure someone will post it on Facebook." Angelica sighed, her expression darkening. "Daddy didn't look well at all when they put him in the ambulance."

"No, he didn't. But I'm going to remain hopeful that this is just a speed bump in the road and that he'll be up and about in no time."

"And out of our hair?" Angelica asked quizzically.

Tricia didn't have an opportunity to answer.

"Miles family?" called a voice from the vicinity of the ER's reception desk.

The sisters stood and hurried over to meet the lab-coated woman. "Family of John Miles?"

"That's us," Tricia said. "We're his daughters."

The doctor eyed their attire, but said nothing. "I'm Dr. Petrov," she said with a faint Russian accent. "Your father has suffered a mild heart attack."

"I knew it," Angelica muttered.

"But the damage doesn't appear to be too great. With a change in diet, some regular exercise, tender loving care from his family, and follow-up with his regular physician, he should make a good recovery. We'll be keeping him overnight, but you can take him home tomorrow."

The sisters looked at each other uneasily.

"Can we see him?" Tricia asked.

"Certainly. If you'll follow me."

They trailed behind the doctor to a cubicle with a multicolored drape. The doctor pulled it aside and let them enter. Despite the backdrop of monitoring equipment and IVs, John lay back on the gurney looking none the worse for wear. Certainly his color had improved since he'd collapsed in the Sheer Comfort Inn's kitchen.

"Princess! Angelica!" he called, his voice sounding pretty much normal. "I'm sorry I gave you such a scare."

"You certainly did," Angelica said, and stepped closer to the bed to give her father a quick peck on the cheek, although from the look in her eyes, all had not been forgiven. Tricia moved to the other side of the gurney and kissed his other cheek.

"The doctor says you can leave tomorrow," Tricia said.

"But where will I go?"

"I've had an amazing piece of luck," Angelica said with what sounded like great reluctance. "My reupholstered couch was delivered just this morning."

"You can hardly ask a sick man to sleep on a lumpy old couch," John said, his voice dripping with faux sadness.

"Of course not," Angelica said. "You can have my bed."

John's answering smile was triumphant, and not at all lost on Angelica.

"They're going to find me a room for the night," John said. "But I thought I should tell you that I left my suitcase on the back porch at the inn."

"We'll retrieve it," Angelica promised.

"Where are your clothes?" Tricia asked.

"In a white bag. I think they stuffed them under this bed."

Sure enough, Tricia found the bag. *Stuffed* was the right word. They'd been tossed in with no regard for wrinkles. "I'd better fold these, otherwise you'll look like a hobo when you leave tomorrow." She turned away, emptied the bag onto the lone guest chair in the cubicle, and folded his shirt, underwear, socks, and lastly his pants—but not before shoving her hand into his pocket and extracting his wallet. She looked over her shoulder, making sure Angelica and her father were engaged in conversation before she checked the contents.

Sure enough, she found not one but six pawn tickets. Poor Fred. The wallet also contained a fistful of twenty-dollar bills.

Tricia folded the pants, putting them back in the bag, but kept the wallet. "Daddy. It's not safe for you to be separated from your wallet. I'll put it in my purse for safekeeping."

"Thank you, Princess."

A nurse stepped into the cubicle. "It's your lucky day, Mr. Miles. We've already got a room waiting for you."

"The service sure is great in this hotel," John said and laughed.

"As soon as we can snag a couple of the guys, we'll be taking you up there. In the meantime"—she turned back to her patient—"I need to take his vitals. If you ladies will excuse us."

"Sure thing," Tricia said, already backing out of the room.

"We'll hang around until you're settled in your room, Daddy," Angelica promised, following her sister.

The nurse pulled the curtain, and Tricia stood there just looking at it.

"He sure doesn't look like a guy who just had a heart attack," Angelica commented.

"The tests don't lie."

"I suppose not."

Tricia held out the pawn tickets. "As soon as we make sure Daddy's tucked in for the night, we've got a stop to make before we go home."

"Why do I get the feeling I'm not going to like this?"

"Like? I have a feeling we're both going to hate it."

It was late afternoon by the time Tricia and Angelica walked into the U-Trade pawn shop in Nashua. Tricia figured her father would have either had to take a cab or, more likely, a much cheaper bus ride from

Stoneham to the state's largest city to visit the money monger where John had hocked not only Fred's father's watch but other items as well.

"I'm terrified Daddy stole something I can't replace," Angelica admitted.

"Since the tickets are only dated yesterday, there's a good chance the items haven't been sold and we *can* recover them," Tricia said.

Angelica held up her left hand, crossing her fingers, while she clutched the car's steering wheel with the other and headed east. "I do wish we could have gone home to change . . ."

"Yeah, well, we couldn't. Not unless we wanted to wait until Monday to find out what Daddy's been up to."

"I've never even been *in* a pawn shop. How icky are they?"

"I don't know. From what Pixie's said, there are TV shows about them, but I've never seen them."

"So you think it will be a safe place for two unescorted women?"

"Are you expecting to be attacked or something?"

"No, it's just that . . . it all sounds so sordid. Six months ago, I would have argued that Daddy didn't even know what a pawn shop was for. Now—I don't even feel like I know a thing about our father."

"I'm in agreement with you there," Tricia said.

They drove along Nashua's main drag, with Tricia keeping a sharp eye out for three gold spheres hanging from a bar. "There!" She pointed them out, and Angelica turned at the next side street to find a parking space.

They got out of the car, heading back for the main thoroughfare. "What do we do when we get there?" Angelica said.

Tricia pushed her sunglasses up on top of her head as though they were a headband. "Proffer the pawn tickets and see what they want for us to recover the items."

"What else do you think Daddy stole from Fred?"

"I have no idea."

The large plate-glass windows of the squat brick building sported a plethora of neon signs proclaiming, DIAMONDS, WE BUY GOLD, and ANTIQUES. Tricia pushed through one of the heavy double glass doors and was surprised to see the place looked like a store, with high-end bicycles hanging from the ceiling, cases filled with estate jewelry and other collectibles, and shelves filled with all kinds of interesting-looking merchandise. A few people stood at the long glass counters at the back of the shop, speaking with employees, and mounted near the ceiling, covering the showroom from all angles, were a number of surveillance cameras.

"It's not what I expected," Angelica muttered.

Tricia charged ahead, aiming for the sales counter. A burly white man with a salt-and-pepper beard and a blue bandana tied around his head leaned forward on the glass. "Going to a costume party, girls?"

"We're on the way home, actually," Tricia fibbed. "I hope you can help us. Our father was in here yesterday." She produced the pawn tickets. "We'd like to get his things out of hock."

"There'll be a charge."

"We figured as much," Angelica said, already reaching for her wallet.

"I'll be right back." The man disappeared behind a curtained doorway.

"Do you think we'll have enough room in the car to put everything?"

"Since Daddy probably came here by bus, I'm betting it'll be small stuff—things he could stuff in his pockets, like Fred's watch."

Angelica nodded, and her gaze went to take in their fellow customers, who were dressed a lot more conservatively than the two of them.

It didn't take long for the man to return with a small plastic box. He withdrew each item, matching them with the tickets. As expected, one of them was a man's watch, but there was also a number of other pieces of jewelry, including a gold ring.

"Good grief. Did Daddy hock his wedding band?" Angelica asked.

Tricia picked up the piece. "It's too small to fit him."

"Mother's?" Angelica asked.

Tricia squinted at the names engraved on the inside of the ring and felt the blood drain from her face. She had to clear her throat before she could speak. "Yes, it's Mother's," she said hurriedly. She examined the rest of the jewelry. A pair of what looked like diamond stud earrings, a tennis bracelet, an opal broach, and a diamond engagement ring—which was definitely not the one her mother had been wearing on her left hand for the previous five decades.

"What do we owe you?" Tricia asked as Angelica inspected the booty.

"Two grand ought to do it."

"Two grand!" Angelica echoed, and nearly dropped Fred's father's watch.

"Hey, we gotta make a living," the man said. "Of course, there's no price one can put on family heirlooms."

No, there wasn't. But the families that had once rightfully owned the items on display had not been her own.

"Pay the man, Angelica. We've got places to go."

Angelica reluctantly handed over her credit card and watched as the man rang up the sale. Angelica signed the receipt and their "purchases" were boxed up. Tricia took charge of the plastic bag the man handed her.

"If your father needs money in a hurry anytime soon, remind him we're always glad to do business with him."

Neither Tricia nor Angelica commented, and they headed straight for the door. They didn't speak until they were well away from the store.

"That wasn't Mother's engagement ring—or wedding band," Angelica said tartly.

"No, but it was engraved."

"And whose name was inside?"

"Carol Talbot's."

SIXTEEN

"What?" Angelica practically screamed.

"Shhh! Wait until we get in the car," Tricia admonished, leading the way.

Once there, Angelica hit the button on her key fob and unlocked the car's doors. The sisters got in, and Angelica immediately started the engine, opening the windows until the air-conditioner was ready to spew an icy gale their way.

"Carol's wedding ring?"

Tricia nodded. "And, except for Fred's watch, I'm betting the rest of the jewelry belonged to her, too."

"But how in the world would Daddy have gotten hold of it?"

"Two ways; either he broke into her home, or he had a key."

"How likely is that?"

Tricia shook her head, still in shock—and maybe a little denial—that her father was nothing but a common thief. And stealing from the dead made the offense that much worse.

"What are we going to do about this?"

"As I see it, we have two choices. We can either go right to the Stoneham Police Department and hand the stuff over, or—"

"Please don't tell me you're going to suggest we try to sneak into Carol's home and plant the stuff."

"Okay, I won't."

Angelica's eyes narrowed. "That *isn't* a viable suggestion."

"Why?"

"Her neighbors, for one. If they see us sneaking in, we're dead meat."

"They obviously didn't see Daddy sneak in. No doubt he did it under cover of darkness, which is what I would suggest we do as well."

"Why do we have to do *anything*?"

"Because . . . because . . ." Tricia thought about it. Maybe doing nothing did make the most sense.

"We could just ditch the stuff that belonged to Carol."

"Throw it away?"

"It isn't doing anybody any good," Angelica pointed out. "As far as we know, Carol was childless. *She* was an only child. Perhaps she had no heirs."

"I suppose I could ask Grant about it. Perhaps he and his officers found a will when they searched Carol's house."

"That would be a good time to ask if he or his men found anything missing. Like, say, the lack of a jewelry box."

"The stuff we just acquired wouldn't fill such a box."

"Maybe it was a small box—or maybe Daddy just threw away anything he thought had little or no value. We could ask him."

"I'm not sure that's a conversation I want to have. How would you start it? 'Tell me, Daddy, when did you become a cat burglar?' Would he even answer such a question?"

"We'll never know until we ask," Angelica said.

"*You* ask."

"I just might."

And then another terrible thought crossed Tricia's mind. "What if Daddy left fingerprints at the scene?"

"It's been four days since Carol died. Surely if they had prints they would have come after him by now, especially as he already has a criminal record."

"Sometimes getting comparison prints from another state takes time—much longer than those TV crime shows would have you believe. And Grant *has* been pursuing Daddy. He just hasn't caught up with him yet. Who besides us and Pixie and Fred knew where he's been staying?"

"Everybody's going to know where he's staying once he gets out of the hospital—unless he just plain runs away."

"Which brings me to another consideration that needs to be voiced."

"And that is?"

"You invited Daddy to stay with you."

"Reluctantly, but yes."

"Except it's three flights up to your apartment. Don't you think that's a little too much exercise for a man recovering from a heart attack?"

"Oh, dear. I hadn't thought of that."

"We're going to have to come up with some alternate plan, and pretty darn quick, as we're supposed to pick him up in the morning."

"I don't want him staying in any of my establishments. It's one thing for us to lose something precious—I don't want anyone else suffering such a loss. My God, think of the possible lawsuits."

"What about one of the Brookview's bungalows?"

"They're all booked for the next week—including yours."

"I guess Miss Marple and I could find other accommodations."

"It's too bad the old house the Chamber was using isn't habitable."

Nigela Ricita Associates had bought the house and used it as the Chamber's temporary headquarters, and had since moved into a newly constructed building down the street. The little house had been transported to a lot on the edge of town. While it had been settled on its new foundation, it still needed a lot of work before the real estate end of Angelica's business could hook it up to utilities and put it on the market.

"And shouldn't somebody look after someone who's had a heart attack? I mean, we can't just dump him anywhere—can we?"

"It does sound rather callous," Angelica agreed.

"You know, hospitals have social workers. Maybe we can talk to one before we fetch Daddy."

"Good idea. But you know what the real solution is?"

Tricia shook her head.

"We need to get Mother and Daddy back together again."

"Do you really think that's possible?"

"She put up with him for over fifty years—maybe she missed him during the past few months."

"How would we even find her? Connecticut isn't as big as Texas, but it may as well be, since we have no idea where to look for her."

"I'm sure we could track her down. She still has plenty of friends around North Haven."

"Like whom?"

"Bunny Murdock."

"Her old grade school friend?" Tricia asked. She'd never been fond of the woman, whom, because of her nickname, she'd always considered to be a *dumb* bunny.

"Last I heard they were still in contact," Angelica said.

"How long ago was that?"

"Maybe a year? You know how Mother loves to play bridge. I'm sure the first thing she did when she returned to the States was figure out where she could round up enough old pals to play a few hands."

"It's a start," Tricia conceded. "How about tomorrow?"

"I'm up to my eyebrows in work. Is there a chance you could call her?"

Tricia scowled. "Bunny's such a flake."

"But she always seemed to like you—probably because Mother didn't."

Thanks for rubbing that in, Tricia thought. "I suppose I can. The guys won't be working on my apartment reno tomorrow. I'll try to track her down then."

"Great idea."

"But if I get the number, you're going to have to be the one to talk to Mother."

Angelica sighed. "Okay. But she may hang up on me. The situation wasn't exactly happy the last time we spoke."

"There's nothing we can do about that now. Maybe I can get Bunny to tell me about the breakup."

"Reticence has never been Bunny's strong point," Angelica observed.

Tricia nodded.

The air-conditioning had finally come up to speed and Angelica put the car in gear and pulled out onto the road.

"In the meantime, who should hang on to Carol's jewelry—you or me?" Tricia asked.

"You?"

"Why me?"

"Because you're used to all this intrigue—and I'm just an innocent bystander," Angelica said.

"There were surveillance cameras all over that pawn shop. Depending on how good the video is, we both could be directly traced to the stolen items."

"Damn! What if we cleaned it up—made sure there're no fingerprints on anything, and then mailed the items to Chief Baker?" Angelica asked.

"Haven't you ever looked at a postal receipt? Everything that goes through the postal service has an ID number."

"Not letters."

"No, but any kind of package does. Besides, just like everywhere else, most post offices have surveillance cameras."

"What if we drove to some little Podunk town and mailed them?"

"You mean even smaller than Stoneham?" Again Tricia shook her head. "I don't think so."

"Well," Angelica said, sounding utterly defeated. "There's always the option of flushing the stuff down the toilet."

"Then you'd better hope it doesn't get clogged."

Angelica heaved a sigh. "I was just not cut out for a life of crime."

"That's for sure."

They drove in silence for several minutes before a disheartened-sounding Angelica spoke again. "What do you want to do for supper?"

"You mean besides drink heavily to forget?"

"Now that I've restocked the fridge at Booked for Lunch—to the tune of four hundred and thirty-seven dollars and change—there's plenty to eat."

"Maybe we deserve something better than luncheon fare," Tricia suggested.

"I'm not up to cooking tonight," Angelica admitted.

"We're in Nashua. There're a lot of nice restaurants here. In the mood for seafood?"

"Let's get our priorities straight. We're either going to drink heavily to forget or eat out. I'm not going to risk a DUI arrest."

"Okay, okay. It was just a thought."

"But . . . we could call the Brookview. For an outrageous amount of money, they will deliver."

"You own the place. Can't you get it comped?"

"Nigela Ricita owns the place. I'm just another customer as far as everyone else is concerned."

Sometimes Tricia forgot that little fact.

"Okay, then, let's go to your place and order the best thing on the Brookview's menu."

"I thought you already tried the truffled lobster risotto."

"Okay, then the *second*-best item on the menu."

At least Angelica managed a smile. "I like the way you think."

SEVENTEEN

Tricia pulled her car into the municipal parking lot early that Sunday morning—*early* being a relative term—and with only the teensiest bit of a hangover. Thank goodness there would be no construction work done on that day.

Since her shop didn't open for another hour, she wanted a sneak peek at the progress being made in her apartment and didn't want to run into Jim Stark or any of the other laborers, who made her feel like she was an intruder on her own property. Since it was to be a quiet day, she'd again brought Miss Marple along. Tricia parked her car, extracted her cat's carrier, and locked the vehicle. Mary Fairchild had pulled into the lot just after her, so she waited so they could head down Main Street together. Mary took a big bag of what looked like knitting yarn out of her backseat, shut and locked the door, and caught up with Tricia.

"Hi, Mary. Beautiful day, isn't it?"

"It sure is—just another day in paradise."

At that moment, Tricia's definition of paradise would have been waking up in her own home, in her own bed, and no construction again—ever!

They headed for the sidewalk.

"Can I carry something for you?"

"Oh, no, I'm fine," Mary said, as she tossed her long purse strap over her shoulder. "That sure was a nice shower you and Angelica threw for Pixie yesterday. It's too bad you couldn't have stayed for the whole thing."

"Emergencies happen," Tricia said simply. She didn't want to dredge up the whole thing, but Mary wasn't going to let it go.

"How is your father?"

"Better. Thanks for asking."

"That's good." A rather sly smile crept across her lips. "How have *you* been feeling lately?"

"Quite well," Tricia answered cautiously.

"That's good. All recovered from the loss of your ex-husband?"

Where was this conversation heading?

"Uh, yes."

Mary nodded. "It's hard to get over a broken heart, and it's so nice when you fall in love with someone you know is going to change your life for the better." Her gaze wandered down to the small diamond solitaire on her engagement ring, and again Tricia thought she looked unhappy about its size. "I'm not the only one who seems to have found a new love. Chauncey and I went bowling in Milford last night and ran into Chief Baker and his new girlfriend at Left Hook Lanes. She's very pretty—and *young*."

"Well, how nice," Tricia said, even though it was a struggle to keep her voice from cracking. She slowed her pace. Not that she cared if Grant Baker found someone new. More power to him—or rather to her, since it was unlikely the man would ever make a commitment. Besides, she was happy with the way her life was unfolding.

For the most part.

"They seemed pretty serious. I wonder why the chief doesn't bring her to Stoneham."

"No bowling alleys?" Tricia suggested.

"Maybe."

"And here I am at my store. It was nice to see you again, Mary. And thanks for helping to make Pixie's shower so much fun."

"Not a problem. Bye."

Tricia watched her neighbor carry on down the sidewalk. Had she taken just a little bit of pleasure in letting Tricia know that Grant Baker had finally moved on? They hadn't dated for years. It didn't bother Tricia in the least that he was with somebody new.

Oh, yeah? Then why had her stomach done a little flip-flop at the news?

Because it was a surprise—that's all, Tricia reassured herself.

She unlocked the door and let herself in. She set the carrier on the floor and opened its door. After a brief hesitation, Miss Marple ventured out, looking around. The cat seemed happy to be back in familiar—and quiet—territory.

After getting her cat a bowl of fresh water, Tricia closed the door to the stairs behind her and crept up the steps. The entire second floor was still in disarray, with wood shavings and other dust covering every flat surface. For all the noise they'd been making, there didn't seem to be much improvement from the last time she'd seen what she thought of as "the big mess." However, the bones of the custom cabinet that was to house the most valuable of her vintage mystery collection had been constructed, taking up most of the north wall. It would be the focal point of the room, and even though the glass doors weren't anywhere in sight, it was a sign of good things to come, giving her a much-needed shot of hope.

Climbing the steps to the third floor, she noted that the gate to what would be her master suite still hadn't been installed. Crossing the expanse of still-scuffed wooden floors, she ducked into the bathroom. Ceramic tile had been applied to the shower stall and travertine graced the floor, but the walls were still absent. Why did everything move so slowly? On TV, they could gut and rebuild a home in less than an hour!

She gazed around the wide expanse that was to be the new bedroom and sitting room. She'd shared intimate moments with two different men in that space. Men who'd gone on to relationships with other women. And it wasn't the guys who'd walked away from both relationships; it had been Tricia herself—and with good reason.

And she really *was* happy with her life. Well, maybe not during the whole renovation process. Being forced to stay somewhere else for goodness knew how long was jarring, but she was made of tough stuff. As Ginny and Angelica had repeatedly reminded her, she was going to be deliriously happy with the changes in her living space—when it was finished.

Tricia headed back downstairs, but she took her shoes off before entering the store. She wiped them off before heading back to the front of the shop and the cash desk. Haven't Got a Clue had more than enough dust in it, and she feared for the health of her vacuum cleaner, which was getting a great deal of use since work had begun upstairs.

Miss Marple had taken up residence on the little shelf above and behind the cash desk and was already happily napping, and with time to kill, Tricia pulled out the slip of paper with Bunny's phone number on it, picked up the vintage phone's heavy black receiver, and dialed.

"Hello?"

"Bunny? It's Tricia Miles."

"Good grief! Talk about a voice from the past. What's it been—ten years since we've spoken?" the older lady asked.

"Probably longer," Tricia admitted. "I hope you're well."

"Well, I've got this sciatica problem," Bunny said, and then launched into a long and extremely detailed list of her past and current ailments and all the different treatments she'd sought to no avail. Tricia muttered an occasional "Oh, dear" and "That's awful" when she could get a word in edgewise. She'd counted the squares of tin on the ceiling above her, wiped down the counter, and made at least twenty circuits around the cash desk by the time Bunny finally wound down.

"Of course, I heard the sad news about Christopher, but I didn't know where to send a card."

"I'm still in Stoneham. I own the mystery bookstore, Haven't Got a Clue."

"Is that so?"

Tricia had to bite her tongue. She'd only owned the store for six years. Apparently it wasn't a subject that came up when Bunny and her mother conversed.

"So have you had to testify against the horrible man who killed him?"

Tricia sighed. "The trial is set for the fall. I can't say I'm looking forward to it."

While Bob Kelly's lawyers had done everything they could to delay the trial, what they hadn't been able to do was get a judge to give Bob bail, for which Tricia was grateful. At least she didn't have to worry about running into him at the supermarket or dentist's office.

"So, what do I owe the pleasure of this call?" Bunny finally asked.

"I understand my mother has returned to North Haven."

"Oh, yes! Sheila's got a gorgeous condo not far from where you grew up. You mean she didn't give you her address?"

"It must have slipped her mind," Tricia fibbed, knowing full well her mother could care less if Tricia knew where she lived and what she was up to these days. "Angelica and I would like to contact her.

You see, it's just come to our attention that she and Daddy are now separated."

"And long overdue, if you ask me," Bunny muttered.

Tricia hadn't. "Angelica and I would like to get Mother's perspective on the subject."

"How is dear Angelica? Sheila tells me she's quite the entrepreneur and fabulously successful with her restaurant, store, and bed and breakfast."

Funny how Bunny knew all about Angelica and nothing about Tricia.

"Yes, she is," Tricia admitted, changing tacks. "In fact, it was Angelica who asked me to call you. She's so terribly busy—but she desperately wants to touch base with Mother, and—"

"Let me get that phone number right now." Bunny evidently put the phone down, for Tricia heard a loud *clunk* and then the rustle of papers before Bunny came back on the line. "Here it is."

Tricia took down the number just as the shop door opened and Pixie entered amid the jingling bell.

"Oh, dear—look at the time. I'm afraid I need to say good-bye, because it's time for me to open my shop. It's been lovely to speak with you, Bunny."

"Oh, but Tricia—!"

"Good-bye, and thank you."

Tricia pressed the rest buttons on the phone and then hung up the receiver.

"You didn't have to get off the line on account of me," Pixie said.

"Believe me, I've been looking for an excuse for the last twenty minutes."

Pixie's eyebrows rose. "Anybody interesting—and male?"

Tricia sighed. "No such luck." She grabbed her purse and began to rummage through it. "I'm dying to hear how the rest of your shower went yesterday after Angelica and I had to leave—but first I want to give you this."

"Another present?" Pixie asked hopefully, but as Tricia placed the man's watch into her open palm her smile faded.

"It's Fred's watch. I was able to track it down. Would you mind giving it to him?"

"Not a problem," Pixie said, pulling the expandable watchband over her right wrist. "Did your father hock it?"

Tricia nodded. "I'm terribly sorry."

Pixie shrugged. "Hey, my old man was a thief who did time. It's kinda embarrassing, but now that he's been dead twenty years, nobody but me remembers."

Was it going to take two decades for Tricia to live down this humiliation?

"Is your father okay?"

"Yes, thanks for asking. He's supposed to be released today. Angelica was going to go to the hospital and talk to a social worker to find out what our options are."

"Sorry to say, but I think you're stuck with the old guy."

"Yes, well, I'm sure Angelica will phone as soon as she figures out what's going to happen."

Pixie nodded, and Tricia changed the subject. "So how was the cake yesterday?"

"Oh my God—it was delicious!" Pixie nearly squealed, and launched into a detailed description of it and every other aspect of the bridal shower Tricia had paid for and had to miss. But unlike her conversation with Bunny, Tricia actually enjoyed listening to Pixie's monologue, which was punctuated with more than a dozen utterings of "thank you."

"I bought a couple of boxes of pretty thank-you cards with pansies on the front and I plan to write all my notes tonight to everybody who came and for all the wonderful presents. I brought them along with me today . . . in case things get slow."

Tricia smiled but didn't have a chance to comment, as a customer entered the shop and Pixie became all business. The telephone rang just then, and Tricia picked up the receiver. "Haven't Got a Clue—"

"It's your sister," Angelica sang on the other end of the line.

"What's the news on Daddy?"

"As we feared, they're discharging him," Angelica said, sounding not entirely happy about the situation. "I spoke to the resident on duty and was told he was doing remarkably well. He can be left on his own, but has to avoid stairs—so you were right; he can't come stay with me. The other bungalows at the Brookview are booked solid for the rest of the week."

"Does that mean I have to move out?"

"I can give you a lovely room at the Sheer Comfort Inn."

"What about Miss Marple? I don't think she'd enjoy being cooped up in such a small space all day and night. It's so noisy here during the week, she doesn't enjoy coming to the shop."

"I thought of that. I just got off the phone with Grace. She and Mr. Everett would be more than happy to take care of Miss Marple until things settle down."

"Oh, that would be wonderful. She already adores them both." As though the cat knew she was being spoken about, Miss Marple jumped down from her perch to the cash desk and rubbed her head against Tricia's shoulder. She'd have to get out the lint roller when she got off the phone.

"Is there a chance you could go over to the Brookview now and pack up? I can take Daddy out for brunch, and that should give you about an hour."

Tricia sighed. "Pixie's here, so I guess I can do it. I'll give Grace a call this afternoon and ask if I can drop off Miss Marple after the shop closes."

"Sounds like a plan."

"I spoke to Bunny and have Mother's number. Are you game to call her?"

It was Angelica's turn to give a martyred sigh. "Yes. But I think I should do it this evening. That way I can fortify myself with a good, stiff drink. And it wouldn't hurt for you to be present. I can put the call on speaker. You don't have to join in the conversation, but at least if you're there I won't have to repeat everything."

"Then you'd better make a pitcher of martinis," Tricia agreed.

"That was part of my plan. Meet me at my place around six."

"See you then," Tricia promised. She hung up the phone just in time to ring up the customer's sale. Pixie really was an excellent saleswoman. She'd convinced the woman to buy the first book in at least five different series, as well as reprints of a number of books by Josephine Tey. Once they'd said a cheerful good-bye to their happy buyer, Tricia gathered up her purse.

"That was Angelica on the phone. She's installing our father in my bungalow at the Brookview, and I'm moving to the Sheer Comfort Inn. I hope to be back in plenty of time to close the shop."

"Don't worry about it. I'm fine here on my own. If it gets slow, I can always dust, vacuum, or write my thank-you notes," Pixie said cheerfully.

"You're a doll," Tricia said, and hurried out the door. She had a lot to accomplish during the next couple of hours.

Tricia was dismayed to discover she'd accumulated a lot of stuff during her enforced relocation and had underestimated the equipment necessary to ensure a happy cat. It took two trips to transport her possessions to her new digs in order to make the bungalow at the Brookview available for her father, and another carload of stuff to accommodate Miss Marple for her stay with Grace and Mr. Everett. Angelica had arranged for the room to be cleaned and the sheets changed, and Tricia felt guilty for keeping the chambermaid waiting almost ten minutes as she finished gathering up the last of her belongings.

Her guilt was reinforced when she dropped her cat off at the Harris-Everett home, but Miss Marple didn't seem at all concerned and was already firmly entrenched on Grace's lap, purring like a well-oiled machine, as the door closed on Tricia's back.

It was ten minutes to six when Tricia arrived at Angelica's, and once again Sarge greeted her with the unbridled enthusiasm only a dog can muster.

"Calm down!" Tricia implored, and laughed. "You're liable to rupture something vital!"

"Hopefully his vocal cords," Angelica said, but it only took her command to "Hush!" and the barking abated. Sarge really was a well-trained canine.

Angelica was clad in a flowing caftan, which meant she was already in for the evening. She turned to the refrigerator and removed the pitcher of martinis, then retrieved the frosted glasses from the freezer. "I've waited *all day* for this."

"Did Daddy give you a hard time?"

Angelica poured, setting the olives skewered by frill picks in the glass with a flourish. "He gave me no trouble whatsoever, which raised my hackles. I told him to order from room service and told the desk to approve any movies he wants to watch."

"Even X-rated?"

"If it keeps him quiet and in one location. But I had them limit his calls. If he needs help, he'll have to call the desk. I don't want him calling anyone on an outside line, because goodness knows what other trouble he could get into."

"Thanks for taking care of all that," Tricia said, wondering if she'd reached her guilt quota for the day.

They clinked glasses and then drank deeply. Tricia was the first to speak. "What if Mother isn't home when you call?"

"Then I'll leave a message. And try again once every hour until I do get her, because Daddy needs to *go home*!"

If anyone could make that happen, it was Angelica.

Tricia handed over the slip of paper she'd written on earlier that day. Angelica took another fortifying swig of her drink and picked up her cell phone, punching in the number and the speaker function. It rang three times before the call was answered.

"Hello?" came a voice the sisters knew well, and that sounded remarkably happy.

"Mother? It's Angelica."

"Oh." The happiness had immediately evaporated. "Why are you calling?"

"Just to see how you are. Well, I hope."

"Yes."

Silence ensued.

"That's—that's great. I'm fine, too. And so is Tricia."

More silence.

"How did you get this number?" Sheila asked, sounding annoyed.

"The Internet is just full of interesting information," Angelica lied.

"But I paid to make sure my number was kept private."

"These days, everything is fair game," Angelica fudged.

Yet more silence.

"What do you want?" Sheila asked bluntly.

Angelica took another fortifying sip of her drink before answering. "It's Daddy."

Again, silence.

"He came to visit us earlier this week, and yesterday he had a heart attack. I thought you should know."

Even more silence.

"Mother?" Angelica prompted.

"Will he live?"

"Yes. Thankfully, it was pretty minor. But he needs loving care and time to recover."

"And *you* don't want to give him that," Sheila stated bluntly.

"That's rather a cold statement," Angelica countered.

"But true," her mother asserted.

Tricia picked up the martini pitcher and topped up Angelica's glass. She was going to need it, going head-to-head with their mother.

Angelica took another healthy swig of her drink before answering. "It seems that Tricia and I have been kept in the dark about Daddy's . . . proclivities."

Silence yet again. This was getting tiresome.

"Your father was always a rogue," Sheila finally exclaimed. "It was what first attracted me to him."

"And it must have been enough to entertain you, since your marriage endured for five decades."

"If nothing else, your father always managed to make me laugh."

"And why did you stop laughing?" Angelica pressed.

"Bermuda," Sheila answered simply.

Bermuda. Where Angelica had insisted they talk about the painful past. Her mother had berated Tricia and refused to engage in such a conversation—which had been too much for Angelica to endure. It had made Tricia infinitely sad, and yet incredibly indebted to and in awe of her older sister.

"I suppose Tricia is standing beside you listening in," Sheila accused.

"Why shouldn't she?" Angelica asked.

"Hello, Mother," Tricia said, but wasn't acknowledged in return.

"Let's get back to your father," Sheila said succinctly. "I assume you want to ship him back to me."

"If nothing else, you've taken care of him for most of his life. And from what we've gathered, bailed him out of trouble as well."

"I think after doing that for half a century I've had my fill."

"Why are you angry with Daddy? Just because he stuck up for Tricia?" Angelica demanded.

"Yes."

Sheila couldn't have hurt Tricia more if she'd stabbed her in the heart.

"Do you know how unreasonable you are?" Angelica accused.

"I don't care," Sheila declared.

Angelica swung her gaze to Tricia and then back to the cell phone sitting on the kitchen island.

"I'm sorry you feel that way, Mother. I think this conversation—and our relationship—is over. Have a happy, lonely life. You reap what you sow," Angelica said, and stabbed the end-call icon.

"Oh, Ange. I wish you hadn't done that."

Angelica's cheeks flushed, and the hand holding her drink shook just a little. "I can't imagine anything Antonio could do that would ever, *ever* make me angry enough to cut him out of my life, and he isn't even my flesh and blood."

"He's very lucky to have you on his side," Tricia said quietly.

"There's such a thing as unconditional love. That's what I feel for him, for Ginny, for Sofia, and especially for you. You are my sister, and there's nothing I wouldn't do for you."

"Oh, Ange," Tricia said again, and suddenly the sisters were in each other's arms, tears streaming down their cheeks.

It was Angelica who finally let go, reaching for the paper towel roll that hung from under one of her kitchen cabinets. They blew their noses on the rough paper, wiped their eyes, and tossed the toweling into the trash can.

Sarge was suddenly standing at their feet, quietly whining.

"You are just the best boy," Angelica said, turned, and reached for a dog biscuit in the jar she kept on the counter. She tossed it to the dog, who caught it in midair.

Despite her heartache, Tricia managed a soggy laugh, but unfortunately she sobered pretty darn quick. "This still leaves us with the problem of what to do with Daddy."

Angelica sighed. "Yes, it does. The social worker said that he had been evaluated and been found to be mentally competent. That you and I don't have to worry about him and can"—she waved a hand in the air—"set him free."

"To get into what kind of trouble?" Tricia asked.

"There's not much we can do. We have no power of attorney. He's a free man. He can do as he pleases."

"Including stealing from our friends and doing who knows what else that's against the law," Tricia said bitterly.

"We can't let him define who *we* are," Angelica said. "You and I are a force for *good* in this village, and that's the way I want it to stay."

"You've paid a pretty hefty price to keep it that way, too," Tricia said.

Angelica shook her head. "I've always made sure any business endeavor I've been a part of is aboveboard and honest, and I don't intend to change."

Tricia shook her head. "How did neither of us know that our father was a"—it hurt to say the phrase—"con man?"

"Because both you and I only want to believe the best of everybody we meet. To learn that our father can't reach that criteria has been sobering to say the least."

"So what do we do now? Encourage him to leave Stoneham to wreak havoc on some other community?"

"I don't know. If Mother couldn't rehabilitate him in half a century, I don't think there's a chance in hell you and I will do any better."

Tricia shook her head. "Poor Grandma Miles. It must have broken her heart to know her son was a ne'er-do-well."

"And now another generation feels the same way," Angelica said tartly.

There didn't seem to be much to add to that conversation.

Tricia drained her glass. Her stomach growled. "What are we going to do about supper?"

Angelica shrugged. "We are both in need for comfort food. I've got eggs and bread. I could make either omelets or French toast."

Tricia smiled. "I don't think I've had French toast in at least a decade."

"There's bacon in my freezer, and I have a half-gallon jug of New Hampshire's finest Grade A amber maple syrup in the cupboard. It sounds like French toast might just fit the bill."

"Sounds like heaven to me," Tricia said, smiling.

Again, Sarge whined just a little, his little brown eyes filled with nothing but the unconditional love Angelica had mentioned just minutes before.

Angelica turned to crouch before one of her cupboards, taking out a couple of shiny frying pans. "Are you game to help?"

"I've never actually made French toast before. I'd sure like to learn."

Angelica smiled. "It's not rocket science."

"Then let's make it together," Tricia said, grinning. She wasn't sure if she'd ever seen such a happy expression on her sister's face.

EIGHTEEN

Tricia arrived at Haven't Got a Clue early the next morning—but not early enough to beat the construction workers. A huge pile of drywall had arrived and was being hoisted by a JLG lift into the hole where there had once been a window. New energy-efficient windows were also on the to-be-done list of upgrades. The plans also called for a balcony with French doors leading to it to be added to the second floor overlooking the alley. True, the view wasn't spectacular, but it would be nice to have some kind of outdoor space—although the way things were going, Tricia wasn't sure she'd get to enjoy it this summer.

She found herself looking out the window, waiting for Mr. Everett to arrive. While her new digs at the Sheer Comfort Inn were cramped, she missed her cat something fierce and was eager for a full report on how Miss Marple had fared during her first lonely night away from Tricia.

When he came into work, Mr. Everett entered the store with not only a smile on his lips, but whistling a happy tune: "High Hopes," another tune off one of the CDs Pixie had brought into the store.

"My, but you're in a good mood today," Tricia said by way of a greeting.

"It's a beautiful morning and enough to make one glad to be alive. I'll just get my apron and then I'll get the coffee going?" Mr. Everett said, and headed toward the back of the store.

"Wait!" Mr. Everett turned back to face her. "How did Miss Marple make out last night?"

Mr. Everett positively grinned. "Splendidly." He moved closer to the sales counter. "She took turns sitting on our laps all evening." He leaned in closer. "But I do think she's partial to me."

It was the first time Tricia had ever heard Mr. Everett brag.

"Did she eat her dinner? I'm worried that disrupting her routine may have an adverse effect on—"

"She ate every bite last night, and tucked in with gusto this morning."

"I'm so pleased. Did she sleep in her carrier?"

He shook his head. "We usually sleep with the bedroom door closed, but Grace was afraid Miss Marple might be lonely in the night, and we left it open a crack. When we woke up this morning, that darling cat was nestled between us, purring happily."

Tricia's stomach did a little flip-flop. "She didn't miss me?"

"Not a bit," he said quite cheerfully, which didn't make Tricia feel any better. "You know, I haven't had a pet since my dog, Nipper, died when I was ten. It was too painful. But having Miss Marple in our house has made it seem more like a home."

"It's a well-known fact that having a pet is good not only for your soul, but for your health as well."

"I've read that, too," Mr. Everett said, nodding. "Of course, at our ages, we're much, much too old to even think of adopting a pet."

"Not necessarily," Tricia said. "There are many elderly pets who've been abandoned and are in need of loving homes."

"Yes, but like when I lost Nipper, it would be very heartbreaking to have to say good-bye."

"That's true," Tricia admitted. "But just think; you might fill an older animal's last days with pure joy. And isn't that a better way to go than in a cage or to be euthanized?"

Mr. Everett's happy mood seemed to have completely evaporated.

"I'm sorry. I didn't mean to lecture you."

"What you've said makes a lot of sense. I shall think long and hard about it, but I can make no promises. For now, I shall simply enjoy Miss Marple's company for as long as she stays with us."

"And I know she couldn't be in better hands."

The ghost of a smile returned to the elderly gentleman's lips. He nodded and turned, heading for the back of the store once again, and again he started to whistle.

The phone rang and Tricia picked up the receiver. "Haven't Got a Clue, this is Tricia—"

"And it's me, your sister," Angelica said. "Do you have any lunch plans?"

"Just the usual—meeting you across the street when the Booked for Lunch crowd thins out."

"I spoke to Daddy just now, and I think we should have lunch with him. We need to figure out his future."

"I want to grill him about the"—she glanced askance to see if Pixie was listening in as usual before remembering that she hadn't yet arrived for work—"you-know-what."

"You might want to call the chief to see if he's going to arrest Daddy."

"Well, at least that *would* get him out of our hair."

"I would prefer that he quietly leave town. I want your opinion on that—and if we agree—"

"I would be glad to pay my fair share to resettle him."

"You know, that's a good idea. I wonder what it would cost to have him move into the development where Mother lives."

Tricia smiled in spite of herself. "You know, that's a very good idea."

"I'm sure Daddy has plenty of friends in North Haven. Maybe he can play cards or golf with his old buddies. That would be enough for him."

"It can't hurt to ask."

"Great. I've booked the Brookview's private dining room so we won't be disturbed and can talk freely."

"Good idea."

"Shall I pick you up at one?"

"I'll be ready."

"Fine. See you then."

Angelica's suggestion that Tricia call the chief was a good one, but before she had an opportunity to do so, he showed up at Haven't Got a Clue, and she knew without a doubt that it wasn't a social call.

"Hi, Grant. I bet I can guess why you're here."

"I'll bet you can. Where would you like to go to talk?"

Tricia felt like she'd left the premises—abandoning her employees—far too often during the previous week.

"Would you like to see how my renovation is progressing?"

For the first time in what had seemed like an awfully long time, the chief actually smiled. "Yeah. Lead the way."

"I'll be back down in a few minutes," Tricia told Mr. Everett, and started toward the back of the shop with Baker following close behind.

They climbed to the top of the building and entered the large expanse that was to be Tricia's new master suite. "Wow," Baker said, his voice hushed. "You really *have* moved on."

She wasn't sure what to make of that statement, but figured this might be an opportunity to clear the air. "So have you, apparently."

"What does that mean?" he asked, sounding wary.

"I understand you've got a new lady friend."

"Joanna," he said simply. "We've been seeing each other for about a month now."

"Congratulations."

"I understand you're still *not* seeing anyone." Was that a taunt?

"No. I've got a lot on my plate right now, what with the reno and all."

"And your father visiting," he added rather pointedly.

"Yes." She thought about elaborating, but decided to wait. She didn't want to talk about such things in a space where the two of them had been intimate on so many occasions. So instead, she walked him through the space, telling him about the improvements that had yet to be made, and then they went down to the second floor, where they could at least lean against the kitchen island while they talked.

"I don't know if you know it, but my father had a heart attack on Saturday afternoon."

"That was how I tracked him down. The EMTs filed a report."

"Angelica picked him up from the hospital just yesterday."

"He's staying at the Brookview Inn—the bungalow *you* previously rented," Baker said. So he already knew what was going on.

"Yes. I got tossed out to make room for him. I've had to farm Miss Marple out to Mr. Everett for the duration." Gosh, it actually *hurt* to say those words.

"Now that your father has reappeared, I need to speak with him. I'd like you to arrange that."

"Angelica and I are having lunch with him at the Brookview's private dining room this afternoon. He and our mother have separated, and we've got to figure out what to do with him. We thought a nice assisted-living site might be good for him."

"You mean to keep him out of trouble."

Tricia sighed. "Yes, that's a major concern."

"I don't want him leaving the village until we clear up the Talbot murder case—or at least until I'm sure I can trust whatever it is he'll tell me about his relationship with the deceased."

"I understand that. I imagine it'll take several weeks to get him established somewhere else."

"And far away from Stoneham."

"Angelica would like to engineer a reconciliation between our parents," she said.

"If anybody can accomplish it, it's her," Baker agreed. Tricia wasn't sure he'd ever liked her sister, so it was a rare compliment.

"How's your investigation into Carol's death going?"

He took a moment, seeming to mull over his answer before speaking. "Slowly. We know someone broke into her house on the night she was murdered."

Tricia felt every muscle in her body stiffen. "Oh?"

"The neighbors called to report seeing lights inside, but before a patrol car could get there, whoever had been there was gone."

"Was it forced entry?" Tricia asked.

"No."

"What was missing?"

"The place wasn't ransacked, and the intruder took care, because every flat surface in the house seemed to have been cleaned of fingerprints. We had a hard time finding even those of Mrs. Talbot."

That seemed odd. Tricia's father had arrived in town only hours before Carol's murder. If, as he'd boasted, he had been Carol's lover some five months before, it was possible that his fingerprints might still have been found in her home—but only if they'd gone there for their trysts. Had John decided to go back and make sure he'd obliterated all evidence he'd ever entered the home and then stolen Carol's jewelry as an afterthought?

It was a sobering notion.

"Will you be hauling Daddy off to police headquarters this afternoon?" Did that mean they'd need to hire a lawyer for him?

"We aren't going to accuse him of murder. We'd just like to know what his relationship was with the deceased."

"I could answer that, but I suppose it's better if you hear it from Daddy."

"If you tell me now, I'll have a place to start."

Tricia mulled over the rather damning answer. If she told the chief what she knew, her father would know that either she or Angelica had spilled the beans—and there went any trust he had in them. And yet, not only had he abused their trust, he'd repeatedly stolen from Angelica.

"I do know—and so does Angelica—but I think it should be Daddy who tells you what we were told in confidence. That said, if he lies to you, then I will tell you everything he told me, with one caveat: that it, too, could be a lie."

"That sounds fair. Do you mind if I call you after I speak with him? Or, if you'd like, you can be there *when* I speak with him."

"That might be the best option."

"Okay. What time did you say you were having lunch?"

"One. If you could give us an hour and then show up, that would be more than fair."

"Okay. I'll be there at two o'clock." His gaze bore into hers. "I know this is very hard for you, Tricia. You and Angelica have always presented yourself as honest and trustworthy. It's got to be like a stab in the heart to find out that your father isn't the man you thought he was."

He had that right.

"I need to get back to work," Tricia said.

"So do I."

They left the dirty, unfinished space, and Baker trundled down the stairs after Tricia. He barely said good-bye before he was out the door.

Pixie had arrived for work and was stationed behind the cash desk. "Well?" she asked eagerly.

"Well, what?" Tricia said.

"Are you two getting back together again?"

Tricia understood where Pixie was coming from. She was in love. She wanted the whole *world* to be in love, too.

"He's got a girlfriend."

"What?" Poor Pixie actually sounded distressed.

"At last he's moved on, and it's a great relief for me."

"Oh. Well, I'm sorry about that."

"Don't worry, Pixie. If I'm meant to fall in love again, it'll happen."

"I guess you're right. I sure as hell never thought I'd meet a great guy like Fred and fall in love. And I never in a million years thought I'd ever get married." She smiled, and her thumb rubbed the engagement ring on her left hand. "But there is just one thing I'm not gonna do, and that's change my name to Pillins." She shuddered. "I don't like that name. I like being a direct descendent of Edgar Allan Poe. It's good for the shop."

And it was extremely unlikely she could be Poe's descendent, since the man had never procreated. Well, not that anyone knew, at least.

The bell over the door tinkled, and a man and woman entered the store. Pixie went straight into her well-practiced, and extremely successful, mystery-buff saleswoman shtick. Tricia had no doubt that, if given half a chance, the woman could sell vintage mysteries to whales under the ocean.

Tricia retreated behind the cash desk, feeling a little discombobulated. Did Baker already suspect John Miles had been in Carol Talbot's home after her death? Would Baker be able to tie the stolen jewelry to John? And how could she explain the fact that she and Angelica had retrieved the loot and that it was still in her possession?

Oh, what a tangled web, Tricia thought, and dreaded what might befall them all.

NINETEEN

Angelica's car showed up across the street at ten minutes to one, and Tricia grabbed her purse and hurried out the door. She crossed the road and jumped in the car. Angelica stepped on the accelerator and the car took off.

"You're early," Tricia said as she buckled up.

"Sorry. Better early than late. Especially when I've got this terrible fear that Daddy may have escaped."

"Really?"

"He was still in his room as of ten minutes ago. I had Antonio tell the staff to watch him."

"Were they told why?"

"Just that he's been ill. They don't have to know the rest of the sordid details."

"And speaking of sordid, I spoke to Grant this morning."

"Oh?"

"He's going to suddenly appear at the private dining room at two o'clock to talk to Daddy. He invited us to sit in."

"I think that's a good idea."

"Yeah, although with his background, I'm sure Daddy knows when *not* to speak to a policeman so that he doesn't incriminate himself."

"Just lovely."

"Worse than that, Grant knows somebody was in Carol's house the night she died."

"What do you mean?"

"Neighbors reported seeing lights on."

"The ones we spoke to or someone else?"

"I have no idea."

Traffic was less than light, and they arrived at the Brookview in less than two minutes. Angelica parked the car and they walked to the bungalow to collect their father.

They knocked on the door, but there was no answer. "Oh, no," Angelica groused. "I sure hope he hasn't absconded."

"You said he was here only minutes ago."

Angelica looked around, as though to see if anyone was watching, and then rummaged through her purse and came up with a key ring Tricia had never seen before. "What's that?"

"My master set. I can get into any door in any establishment I own—not that I do. I have it for emergencies. I'd much rather open a door than have someone—like the police—kick it in."

She found the appropriate key, shoved it into the lock and the door magically opened.

It was obvious that the room was empty, but Angelica charged into the bathroom just to make sure.

"Now what?"

"We check inside. My hope is he's already gone to the private dining room and has ordered a drink—or two."

They walked across the parking lot and entered the Brookview's back entrance, walking down the corridor to the lobby, where they paused at the reception desk. "Hello. I'm Angelica Miles. I've reserved the private dining room for one o'clock."

"Yes, your other party has already shown up."

She offered a grateful-looking smile. "Thank you."

The sisters turned right and headed for the private dining room.

The door was closed, and Angelica knocked before they entered.

"Come in, come in, my darling girls," John said in welcome. He sat at one of the upholstered chairs off to the side. Before him on the side table sat a sweating glass of amber liquid—no doubt Scotch on the rocks.

"Should you be drinking so soon after your health scare?" Tricia asked.

"If not now—when?"

"When indeed," Angelica grated, but then she strode to the little button on the wall that would alert the waiter who was to serve them. It was like she'd hit speed dial, for the man appeared in only seconds.

"Hello, I'm Danny. How can I help you?"

"My sister and I would like a couple of glasses of Chardonnay," Angelica said without consulting Tricia. That she'd ordered wine meant she intended to make sure they kept their wits about them during the ensuing conversations.

"Very good. And will you be ordering now?"

"Not yet. We'll need a little time."

"Very good," Danny said, and backed out of the room, closing the door after him.

The sisters turned their attention back to their father. "Daddy, you know we love you, but you can't stay here in Stoneham," Angelica announced with no preamble.

"And I don't want to," he said and reached for his drink. "Talk about a backwater," he mumbled into his glass.

"But?"

John set his glass back down. "As I told you before; I'm short of funds."

"How much do you need?" Angelica asked, her tone icy.

John shrugged. "Ten or twenty thousand—"

"What on earth for?" Angelica nearly bellowed.

"To get established in a new locale."

"What's wrong with North Haven? You've got friends there. You've got—"

"Family? My family is all gone. The only person I know there is your mother—and she has made it clear that I am no longer welcome in her home and in her bed. And by the way, all the years we were married she made it clear that it was always *her* home and that I was nothing more than a boarder."

"Then why did you stay?" Tricia asked.

"Where else was I going to go? I suppose it was a comfortable life. I played golf. She occasionally let me dabble in business dealings, but she always held the purse strings, making me feel like some kind of a vestigial organ."

Not the analogy Tricia would have chosen.

"You do realize that the police have been looking for you?"

"I haven't exactly been hiding."

"But you haven't exactly been accessible, either."

"What could they possibly want with me?"

"A woman slapped you in front of dozens of witnesses less than thirty minutes before she was found dead. Naturally the police want to know why."

John again reached for his drink. “I asked if I could stay with her. She was still miffed I’d left without consulting her back in January, and she smacked me. I didn’t hold it against her.”

“The police seem to feel otherwise,” Tricia added, but before she could say anything else, Danny had arrived with a tray and their drinks. He set the glasses on napkins on the cocktail table. “May I present you with our menu?”

“We know where they are. We’ll call you when we’re ready to order, thank you,” Angelica said.

Danny nodded and again backed out of the room, closing the door.

“Now, where were we?” Angelica said, and picked up one of the glasses, taking a swig.

“Talking about Carol—and Daddy.” Tricia turned her attention back to her father. “I found the pawn tickets in your wallet on Saturday.”

“Pawn tickets?” he asked, his expression guileless.

“Yes. For Fred’s father’s watch, and Carol’s wedding band and other pieces of jewelry.”

“You should be ashamed of yourself. First you try to rope Fred into fencing stolen cold cuts—which you appropriated from me!” Angelica cried, her voice cracking, “and then you stole the man’s father’s watch.”

“Borrowed,” John insisted. “I only needed a little cash advance. I fully intended to reclaim it at the earliest opportunity.”

“And when would that be? When hell freezes over?” Angelica asked.

“Ange, Ange,” Tricia chided, and guided her sister into a chair. Then she picked up her own glass and took a healthy sip. “So when did you steal Carol’s jewelry?”

“Steal?” John repeated as though puzzled.

“I can’t think of a better explanation,” Tricia said.

“I borrowed it.”

The man truly was in denial.

"How can you borrow something from a dead person?"

"She wasn't using it. And I intended to make full restitution."

"To whom?" Tricia insisted.

"I'm still waiting for you to make restitution to me," Angelica grated.

"Yes, well, that's what I intended. However, the loan I was able to obtain—"

"You mean from the pawn shop?"

"Er, well, yes. It was considerably lower than I'd anticipated. It would have been an insult to offer you such a paltry sum."

"Believe me, I wouldn't have been insulted."

"Daddy," Tricia began, "won't you please tell us what's going on with you? And perhaps it might be best to come clean about the past, too."

"The past?" he asked innocently.

"Yes. Tricia's good friend—the chief of police—said you have a rap sheet as long as our arms."

"Why are you friendly with the law?" he asked suspiciously.

"In case you haven't heard, it's Tricia's hobby to find dead bodies and help the police solve crimes."

"I was wondering about that," John admitted. "Carol did mention you seem to make a habit of it."

"That's beside the point. You still haven't told us the whole Carol story."

"There's not much else to tell."

"How about how you entered her home?"

"Uh, I knew where she hid the spare key."

"Is it still there?"

"Unless someone else took it, it should be."

"Tricia!" Angelica warned.

"I'm not planning to follow in Daddy's footsteps," Tricia said, but at that point she wasn't exactly sure it was the truth.

Angelica shook her head, turning her attention back to their father. "What are we going to do with you?"

"You don't have to do anything. Except perhaps buy me a bus ticket to Boston. I've got connections there."

"What kind of connections?"

"Nothing you'd be interested in. Friends. Business associates. Colleagues."

"Crooks?" Angelica supplied.

John frowned. "Nothing of the sort."

"That wouldn't be a very good idea," Tricia said, "not after that scare you gave us with the heart attack."

"The doctor said it was very mild. If I take care of myself, I should be one hundred percent in a couple of weeks."

"And how are you going to take care of yourself when you're on the road or bumming space with these so-called business associates and colleagues?" Angelica asked.

"Have you got another solution?" John pointedly asked.

Tricia looked to her sister to explain.

"We're not willing to give you a load of money that can be frittered away, but we are open to setting you up in some kind of living arrangement."

John sipped his Scotch before speaking. "I'm listening."

"We thought some kind of retirement community."

"With a bunch of old fogies!" he protested.

"Look in the mirror; *you're* an old fogy," Angelica said. "We're talking about a nice place where you wouldn't have to worry about cooking, cleaning, and doing laundry. Kind of like the arrangement you had with Mother, only without the sex."

"And there wasn't nearly enough of that these past few years, either."

Tricia put her hands over her ears. "That's far more information than either of us needs to know!"

John went back to sipping his Scotch.

"Well, what do you say?"

"I don't want to live in Stoneham—or even New Hampshire. There's not much to do here."

"We were thinking Connecticut."

"North Haven?" he asked, not sounding at all pleased.

"It's either there or here. Those are the only choices."

John scowled. "Why don't you give me ten thousand bucks and let me take my chances?"

Angelica, the hardened businesswoman who was used to negotiating contracts, shook her head. "It's tough love time, Daddy."

John scowled. "Then I don't suppose I have much choice."

Again, Angelica shook her head.

"I don't want to be dumped in some fleabag—and I'll need transportation. A nice Cadillac should do."

"We can discuss the particulars later. That is, if you aren't arrested for murder," Angelica accused.

John waved an impatient hand in the air. "You worry too much."

"You don't seem to worry at all," she countered.

"That's because I'm innocent."

"And how many times have you uttered that phrase during your lifetime?" Angelica muttered.

Tricia looked at her watch. If they were going to eat before Baker showed up for his interrogation, they had better think about ordering. She marched over to where the menus were kept, grabbed three, and handed them out. "Lunchtime."

They perused their choices, and then Tricia pressed the button to summon Danny.

When he arrived, they ordered, and with a nod Danny exited.

For a couple of long, awkward minutes, no one spoke. They sipped their drinks without making eye contact.

It occurred to Tricia that the man she'd adored—her father—not only had feet of clay but was no longer the man she'd thought she'd known for her entire life.

"Daddy," she began, "you need to tell us who you are. I feel like I don't know you. I don't know what you love—or who. I really don't know anything about you."

"Oh, Princess, you sound so disappointed."

"I am. I always thought my daddy was a great man, a kind man. An *honest* man."

John shook his head. "Princess, I'm the same man who read you stories. Who tucked you in at night. Who was there at your dance recitals."

"But what else did you do—who else were you?" Angelica queried.

John shrugged. "I've always been a free spirit. I think that's what first attracted your mother to me. I always hovered around a flame, and she found that exciting . . . until she didn't."

"Do you miss her?" Angelica asked.

John took several long moments to think about it. "Yes, I do. But she's made it clear to me that her feelings have changed."

Because he had defended Tricia.

Good grief; that made Sheila sound like a horrible excuse for a mother. And even if she was, Tricia still loved the woman and always would. She was her mother, after all. But that didn't mean she had to like her.

How sad.

How terribly sad.

And so they sat in virtual silence until their lunches arrived. And even then, they didn't say much more.

The three of them picked at their entrees, not hungry for food—but Tricia was hungry for something more elemental.

Understanding.

Danny had cleared the dishes away and asked if they'd wanted coffee or dessert, which they'd all decided against, when another knock on the door broke the quiet.

"Come in," Tricia said.

Chief Baker entered. John took in his dark blue policeman's uniform and shot angry glances at both his daughters.

"Daddy, this is Grant Baker—Stoneham's chief of police," Tricia said.

"Your old boyfriend," John accused.

Baker shot an angry look at Tricia, but said nothing.

"Do you know why I'm here?" Baker asked John.

"Because Carol slapped me mere minutes before she died, you think I may have killed her."

"Yes."

"Sorry to disappoint you, Mr. Cop, but my feelings for the woman could be summed up in two words: easy lay."

"Daddy!" Angelica protested.

John shrugged. "Carol and I were intimate when I was here back in the winter, but apparently she wasn't interested in taking up where we left off."

"So she slapped you?"

John nodded. "It's as simple as that."

"Where have you been staying in Stoneham?"

"Actually, I was in Milford until I had a heart attack on Saturday. Now I'm staying here at the inn in one of the bungalows."

"For how long?"

"That's up in the air just now."

"I would prefer you to stay in the area until I can corroborate your movements."

"How long will that take?"

"A few days, at least."

John merely shrugged.

"Where were you when Carol Talbot was murdered?" Baker asked.

"Probably on my way to Milford. I snagged a ride."

"And where did you go?"

"To an apartment building on the highway."

"Who lives there?"

"Fred Pillins. He's Pixie Poe's fiancé," Tricia answered.

"I'm talking to *him*," Baker said rather testily.

"Yes, and if you didn't sound so prissy, you might get more cooperation from everyone," Angelica said.

"You can leave," Baker said.

"No, you interrupted *our* lunch. *You* can leave," Angelica said.

"Would you rather I speak to your father at the police station?"

"If you do, it won't be without a lawyer present."

"I don't need a lawyer," John protested. "I'm innocent."

"There are other things you might not be innocent of."

"Such as?" John asked.

"Trying to fence stolen cold cuts."

"Did anyone report food stolen?" Angelica asked.

"No. But Statewide Waste Management reported a Dumpster full of rotting cold cuts at a certain apartment complex along the highway. They found it suspicious and thought the Milford Police might be interested. They shared that information with me."

"How very odd," John said.

"One of the neighbors saw a man of your description tossing the food into the Dumpster."

John made no comment.

Baker glared at both Tricia and Angelica, as though daring them to say something. Neither did.

"What else have you been up to since your return to Stoneham?" Baker demanded.

"Mostly watching bad TV. The apartment I was staying in has a rather uninteresting cable package. And then I had the heart attack. I'm sure the hospital in Milford can attest I was there."

"Yes," Baker grumbled. "Will you be staying here?"

"For a while. My darling girls are keen to ship me back to Connecticut as fast as they can make arrangements."

"We are *not* shipping you off," Tricia said. "We're going to find you a nice place to live." She turned to Baker. "I'm sure it won't happen for several weeks."

"More's the pity," Angelica muttered.

"And I'm currently without funds *and* personal transportation—unless I walk—so I'm pretty much stuck here at the Brookview," John lamented.

Baker consulted his notebook before slapping it shut. "If I have more questions, I'll look you up there or call."

"My phone only seems capable of calling the desk." John shot a withering glance at his daughters. "I don't know if incoming calls can be accommodated."

"Of course they can," Angelica said. "They'll go through the front desk."

"I'll be in touch," Baker said, before turning and exiting the room.

Once he'd gone, John glared at his children once again. "I feel like I was set up."

"Not at all. We knew Chief Baker wanted to talk with you and thought it would be prudent to be here with you at the time."

"May I go back to my bungalow and watch more bad TV?"

"Of course."

"But first"—John pulled a piece of Brookview stationery from his left pants pocket—"I need a few things. Since I'm being held hostage here against my will, perhaps one of you would be so good as to get me what I need."

"I'll do it," Tricia said. After all, Angelica had been footing the bill for just about everything else John had needed—or appropriated.

"I'll go pay the lunch check," Angelica said, picking up the leather holder Danny had left earlier, and she exited the room.

Tricia hung back and glanced at the list John had given her. The handwriting was familiar, but not as steady as it had once been. Tricia looked back at her father's careworn face, and a pang of sadness constricted her heart. It was an old man who sat before her.

"I'll get these things and drop them off later today," she promised.

"Thank you."

She offered him a hand up, which he accepted.

They caught up with Angelica, who folded her credit card receipt, stuffing it into her purse. "We'd better get going. Tricia and I both have businesses to run."

"We'll walk you back to your bungalow, Daddy," Tricia said. Angelica led the way out of the lobby and back through the inn to the back entrance. They crossed the parking lot without a word.

"I don't know if I'll be back to see you again today, Daddy," Angelica said.

"I won't miss you," John muttered.

Angelica didn't comment, and neither did she react to his words.

"See you later," she said as John dug for the room key in his pants pocket.

"I'll be back with your things in a little while," Tricia promised, and leaned forward to kiss his cheek.

"At least one of my children still cares about me," John muttered as Angelica continued on to her car.

"She's just upset with you, Daddy, and with cause."

He shrugged.

Tricia waited until he entered the bungalow and closed the door before hurrying after her sister. Angelica was already in the car with the engine running.

Tricia got in. "Are you okay?"

"Why do you ask?"

"You seem upset."

Angelica eased the shift into reverse and backed out of the parking space. "I am. I'm upset that Daddy could be so flippant about the trouble he's caused. That he doesn't seem to care that he keeps making us look bad. And that he's a suspect in a murder case."

"You don't really think he killed Carol, do you?"

"Of course not. But that doesn't mean the chief won't try to pin her murder on him." She steered out of the parking lot and headed back toward the village. "It's bad enough my ex is a killer," she said, referring to Bob Kelly. "But I don't know how I'd live it down to find out my father is a murderer, too."

"What did you make of Daddy's comment that Carol was"—she didn't want to use the same term her father had used—"open to having sex with him—and boy do I wish I didn't know about that."

"Daddy's a *man*. They *love* to brag about their prowess. But I must say, I'm rather amazed he's still interested. Do you think he uses Viagra?"

"I don't know or care!"

Angelica smiled. "Most children don't want to think about their parents having sex—but that's how we got here."

And again, Tricia wondered if it was John who was Angelica's biological father. She scrutinized her sister's face. She definitely had the

Miles nose. Okay, so she probably *was* John's daughter—unless he had a brother they'd never known about. But that didn't mean he was married to their mother at the time of her conception. It was something she needed to ponder. Maybe she should do some genealogical research to find out just what year her parents had married.

Then again, who cared? The past was the past.

Only it wasn't for her mother.

"Do you want me to drop you off at your store?"

"No. I may as well head straight to the drugstore to get the things Daddy needs, so you can drop me off at my car."

"Right."

A minute later, Angelica pulled into the municipal parking lot, steered over to Tricia's car, and parked two spaces away.

"What do you want to do about dinner?" Angelica asked.

"Are you up to cooking?"

"Yes. I always feel better when I'm preparing food."

"What will we have?"

"What else? Zucchini in some way, shape, or form."

"Sounds okay to me."

"Great. I'll see you after you close your store," Angelica said.

"Right."

The sisters parted, and Tricia got into her own vehicle, which was stifling hot. She started the engine and opened the windows before taking off.

As she pulled out of the lot, she noticed activity on the village square. Ginny stood on the sidewalk near a truck from R & A Tents and Awnings, speaking to a man who was probably the driver. Ginny caught sight of her and waved. Tricia waved back.

The first annual Stoneham Wine and Jazz Festival would start in only two days. Poor Carol Talbot was dead—never to witness or be a part of the fun.

It was a sobering thought. Tricia had already had too many sobering thoughts that day. She turned on the radio and Katy Perry belted out her latest hit. Still, thoughts of Carol Talbot seemed to shadow her thoughts, and she wondered when the dead woman would stop haunting her.

TWENTY

**The parking** lot of the big chain drugstore in Milford was nearly empty when Tricia parked her car. She got out and headed into the store. Once inside, she opted for a cart instead of a basket. John's list of things he wanted was fairly extensive.

She read the overhead signs and located the aisle that stocked shaving cream. It had been a long time since she'd purchased that item. Her former husband, Christopher, hadn't been fussy, but her father had requested a specific brand, as well as a new razor and blades. Ouch! They were expensive! She found them, then the toothpaste, an arthritis-strength pain reliever—was he hurting and hadn't mentioned it?—as well as other sundries. Last on the list was a bag of peppermints. She'd forgotten that her father often had a stash of peppermints on him at any given time. Her mother would never let her eat them. She said they promoted tooth decay, but her father liked to sneak them to Tricia whenever her mother was out of earshot.

With the list exhausted, Tricia steered her cart toward the cash desk and was surprised to see Carol's neighbor manning the register.

"Hi," Tricia called, noted the name tag on the woman's smock, and added, "Ellen. Remember me? We spoke last Wednesday evening."

The woman studied Tricia's face for a moment before recognition dawned. "Oh, yes. You were with the woman who had the Bichon Frise—Sarge."

"That's right. I'm Tricia Miles. I run the mystery bookstore, Haven't Got a Clue, in Stoneham."

"I read romances—and the steamier the better," Ellen said with a crooked smile.

"Do you patronize the Have a Heart romance store in Stoneham?"

Ellen shook her head. "I have an e-reader." She left it at that.

Tricia started taking the items out of her cart and putting them on the counter. "Shopping for a friend?" Ellen asked, ringing up the shaving cream.

"My father, actually. He's visiting Stoneham."

"That's nice. All our relatives live out of state."

"Just like Carol's," Tricia commented idly. "I heard she was originally from Indiana."

Ellen's expression soured. "I guess."

"I was wondering what would happen to Carol's house."

Ellen shrugged.

"I understand her husband had quite a collection."

"What?" Ellen asked sharply.

"That he collected baseball cards or something."

"Oh, yeah," Ellen said, and went back to ringing up the sale. "I saw it. It wasn't all that great."

Tricia nodded. "Do you know if there'll be a funeral service for Carol?"

Again, Ellen shrugged.

Her lack of interest in her neighbor seemed a little odd, considering she'd been willing to talk about Carol less than a week before. Tricia tried again. "It won't seem the same without her at the pub tonight. There's a tournament. She was one of our best players."

"Look, I don't really want to talk about *her*." The emphasis she put on that last word was distinctly unfriendly.

"Sorry. I just thought that as you and she were friends—"

"She may have been my friend at one time, but no longer."

Of course not; Carol was now dead. But had Ellen had a change of heart before or *after* that death? Tricia thought she knew the answer to that question.

"I'm sorry. I just thought—"

Ellen didn't let her finish the sentence. "That'll be forty-six dollars and sixty-seven cents."

Tricia pulled out her credit card and swiped the machine on the counter. Ellen handed her the slip to sign and waited impatiently for Tricia to hand it back. She gave Tricia the final receipt and shoved the three plastic bags Tricia's way.

"Thanks for shopping with us today." A dismissal if ever Tricia had heard one.

"It was nice talking to you," Tricia said, but Ellen folded her arms across her chest and just looked at her. Tricia plastered on a faux smile. "Bye."

Still nothing.

Tricia gathered up the bags and exited the store. And she wondered why the subject of Carol Talbot was suddenly off-limits with Ellen.

It took about fifteen minutes for Tricia to drive back to the Brookview Inn. She got out of her car, gathered the bags, locked the car, and headed for bungalow two. Transferring the third bag to her left hand, she knocked on the door. "Daddy. It's Tricia."

No answer.

Maybe he was in the bathroom.

She waited thirty seconds before knocking again.

Still no answer.

Feeling a bit panicky, she walked over to the window, but the drapes were drawn. What if he'd had another heart attack? What if he hadn't been able to summon help and was lying on the floor helpless—or worse!

Angelica had a master key to all the rooms, but she was back in the village.

Tricia hurried to the main building, ran up the steps, and then jogged to the front desk, with the can of shaving cream banging against her leg like a truncheon, but no one was standing at reception.

"Hello! Is anybody here? I need help!"

Still no one appeared, so Tricia dropped the bags on the floor and hurried over to Antonio's office. She banged on his office door, then tried the handle. It was unlocked.

She shoved her head inside his office. Antonio was on the phone, but said to his caller, "Just a moment. Tricia, what's wrong?"

"It's Daddy. I went to the store to get him some things he needed not half an hour ago and now I can't get him to answer the door. I'm worried he might have had another heart attack."

"I'm sorry," he spoke into the phone again. "I'll have to call you back, I have an emergency." He hung up the phone and rose to his feet. "Bungalow two?"

"Yes."

They hurried out into the lobby, where Tricia bent to grab the bags and her purse. Antonio took two of the bags and took off down the hall, with Tricia trailing behind.

By the time she caught up with him at the bungalow, he'd already opened the door and entered and was nowhere in sight.

"Antonio!"

He came out from the bathroom, shaking his head. "There's no one here."

"But that can't be!"

Antonio shrugged.

Tricia set the bags down on the coffee table and looked around before she headed for the dresser. Yanking open a drawer, she saw that John's clothes were still there, but there was no other sign of him.

"I don't understand it. He's got no money, and no transportation." She remembered what her father had said earlier; that he was a prisoner there. She hadn't spied him walking on the sidewalk when she'd steered for the inn, and it was a good fifteen-minute hike to the village. Where could he have gone—and more importantly, why had he left?

"Not again," Angelica said with a weary sigh after Tricia had called to say their father had pulled yet another fast escape. "But if his clothes and everything else are still in the bungalow, he *may* still be coming back."

"What should I do?"

"It could be hours—or even days—before he returns. I'd say go on with whatever you had planned for the rest of the day."

"Doesn't that seem rather—" Tricia struggled for a descriptor. *Heartless* wasn't the word; it could be said her father's vanishing act was heartless, when she'd told him she would soon be back from the store—and after dropping nearly fifty bucks for the things he'd requested. Disinterested? Oh, no—she was *very* interested in finding out where he'd gone, and why. She should take a day from Angelica's planner and admit defeat, or at least resignation.

"Okay," she said finally.

"We'll still have a few drinks and a nice dinner together and be grateful we have each other."

"Sounds like a plan. I'll ask the desk to give Daddy a message to call us."

"He's got no outside line," Angelica reminded her sister.

"Okay, then I'll have them call *me* and I'll call him back." *And give him a piece of my mind, too.*

"Keep me posted," Angelica said, and rang off.

Tricia put her phone away and headed for reception to ask for a call when her father returned, while feeling that it was probably a useless gesture. When the shift changed, the message was likely to be lost or abandoned.

On the drive back to Haven't Got a Clue, Tricia kept a watch for her father in case she saw him along the sidewalk. He'd said he couldn't go anywhere except to walk. He had no money for a cab, but she hadn't thought to check his wallet for credit or ATM cards. Some sleuth she was.

Tricia checked her watch as she left the municipal parking lot. It was already after three. What must her employees think of her constantly leaving the shop to run errands—and interference with her father?

Two tour buses were parked at the far side of the lot and the sidewalk was filled with people, but once again when she entered her noisy shop, the customers were few and far between. Pixie was back to wearing earplugs, and Mr. Everett was nowhere to be found.

"He went home," Pixie reported. "He feels guilty working when there's no money in the till. Besides, he said he feels bad leaving Miss Marple all alone. She's used to having company most of the day, and Grace is a docent at the Horticultural Society this afternoon."

Tricia nodded as the sound of banging continued unabated on the floor above. She reached for a pair of the earplugs. Conversation was out of the question under those conditions, and she and Pixie read for most of the rest of the afternoon. It was nearly five when the phone rang.

"Haven't Got a Clue, this is Tricia—".

"And this is Angelica. I'm running late and the Patisserie is going to close in a little while. Could you run down the block to see if they have any Italian or French bread left to go with our dinner?"

"Sure. It's so dead here"—a loud bang overhead sounded as though to negate that remark—"I've got nothing else to do."

"Excellent. I'll see you around six."

Tricia hung up the phone.

Pixie placed the fingers of her right hand against her forehead and struck a pose. "I see another errand in your future."

"Angelica wants me to get a loaf of bread from the Patisserie. I'll only be gone a few minutes."

Pixie waved a hand as though in dismissal. "Like you said, you've got nothing else to do."

Tricia grabbed her purse. "I'll be right back."

Luckily, Nikki had one unsold baguette left and she rang up the sale in no time. But as Tricia left the bakery, she paused, taking in the shop next door: the Have a Heart romance bookstore. On a whim, she decided to pay the owner a quick visit.

Unlike her own store, Have a Heart was quiet. Soft music played in the background while several women perused the shelves.

"Hi, Tricia," Joyce Widman called in greeting. "I don't think I ever remember you dropping by the store before. Did you suddenly change genres?"

Tricia and Joyce had become friendly at the Chamber of Commerce meetings, but this was the first time Tricia had ever actually entered the romance bookstore.

"You can't talk me out of loving mysteries, but I could use a little of your expertise."

Joyce laughed. "I don't think I could call myself an expert on any subject, but I'm willing to take a shot at it. What's on your mind?"

"I was speaking to a reader who told me she was a romance reader—and the steamier the better."

"Oh, yeah?"

Tricia nodded. "Do you carry a lot of hot titles?"

Joyce shook her head. "I sold a few copies of *Fifty Shades of Grey* and its sequels when they first came out, but most of my clientele like contemporary or historical romances."

"So where do people buy the really steamy stuff?"

"Online. Erotica titles sell like hotcakes for e-readers, but I've also heard authors complain that they get returned a lot, too—cutting off their income."

"Why's that?"

"Readers—women *and* men—love the explicit stuff, but they don't always want their friends and family to know they read it."

That made sense. But Ellen hadn't seemed at all ashamed to mention her preference—not that she'd actually used the word *erotica*. It was hard to think of the drab woman as overly interested in sex—but then, perhaps it was just that fact that made her preference understandable.

"Of course, Vamps sells a lot of vintage stuff."

"Vamps?"

"The porn shop up by the highway. I met the owner at one of the Chamber mixers. What's his name?" She looked thoughtful.

"Marshall Cambridge," Tricia supplied. The guy hadn't exactly been welcomed to the Chamber with open arms, but he paid his membership dues and hung out the Chamber shingle, and he had come to a couple of Chamber events when he first joined—but that was about the extent of his involvement with the organization. And he'd quickly become a regular at the Dog-Eared Page.

One of Joyce's customers walked up to the register with her arms filled with books.

"I'd better get going. It was nice to see you. Talk to you more at the next Chamber meeting."

"Bye," Joyce called as Tricia left the store.

Armed with her baguette, Tricia headed back to Haven't Got a Clue, thinking about what Joyce had said. Ellen said she liked steamy reading. Did she only read erotic e-books, or was there a chance she might also patronize a place that sold hard-copy versions of the genre?

Doing an about-face, Tricia headed toward the municipal parking lot to get her car. After all, it was too far a walk to pay a visit to Vamps.

TWENTY-ONE

The Vamps parking lot was empty—for which Tricia was grateful. She really didn't want to be caught dead—or alive—in the place. But it seemed that curiosity always got the better of her, and now that she was here, she knew she had to enter.

Tricia got out of the car, looking around to see if anyone was around to witness her journey into the depths of what she thought might be the depraved, and entered the store. She must have triggered an electric eye, because a buzzer went off. Seconds later, a purple beaded curtain at the back of the shop parted, and Marshall Cambridge stepped into the shop.

"Well, if it isn't Stoneham's village jinx," Marshall called jovially.

Tricia didn't laugh. She *loathed* the phrase. "What can I do for you?" Marshall asked. "Need any marital aids?"

"I'm not married."

"All the more reason to buy a sex toy or two to make your life more interesting."

Tricia still wasn't laughing. Instead, she took in the shop, which housed quite a number of magazine racks with what looked like new and vintage copies of various glossy magazines aimed at men, women—and various combinations of the same. Along the walls were framed pictures of pinup girls—most of them nude—from what she guessed were the nineteen forties and fifties.

"What can I do for you?" Marshall asked.

"I understand that you sell a lot of erotica."

"I do indeed. What are you interested in?"

"I'm not interested in anything of that nature."

"Then why are you here?"

"To ask you a few questions about your clientele."

"If you're looking for names—forget it. I'd be out of business in a heartbeat if I ratted on the villagers who frequent my establishment."

"How about those who are dead?"

"Such as?" Marshall asked warily.

"Dale and Carol Talbot," Tricia bluffed.

Marshall's head seemed to bow involuntarily. She had definitely struck a nerve.

"What do you want to know?"

"I understand Dale had a very nice collection of erotica," she bluffed.

"I wouldn't know. I only dealt with Carol."

That stood to reason; the shop had only been open for a few months, and Dale had died back into the winter. "Were you buying from or selling to her?"

"Buying."

Tricia blinked. She hadn't expected him to actually answer her question. "What kind of things?"

"See these framed pinup illustrations?" Marshall asked. "They're prints from artists like Mike Ludlow, Duane Bryers, and Gil Elvgren. They're not especially valuable, but prime examples of what was available in the nineteen thirties, forties, and fifties."

"How much can you sell them for?"

"I get about fifty bucks each."

Tricia nodded. "What else did Carol try to sell you?"

"She brought in some vintage—Victorian—photographs. Not copies, the real thing. But there's no way I could give her the prices she was asking for the stuff."

"What kinds of things are we talking about—besides photos?"

Marshall shrugged. "Playing cards, books, and magazines."

"Where else could she sell them?"

Marshall shrugged. "Online. She may have also tried to flog them with an auction house. But I did buy a number of the pinups." Again he jerked a thumb over his shoulder to indicate the framed beauties in provocative poses wearing little to nothing over their birthday suits.

"Do you have any photos that are similar to what Carol wanted to sell you?"

"Oh, sure." He turned and opened an old, four-drawer oak cabinet, rummaged around for a bit, then pulled out a file folder of photos. He handed them to Tricia, who thumbed through them, wincing. There was no finesse to these photos. Unashamed women—who'd probably been outcasts in what was then a very straitlaced society—showed off what Mother Nature gave them, and in the most uncomplimentary of poses. You couldn't even call the photos alluring, they were just . . . bad, with an almost textbook aesthetic.

She handed them back to Marshall.

"Not what you expected?"

"No." And not at all what she would have considered erotic. More . . . pathetic. "Collectors actually pay for these?"

"Oh, yeah," Marshall admitted.

"When was the last time Carol came to see you?"

"About a week ago."

"Did you buy anything?"

"The last of her pinup girls."

"I don't suppose she mentioned why she needed to sell the collection."

"Something about her health care not picking up the tab for something. I wasn't really paying all that much attention."

What health care was that? Seeing the psychologist? Often insurance only paid for a certain amount of counseling visits. They expected their clients to shape up PDQ or go without such sessions.

Tricia inspected the man before her. "I'm curious; what made you go into this business?"

"Money, what else? People are always looking for cheap thrills, but these days they can get a hell of a lot of that on the Internet for free. My clientele wants the real thing, and they come to me from all over New England."

Tricia couldn't imagine why.

"Thank you for speaking with me."

"My pleasure. You wouldn't want to pass out some of my business cards to your customers, would you?"

"Sorry, I don't think they'd go over well."

"It never hurts to ask," Marshall said with a shrug.

Tricia bid him *adieu* and headed back for her car.

So, Carol had a collection of erotica she was trying to flog—pardon the pun. Tricia wondered if the collection was still intact—or at least as intact as it had been before Carol's death.

Did she dare ask Chief Baker about it? Had John seen the collection when he'd been rooting around for things of value to pawn? Was he likely to tell if she asked?

Tricia got back in her car and drove back to the municipal parking lot, wondering just how valuable what she'd learned could actually be. And worse—what if it meant nothing at all?

Not long after Tricia returned to her store, the sidewalks cleared, the buses filled with tourists took off, and it was finally time to close the bookstore for the day. And still no one from the Brookview Inn had called to say that John had returned to his bungalow.

The construction workers had already given up work for the day, and Pixie gathered her purse, pulling out her car keys. "Another day closer to my wedding," she said, her tone sounding distinctly dreamy.

"I need to look at the renovation of my home in the same light—only you have an actual date for your wedding and I only have vague threats about when they'll be finished with construction."

"It'll happen," Pixie assured her.

Out the corner of her eye, Tricia noticed a familiar figure ambling up the sidewalk.

Pixie noticed, too. "Well, if it isn't that author guy—Richardson."

Richardson stopped outside Haven't Got a Clue's big display window, seemingly contemplating the items on offer.

"Do you want me to quickly turn the sign on the door to CLOSED?" Pixie asked.

"No. If he wants to come in for a chat, I'm willing to talk."

Pixie waggled her eyebrows suggestively, but this time didn't voice her hopes for an uptick in Tricia's love life. "I guess I'll see you in the morning."

"Have a good evening," Tricia said, and Pixie pushed through the door, pausing only long enough to give Richardson a good once-over before she turned right and headed down the sidewalk.

Richardson walked over to the door and entered the shop. "Are you still open, or am I too late?"

"Too late for what?" Tricia asked.

"To see how your investigation is going."

Tricia shrugged. So far her inquiries seemed to have gotten her next to nowhere. "I've got a few minutes I can talk, but then I've got a dinner appointment." He didn't have to know with whom.

Richardson sauntered over to stand before the cash desk, resting his elbows on the glass top, then his head in his hands. "People around here don't seem to want to open up to a stranger."

"Would you?"

He shrugged as best he could. "Maybe. Maybe not. Are you having any better luck?"

"That depends on your definition of success. To whom have you spoken?"

"If I tell you, it might tip my hand."

"I could say the same thing."

He smiled. "Then it looks like we're at an impasse."

"I guess so," Tricia said, returning the smile.

"I understand I wasn't the only one who got slapped by Carol Talbot the night of the book signing."

"That's true," Tricia said, keeping her voice neutral.

"I understand it was also your father."

"Word gets around."

"May I ask *why* she slapped him?"

"From what I understand, he said something she didn't like."

"And that was?"

Tricia shrugged, declining to answer.

"Is your father around?"

"I can truthfully say that I have no idea where he currently is—but I would very much like to speak to him myself."

Richardson nodded. "Has your friend the police chief shared any news about Carol Talbot's murder with you?"

"I haven't run into him lately," she fibbed.

"It doesn't sound like he's got any idea who may have killed Carol."

Except for possibly trying to pin the rap on my father, Tricia thought sourly. She glanced at the clock. "I really need to get going, or I'm going to be late for my dinner appointment."

"Is there any chance we could meet later for a nightcap?"

"Tonight is darts tournament night at the Dog-Eared Page, and I'm playing."

"What time?"

"Nine."

Richardson smiled. "Then I'll be there to cheer you on."

Tricia smiled, too. "I'd like that." She may as well make nice. Maybe then she could get some information out of him, since he didn't seem inclined to share any just then.

"Great. I'll see you there."

Richardson headed back out the door, waved, and closed it behind him. Tricia walked to the back of the store to check the door to the alley to make sure the workers had locked it, came back to the front of the store, lowered the blinds, then grabbed her purse and the baguette Angelica had requested.

Turning the sign on the door to CLOSED, she locked up and headed for the Cookery next door. The day had been filled with interesting tidbits of information that may or may not be relevant to Carol Talbot's murder, and Tricia wasn't sure what would end up being pertinent. Needing a neutral sounding board, she knew she had a lot to talk over with her sister.

TWENTY-TWO

Tricia's canine welcoming committee was once again waiting behind the door of Angelica's loft when she entered the apartment. Sarge jumped, barked, wagged his tail with wild abandon, and nearly did a backflip in his joy at seeing her once again.

"Calm down—calm down, and I'll give you a biscuit."

Sarge had an extensive vocabulary, and he also knew right where the biscuits were located, so he raced ahead of Tricia to the kitchen in the front of the building.

"Hush!" Angelica commanded, and the dog instantly went silent, but his little butt wiggled as his tail pumped from side to side.

Tricia set her keys and the baguette on the counter, dipped her hand in the lead crystal jar that held Sarge's treats, and came up with two biscuits. She held out her hand until Sarge sat up smartly, then she tossed it in the air and he sprang to his feet, catching his treat and instantly crushing it between his teeth. He munched it down and stood, waiting for the next one. Tricia sniffed the biscuit, unable to fathom its appeal, then tossed it, too.

"Would you like a glass of wine?" Angelica offered. She stood at the counter, once again grating a zucchini.

"No thanks. I want to be sharp during the darts tournament later tonight." Unlike many of the other contenders, Tricia chose not to imbibe until after game play, and often wondered if that alone might be the key to her success.

"I'd almost forgotten about that," Angelica said as she systematically reduced the veggie in her hand to pulp.

"What's on the menu tonight?" Tricia asked.

"Quiche. I know it's another eggy recipe, but who can turn down bacon?"

Once upon a time, Tricia could—but no more.

"So, what's the dirt for the day—besides what you've already dumped on me," Angelica asked.

"I haven't heard from Daddy—or anyone at the inn reporting on his return. For someone with no transportation—or money to pay for it—he sure seems to get around."

"I'll say. Can you get the eggs out of the fridge?"

Tricia opened the refrigerator and took out the carton, placing it on the counter near her sister's work space.

"Just before I came over here, Steven Richardson arrived at my store to pump me for information."

"Oh?"

"He wanted to know why Carol slapped Daddy."

"And you said?"

Tricia shrugged. "I played it cool, but didn't give him the answers he wanted." She frowned. "I like the guy, but I don't trust him as far as I can throw a dart."

"It was rude of him to stand you up for lunch."

"I'm not talking about that. I just get the feeling that maybe he's up to no good."

"In what way?"

"I don't know. The way he spoke—kind of slyly—made me think that *he* thought he'd pulled a fast one on me."

"What do you mean?"

Again Tricia shrugged. "I don't know. But he said he would be at the Dog-Eared Page to watch the darts tournament tonight."

"Will it throw you off your game?"

Tricia took her usual seat at the kitchen island. "Not a chance."

"Anything else worth mentioning?"

"Several things, actually. I ran into Ellen Shields at the drugstore."

"And she is?"

"Carol's neighbor—you know, Sarge's fan."

Angelica nodded, then went back to work. "I suppose you grilled her."

"I did nothing of the kind. We had a brief conversation."

"Did she reveal anything juicy?"

"She seems to have changed her mind about Carol. No glowing reports of her being a good neighbor."

"Why the switch?"

"I don't know. But she admitted she likes to read erotica."

"She said that out loud in the drugstore?"

"Not exactly. But after I got the baguette, I dipped into the Have a Heart bookstore and spoke with Joyce." Tricia told her what the shopkeeper had had to say.

Angelica waved a hand in dismissal. "Oh, everybody and their brother read *Fifty Shades of Grey*, it doesn't mean a thing."

"I didn't read it."

"Well, I *did*," Angelica said.

"And?" Tricia asked, curiously.

She frowned. "It got tiresome. I'd rather read a cookbook. Then at least I might learn something new."

"What?" Tricia practically shouted, appalled at the implication.

Angelica frowned. "Oh, you've got a dirty mind. I've never been into kinky sex, but I know plenty of people who were—and I definitely mean that in the past tense."

"Anybody I know?"

Angelica resumed her grating. "It's not nice to tell tales."

Tricia sighed, reminding herself that her sister was very good at keeping secrets. "Anyway, Joyce reminded me that Marshall Cambridge owns a porn shop down by the highway."

Angelica shook her head and her expression soured, as though she'd just tasted something bitter. "And what does that have to do with Carol Talbot's murder or Ellen?"

"It seems Carol's husband had quite a stash of sexually explicit photos, pinup pictures, books, and magazines. Carol was selling it off piecemeal—perhaps to pay for her psychological counseling."

"Who said she needed counseling?"

"People Ginny works with. Should we get the bacon going?"

"It's in the fridge. Take it out and I'll cook it."

"I can do that," Tricia offered.

"You don't mind?"

"Of course not."

Tricia retrieved the bacon from the fridge, then took one of Angelica's heavy skillets from the cupboard and set it on the stove. She washed her hands before opening the package and laid half the contents in the pan, then turned on the burner. She put the package back in the fridge and washed her hands once more. They continued talking while they worked.

"What else did Marshall have to say?"

"He didn't want to pay the prices that Carol was asking and suggested she might be trying to sell the collection online. I wonder what Grant Baker would say if I mentioned all this to him."

"He'd probably tell you to mind your own business."

That was a distinct possibility. Tricia gave up on that line of conversation. "So how was *your* day?" she asked, and took out a fork so she could turn the bacon when necessary, noting her fingers still felt a little greasy.

Angelica sighed. "Very long. Nigela had to approve some last-minute details for the wine and jazz fest."

"Is Ginny having problems?"

"No, but one of her vendors was playing hardball. She tried to handle it herself, but the guy was a total jerk."

"Oh, dear. She's terribly afraid she's going to disappoint you."

"Pulling this event together was a nearly impossible task, and she's managed it brilliantly. I simply reminded the vendor—in my no-nonsense voice—of our contract, and threatened to never work with him again."

"Couldn't Ginny have done that?"

"She will—next time."

"What else?"

"Much as I love the job, I've got to give up something, and it looks like come fall it'll be the Chamber presidency."

"That's too bad—you've done a wonderful job. Much better than your predecessor."

"We won't speak his name," Angelica said acidly. She'd get no argument from Tricia.

Neither had uttered Bob Kelly's name since the day he'd shot Christopher.

"*You* would make a great president. You shadowed me for months when you volunteered to help out after your shop burned. You'd be a terrific candidate."

"I never thought about it."

"Think," Angelica said, turning her no-nonsense gaze on her sister, before reaching for her wineglass.

It seemed like whatever Angelica wanted—she got. But as Tricia considered the idea, she found it wasn't at all repugnant.

Tricia looked around the kitchen, noting there wasn't a cookbook in sight. "Where's your recipe?"

"I've made so many quiches over the years, I don't even need to consult one." Angelica washed her hands, dried them, and then began breaking eggs into a bowl. "How's that bacon coming along?"

"Nearly done."

Angelica whisked the eggs to a mighty froth, then reached for the pie pan nearby. It looked—and the kitchen smelled—like she'd prebaked the crust. Sarge wandered back into the kitchen and settled beside Angelica, looking hopeful.

"You know it's not time to eat yet. Why don't you go back to your basket to wait?" But Sarge didn't seem inclined to do as she instructed and began to whine.

"You know that tactic doesn't work with me," Angelica admonished, and turned back to work on her quiche.

Tricia turned the bacon for one last time. "I think this is done."

"Oh, good. Bring the pan over here and we can drain the grease before we add the bacon to the egg mixture."

Tricia turned off the burner and grasped the pan's handle with her right hand, but it still felt gummy from the greasy bacon she'd handled, and she switched to her left. As she turned, Sarge leapt to his feet, startling her. The pan tipped, and she went to grab it with her free hand—forgetting how hot it would be. The bacon grease spilled onto the top of her right hand and she cried out, dropping the pan on the floor with a resounding crash.

"Tricia!" Angelica hollered—sounding fearful, not angry—and Sarge took off at a gallop.

Shocked, Tricia just stood there—holding her wrist, gasping. Angelica grabbed her elbow and pulled her toward the sink, and both of them nearly fell on the greasy floor. Angelica turned on the cold water and plunged Tricia's hand under it.

"Oh, oh—that hurts. It hurtsithurtsithurts," Tricia grated, wincing.

"I'm so sorry," an agitated Angelica cried. "You know that Sarge would never mean to—"

"Oh, don't be silly. He just thought he was going to get a treat."

And he had. For they looked down to see the dog had returned and was not only scarfing up the bacon on the floor—but was licking up the grease as well.

"Sarge! Stop that," Angelica ordered, but the allure of bacon was not to be denied, and in no time he'd eaten every piece.

"Well, at least it'll be easier for you to clean the floor," Tricia said, still wincing.

Angelica reduced the flow of water. "I've dealt with a lot of burns. You need to keep that hand under the water for at least ten minutes, and then we can assess the damage."

Tricia's heart sank. The darts tournament! Despite the cool water, the skin on the top of her hand still burned. Would she be able to play at all? She sighed. "What will we do about dinner?"

"There's still half a package of bacon in the fridge. I'll clean up the rest of the mess and get it going. That is, if you can even stand the sight of bacon after this."

"I'm not going to let this little incident put me off bacon for life." She pulled her hand back from the stream and examined it. The skin was bright pink and smarting. She plunged it back under the faucet.

Tricia glanced up to take in her sister's guilt-filled eyes glistening with tears and knew she needed to lighten the tension.

"You know, I think I'll take that drink, after all."

TWENTY-THREE

"You don't have to go," Angelica said, as she and Tricia left her apartment and walked down the sidewalk toward the Dog-Eared Page just before nine o'clock.

"If I don't show up, everyone will think I'm afraid to face the Purple Finch team."

"Well then, you don't have to stay. Just show them your hand and that will shut up anyone who thinks you're faking an injury. You've got a nasty second-degree burn."

Over the years, Angelica had seen—and experienced—a number of kitchen accidents. Tricia trusted her assessment. The hand looked and still felt vile. Tricia kept her arm raised, as letting it hang made the burn throb. It was going to take a while for the skin to heal.

The bar was crowded, as it was every month on darts tournament night. As reigning champion, Tricia always made sure she was there to play—not necessarily to win, but because she enjoyed the competition, and now she was disappointed that it might be a month or more before she could play again.

Michele saw the sisters standing just inside the door and hurried over to join them, catching sight of Tricia's bright pink hand. "Goodness. What did you *do* to yourself?"

"Bacon grease," Angelica answered for her.

"That's nasty. I imagine it's quite painful."

"You've got that right," Tricia said. "Unfortunately, I could hardly hold a fork to eat dinner. There's no way I can play tonight."

"I'm so sorry. It looks like the Dog-Eared Page has lost both its stars this week."

"But only temporarily," Angelica said firmly.

"Yes, quite." Michele looked back at the crowd in the back of the pub. Maybe it was because Carol had died that so many had gathered and it was standing room only. Were those who weren't regulars only there to gawk? As Tricia looked at all their faces, mixed in among her friends and acquaintances, she recognized Ellen's husband among the crowd. Maybe she'd finally learn his name.

"I wanted to let you know that there'll be a toast in Carol's honor before game play," Michele continued. "Would you like to say something?"

"Um," Tricia stalled. "I . . . don't think so. I mean, I didn't know her well at all. In fact, we barely ever said hello to one another." Not that Tricia hadn't tried—and on more than one occasion.

"That's all right. You seem to be in the majority." Michele looked at her watch. "I'd better get things moving."

"Do you want something from the bar?" Angelica asked.

"A new hand?" Tricia suggested.

"Sorry. No can do."

"Then a glass of wine, thank you."

"Coming right up."

Tricia strayed to the back of the room to listen to the pub manager's speech.

Michele elbowed her way through the crowd, but stopped at the bar to pick up a glass of what looked like a gin and tonic in one hand and a spoon in the other. She moved to stand before the darts board on the south wall and clinked the spoon against the glass to gain everyone's attention. Once they'd quieted, she spoke.

"Welcome, everyone, to the Dog-Eared Page's monthly darts tournament," Michele began. "But before we begin, let us remember Carol Talbot. Although she was only a recent addition to the regulars here at the pub, she proved herself to be a worthy darts player."

Everyone listened attentively, but that seemed to be about all Michele had been prepared to say. It was Carol's neighbor who finally lifted his glass of beer and said, "Hear, hear."

"Hear, hear," many of the onlookers said, but for the amount of people in attendance, not nearly enough of them had spoken up.

Tricia watched as the man took a healthy swig of his beer. Funny, his wife had said they didn't drink. She looked around, but Ellen didn't seem to have joined her husband that night.

Michele gave a quick recap of the rules of the games of 301 and 501, and then each of the players who'd signed up for that evening, including the Purple Finchers, stepped forward to take their nine warm-up shots. Surprisingly enough, it was Carol's neighbor who stepped up when Michele called out "Bradley Shields" as one of the opposing players.

"Unfortunately," Michele said. "We've had a player drop out. Tricia Miles has injured her hand and won't be able to play tonight."

The crowd groaned. How many bets had already been lost? A number of people came up to her to offer their regrets, but also insisted on looking at her hand. The skin was puffy and red, with one large blister and a number of smaller ones clustered around it. More than one person winced.

Michele had a job quieting the group, and Tricia decided to move back and away from the play. Now that the tournament was about to begin, a number of tables had emptied. She spied Angelica sitting at one of them and moved to join her.

"I figured you'd like to watch the tournament," Angelica said from her seat that faced away from the back of the bar.

Tricia slipped into the booth and watched as Shields strode up to take his place in front of the board. He threw three darts, garnering what would have been a good score had they actually been playing. No doubt about it; he was good—possibly as good as Carol had been. As they were neighbors, perhaps he and Carol had played the game together on a regular basis.

As usual, Michele acted as the official scorekeeper, as well as the mistress of ceremonies. She called out the names of the other two contenders, and she watched with interest as they threw their practice shots.

For all the hype about how good they were, there really was only one good player on the Purple Finchers team: Bradley Shields. It would be Jamie Henderson against Shields, and Dave Watson, one of the construction workers from Tricia's renovation, stepped up to play against Jim Thorton. Without Tricia and Carol playing, the atmosphere was decidedly testosterone-charged.

Tricia had played against Henderson several times and wasn't surprised when Shields easily defeated him. Watson was better, but not up to Tricia's standard, and he went down nearly as fast.

Tricia turned her attention to her glass on the table and also noticed a small bowl of ice water and a handful of cocktail napkins sitting before her.

"You can soak the napkins and place them on your hand. It'll make it feel better," Angelica advised.

"You always take such good care of me," Tricia said, offering her sister a wan smile.

"That's what big sisters do."

For the next ten minutes, Tricia alternated between watching the tournament and gently blotting the burn with the cold, wet napkins. It did seem to help.

At last Michele announced the winning team, which was no surprise: the Purple Finchers.

Oh well, there was always next time.

The other patrons drifted back to their seats and the music started up again. A rather smug-looking Brad stepped up to Tricia's table. "I'm sorry we didn't have the opportunity to play against each other."

"As am I," Tricia said truthfully.

"Carol said you were the best darts player in the village."

"I'm honored that she thought so. Can I buy you a drink?"

"Shouldn't I be asking that question?"

"Not at all."

"Did you ever offer to buy Carol a drink?" Shields asked.

Tricia frowned. "I don't think so."

Shields shrugged. "Then I think I'll pass."

At his refusal, Tricia forced a smile. "Perhaps we'll get to play some other day, Mr. Shields."

"Call me Brad. And we will play sometime," he said rather smugly, then nodded and headed for the door.

Angelica sipped her wine. "If nothing else, you're still undefeated."

Tricia looked behind her to watch Shields leave and caught sight of Steven Richardson sitting alone at one of the tables up front.

"I want to have a word with Steven." She nodded toward the thriller author.

"Ooh, this could be good. Go right ahead, but only if you promise to tell all later," Angelica said.

"You have my word." Tricia picked up her wineglass and stepped over to Richardson's table. "Is this seat taken?"

He looked up at her. He'd been nursing what looked like a Scotch on the rocks. "Sure."

Tricia took the seat across from him.

"You didn't play after all." She brandished her hand. Stevenson winced. "That looks evil."

"It certainly is." But she didn't want to talk about that. "So, how goes your investigation into Carol's death? Anything new happen since this afternoon?"

"I could ask the same of you."

She shook her head.

"I saw you talking to Brad Shields."

"Yes. I had no idea he was a member of the Purple Finchers—especially since his wife told me he didn't drink. The latter was obviously incorrect."

Stevenson shook his head. "There's something about that woman I don't trust."

"Ellen? Why?"

Richardson shook his head. "Nothing I can put my finger on."

Tricia debated telling him what Ellen had told her earlier that day, but decided against it. How could her choice of reading material possibly relate to Carol's death? "It doesn't seem like you're making much headway in this story. Will you be staying in Stoneham for a few more days or heading back to Boston?"

The corners of his lips quirked upward. "Would you like me to stay?"

Wouldn't you just love to hear me—or anyone—say yes?

Tricia shrugged. "The wine and jazz festival will begin on Wednesday. It's the first time it's being held in the village. It could be fun. Especially if you like music . . . and wine."

"I like both."

"They've scheduled a crepes food truck as part of the festivities. I thought I might give it a try."

"Sounds like the perfect match with a glass of cabernet."

"I guess that depends on what you choose for the filling."

Richardson raised his glass. "Touché."

Tricia nodded and sipped her wine.

Richardson sobered. "Have you heard from your father since we spoke?"

Tricia's lighthearted mood soured, too. "No. But I'm sure he'll turn up sometime soon." Bad pennies always did.

Richardson nodded, then glanced at his watch. "I haven't got my word count for the day, and there's only two hours left."

"Have you started working on Carol's book?"

He shook his head and drained his glass. "No. And if something doesn't crop up soon, it'll have no satisfying ending."

"Let's hope the killer shows his hand soon."

"If he—or she—is smart, they won't."

"Are you insinuating that this might be the perfect crime?"

"Not at all. But it's a fact—some killers do get away with murder."

The way he said it—so casually—gave Tricia a chill. But, sadly, he was also correct.

Richardson maneuvered out of the booth. "Until we meet again."

Tricia raised her nearly empty glass in salute and watched him leave the pub.

There was something odd about that man. She couldn't put her finger on what it was, but knew it would eventually come to her.

She left the booth. Almost immediately another couple grabbed it, and Tricia headed back to where Angelica sat. She'd just ordered another round. "So?"

Tricia shrugged. "Nothing to tell."

"From where I sat, it looked like flirting was going on."

"Harmless banter," Tricia countered. "The man just doesn't do anything for me."

Angelica sighed. "I know the feeling." Then Angelica's eyes widened. "Good grief—Daddy just walked through the door."

Tricia turned to see her father enter the bar, an unlit cigar hanging over his bottom lip, accompanied by a buxom fifty-something woman with a magenta bouffant hairstyle. "What on earth?"

Angelica stood. "Daddy! Daddy! Come and join us!"

John turned at the sound of his name, saw them, and waved. He spoke to his companion, who peeled away and then headed for the bar while John made his way across the floor to join his daughters.

"Girls, girls! It's lovely to see you."

"Where on earth have you been?" Tricia demanded. "You dispatched me to the drugstore, and then had disappeared when I came to deliver the goods."

John sat down beside Angelica, who didn't look at all pleased. "Just after you left, I got a call from a friend about a poker game."

"But you had no money," Angelica insisted.

"He staked me. I won quite a bit, and now I'm no longer dependent on you girls."

"We're *women*," Angelica asserted.

John smiled broadly. "Yes, yes, yes."

Angelica did not take well to condescension. Her gaze was murderous.

"I hope you haven't been smoking," Tricia admonished. "You had a heart attack just three days ago."

"I can take care of myself," John said with annoyance.

"I doubt that," Angelica muttered.

"And now that I've got transportation—"

"What do you mean?" Tricia demanded.

"I bought myself a car—with cash—and now I can come and go as I please. And I do *not* please to be stuck in some old folks' home back in Connecticut to assuage your consciences."

"We're trying to help you," Tricia said quietly, trying to hold on to the temper that, just days earlier, her sister had insisted she did not have.

"I appreciate what little help you've given me," John said pointedly, "but it won't be necessary in the future. I found someone who will love me for myself." He looked toward the bar, where the woman he'd entered with batted her enormous—and obviously fake—eyelashes.

"How long have you known her?" Angelica asked.

John looked at the clock. "About six hours."

"And where are you two going to go?"

John shrugged. "Wherever the wind takes us. That and a full tank of gas. I only came back to Stoneham to collect my things, and then I'll be out of your hair."

It seemed like he meant to add "*forever.*"

Tricia met Angelica's gaze. That was what they wanted, but not this way. But before Tricia could voice an opinion, Angelica spoke.

"I'm sorry you feel that way, Daddy. Tricia and I only want the best for you. But if you feel you must go, you have my blessing. However," she added rather ominously, "please don't expect us to clean up any more of your messes—financial or otherwise."

John didn't back down. Instead, he turned to Tricia. "Do you feel the same way, Princess?"

"I want what's best for you, Daddy. I don't think running away with someone you barely know is the answer. And besides, you haven't exactly cleared your name when it comes to being a suspect in Carol

Talbot's murder. If you leave, it will make you look like you've got something to run away from."

"I didn't kill the woman. I have nothing to worry about." He rose. "Now, if you'll excuse me. I've left Cherry alone far too long."

The sisters glanced back to the bar, where Cherry wiggled her fingers in a wave.

John said no more and joined his new love.

Angelica took an enormous swig from her wineglass before speaking. "Let's just hope that woman doesn't give Daddy a social disease."

"What are we going to do about this?" Tricia asked.

Angelica shrugged. "He's a big boy."

"But you know we're just going to have to bail him out of some new trouble in the not-too-distant future."

Angelica pouted, then looked thoughtful. "We need to go after him with the big guns."

"Oh yeah? What's that?"

"Mother."

Tricia barely refrained from rolling her eyes. "Have you forgotten, she doesn't want him back—and you hung up on her, too."

"Mother may have said she doesn't want Daddy back, but once she finds out about Cherry . . ."

Tricia looked back toward the bar. John had thrown an arm around Cherry's plump shoulder, the two of them looking very chummy indeed.

Was it possible Sheila Miles would fight to reclaim her man?

Tricia wasn't at all sure.

TWENTY-FOUR

Try as she might, Tricia just couldn't get used to the considerably smaller quarters she'd been forced to accept at the Sheer Comfort Inn. The home's top floor—a lovely suite with a soaker tub—had been rented for the week by one of the musicians who was in the village for the wine and jazz fest. He liked to practice the sax until eleven, which was as late as the local law's noise ordinance allowed, but that didn't make him a friend to the others staying in the inn. Also, Tricia had a small dresser and one tiny closet to live with—not nearly enough space to spread out all the stuff she required to live a normal life. Normal? What was that?

Bleary-eyed, she'd driven to her store after consuming an apple-walnut breakfast muffin and a cup of coffee—not that the inn didn't boast more for the day's most important meal, but with every room rented for the jazz fest, the dining room felt crowded and not as welcoming as she'd hoped.

Pixie had arrived at Haven't Got a Clue before her—and so had the construction crew. However, there wasn't as much noise emanating from the floors above.

"They're spreading the joint compound today," Pixie said joyfully as Tricia stowed her purse behind the sales counter.

"How do you know?"

"I saw them traipsing up there with five-gallon containers of the stuff and asked them. You know what this means?"

"Oh, please—tell me it means I can soon finally come *home*," Tricia begged.

"I dunno about that, but it's *quiet* work, and that seems like a pretty good thing," Pixie said, smiling.

Mr. Everett arrived, his usual smiling self. "Good morning!" he called as he approached the cash desk where Tricia and Pixie stood. In his hand he held a white bakery bag. "I stopped to get some bagels. I hope you ladies are hungry?"

"I could eat a horse," Pixie admitted, smiling.

"I'm afraid I've already had my breakfast," Tricia admitted, but from the hopeful look in her employee's eyes, she acquiesced. "But I'll bet I could eat *half* a bagel. What kind did you get?"

"Sesame, poppy seed—for you, Ms. Miles, because I know how much you like them—and an everything for Pixie."

"My favorite," Pixie crowed. "I'll go get the cream cheese out of the fridge. You can pour the coffee, Mr. E."

He nodded, but Tricia spoke up before he could move.

"Is Miss Marple behaving herself?"

"Oh, she's no trouble at all. She charms us by the hour. She played with her toys for quite some time last evening. Stalking them, killing them, and then presenting them to us. She does so enjoy the praise."

It was the cat's favorite game, and Tricia felt a pang of loss for having missed it for the past couple of days.

"Grace has joked that we may not give her back to you."

It was just a joke, but the threat hit a little too close to home at that moment. Mr. Everett seemed to sense her growing anxiety. "Have no fear. It's all in jest, but we will sorely miss that dear kitty when it comes time to part with her."

Tricia gave him a halfhearted smile and nodded.

"Now, I'll just go pour the coffee," he said, and crossed the floor for the beverage station.

The phone rang. Tricia made a grab for it. "Haven't Got a Clue. This is Tricia. How can I help you?"

"Trish, darling, it's your ever-humble big sister. I have news *and* I desperately need a favor."

"News—this early?" Tricia asked, ignoring the latter part of the sentence.

"Yes. I just got off the phone with Antonio. Sometime last night, Daddy made good on his threat and packed his bags and left the Brookview. His room is available if you'd like to move back."

Would she ever—goodness knows she missed Miss Marple something terrible, and she could sure use the space to spread out again. "Yes, please."

"It'll be ready after three this afternoon. If you need help moving back, give Antonio a holler and he'll send someone to the Sheer Comfort Inn to pick up your stuff."

"That would be great. And I'll pick up Miss Marple and take her back there before the shop closes." Happy about that situation, Tricia wondered if she should bring up a potentially explosive topic—then figured, *Why not?*

"Have you had a chance to call Mother yet?"

"Oh, yes—first thing this morning. She played it cool—but she did *not* like hearing that Daddy's been spotted with another woman. I wouldn't be surprised if she showed up later today."

"But what good would that do? I mean, Daddy's left the inn here in Stoneham."

"But he didn't go far. He gave the hotel a forwarding address."

"Oh, yeah?"

"An apartment complex in Milford. Antonio did a Google search. It belongs to Ms. Cheryl MacIntire—Cherry for short."

"Very interesting. Are you going to tell Mother?"

"I haven't decided. What do you think?"

Tricia sighed. "She kept him on a short leash for fifty years. Maybe it's not fair to sic her on him like a pit bull."

"They *are* still legally married," Angelica reminded her.

"Yes," Tricia admitted. The conversation was getting too heavy. She changed the subject. "You mentioned a favor?"

"Yes. For some reason, when Frannie went to the bank to drop off yesterday's receipts, she emptied the entire cash drawer. There's only spare change left. Can you lend the Cookery twenty dollars in small bills until later this afternoon?"

"Of course. I'll run it right over."

"You're a doll. I'll see you at lunch—and by then I'm sure one of us will have more news to share."

"Sure thing. Bye."

Tricia first retrieved her purse and found a couple of five-dollar bills, then opened the shop's cash register and grabbed ten one dollar bills. Pixie approached with the cream cheese, plastic knives, and napkins.

"I've got to go over to the Cookery for a minute."

"Don't worry. Haven't Got a Clue will be in good hands until you get back," Mr. Everett assured her.

Tricia left the shop and hurried next door. Frannie was dusting the front shelves as she entered the Cookery.

"Hi, Frannie. Angelica said you needed to borrow some change."

"Do I—or should I say we?"

"It amounts to the same thing." Tricia counted the bills onto Frannie's open palm and watched as she filled two of the cash drawer's slots with the bills.

"Thanks. I can't think why I didn't leave enough money in the drawer for us to start the day."

"You must have had a lot on your mind."

"Probably." She seemed to think about it for a moment. "In fact—I've been preoccupied thinking a lot about Carol Talbot."

"Your neighbor?"

Frannie nodded. Tricia had almost forgotten that fact. What she also hadn't considered was that Frannie was known as the eyes and ears of Oak Street.

"As it happens, I had the opportunity to meet another of your neighbors last night at the Dog-Eared Page: Brad Shields."

"Oh, yeah," Frannie said, sounding rather bored. "Nice guy."

"I understand Carol used to take care of the Shields's cat when they went out of town."

"She and her husband, Dale, were frequent visitors at the Shields's house. *Very* frequent."

"Oh?" Tricia asked, playing dumb.

Frannie leaned in, speaking confidentially. "Of course, they didn't often visit the Shields's at the same time."

"Oh?" Tricia asked again, only this time she was confused.

"I'm not the only one of the neighbors who suspected there was a little hanky-panky going on."

"Oh!" This time, Tricia uttered the word with surprise.

Frannie nodded knowingly. "A couple of times a week, Carol would head for the Shields's house around nine o'clock at night. She and Ellen often passed each other like two ships in the night."

Tricia merely blinked.

"They'd stay at each other's homes for a few hours, and then—like a couple of synchronized swimmers—they'd pass each other on the way home once again."

"Really?"

Frannie nodded. "This went on for years."

"Wife-swapping right here in Stoneham?"

Frannie shrugged. "Hey, New Hampshire *was* the setting for *Peyton Place*, you know."

Tricia still couldn't believe what she'd just heard. Carol involved in a long-term illicit relationship with Brad Shields, and Ellen with Carol's husband? She shook her head ruefully. And did such an arrangement account for Ellen Shields's taste in reading material? "Like the song says, 'No one knows what goes on behind closed doors.'"

Frannie laughed. "Except for the neighbors."

"Wow," Tricia muttered.

"Of course, it all came to an abrupt end when Dale died suddenly, which some of us speculated happened during one of those regularly scheduled trysts," she said, her Texas accent growing just a little thicker. "After that, there was a noticeable frost between Ellen and Carol. You know how women get when there's a widow on the loose. They want to put up a barrier between their man and every other woman around."

It wasn't just widows who often received that reaction. Tricia had felt the same kind of cold shoulder from a number of her woman acquaintances after she and Christopher had separated and divorced. After that, she could hardly call those females *friends*.

"So what are you saying?" Tricia asked.

Frannie shrugged. "I wouldn't want to cast aspersions on Ellen, but it does seem odd that her competition is suddenly out of the picture."

Odder still that couples in their later years were so sexually active, or was Tricia just being a prejudiced prude? "I thought Dale Talbot had been dead for quite a while, so I'd hardly call it a sudden move on Ellen's part."

"He died a year ago January," Frannie said with conviction.

"Was that when Carol started drinking?" Tricia asked.

Frannie shrugged. "There were always liquor bottles in their recycle bins, but they really started to pile up after Dale died." She leaned closer and lowered her voice. "That's when Carol started buying her booze by the case."

Tricia remembered something Ginny had told her days before. "I heard she was also seeing a psychologist."

Frannie nodded. "Everybody assumed it was because she was a child killer."

A child who killed, Tricia mentally corrected.

"But I don't think so. She nearly lost her job at the library over her drinking, you know?"

"Oh?"

"They didn't fire her, so I'm assuming they made her go to the shrink to get help."

Lois Kerr had been pretty candid, but had never mentioned Carol's alcoholism, although she had alluded to problems Carol was dealing with. Then again, Tricia suspected that Frannie was now just speculating, and she didn't need to be distracted by such innuendo.

She glanced at the clock on the wall. "Goodness, is that the time? Pixie will wonder where on Earth I am." She headed for the door.

"Angelica will catch up with you later to repay the loan," Frannie called after her.

Tricia gave her a smile and vamoosed while the getting was good.

Upon exiting the store, she looked to her left and noted that more trucks, trailers, and other paraphernalia were in the process of unloading and setting up in the village square across the way. The Stoneham Wine and Jazz Festival was about to become a reality. Tricia smiled, then remembered how, a few years past, Bob Kelly, Angelica's predecessor at the Chamber of Commerce, had been jealous of nearby Milford's annual Pumpkin Festival. He'd been so petty he'd gone around smashing pumpkins in protest. Tricia had advised him to start his own festival—which he'd ignored. Angelica—as Nigela Ricita—had instituted such an event, and from the enthusiasm she'd seen and heard from the villagers, it looked like it was well on the way to being a successful annual event.

Gloating wasn't a trait Tricia aspired to, but in this one instance, she wished she could have had that opportunity. Instead, she would participate in the festival, spread the word, and, most of all—enjoy the wine and the music.

But for now, it was time to get back to work.

For the first time in what seemed like weeks, Haven't Got a Clue wasn't wracked with the raucous sound of hammers, saws, and banging. The workmen trundled up and down the stairs, and the heavy sound of footsteps could be heard on the floor above, but the soothing sound of new age music helped to disguise the din, and customers who entered the store weren't driven out by noise. They might just break even for the first time in nearly a month.

It was nearly closing time when the last of the workers left for the day, and Pixie made sure the back door to the shop was securely locked. She returned to the cash desk. "I think this is the first day in a month I haven't left here with a headache."

"Oh no! I'm so sorry. I really never thought it would be so loud," Tricia apologized.

Pixie waved a hand in dismissal. "They're usually gone by the time I get home. I think they're tension headaches. When I go home, I know I'm going to spend the evening with my darling Freddie, and then I feel as though I haven't got a care in the world."

Tricia smiled. It was cute to see Pixie so in love. But then she thought about how shabbily her father had treated Fred's hospitality and knew an apology on John's behalf had not nearly been enough. She would have to think about what she could do to make up for that. She'd ask Angelica.

As Pixie got ready to leave—gathering her purse and her current book—Tricia's gaze traveled out the store's front window. A shiny silver Mercedes rolled by, pulling into an empty parking space in front of the Cookery. She hadn't seen the driver, but she had a pretty good idea who might disembark from the car . . . and she wasn't mistaken.

"See you tomorrow!" Pixie called cheerfully as she left for the day.

Tricia's gaze was still focused on the car, but she managed a vague "Bye" in reply.

She watched as Pixie walked down the sidewalk, heading for the municipal parking lot. The car's driver's side door opened and a woman with shoulder-length blonde hair, dark glasses, and a sea foam green shirtdress got out of the car. She sized up the Cookery before her.

Why did it feel like the day had just gone down the toilet?

Sheila Miles strode toward Angelica's store and entered.

How soon would the phone ring?

Tricia glanced toward the back of the store and made her decision. She locked the door and turned the OPEN sign to CLOSED, then made a mad dash for the stairs to her loft apartment. She'd been waiting impatiently all day to see just what the workmen had accomplished, and she wasn't about to let her mother's arrival cheat her out of it.

Throwing open the door to the stairs, she dashed up to the second floor and peered into what had once been Haven't Got a Clue's storeroom. A smile crept across her lips. The walls in the entire open space were now clad in Sheetrock, the joints filled with compound had had at least one sanding, as evidenced by the thick layer of dust that seemed to cover everything. But one word rang in her mind: *Progress!* Surely this was a huge step in completing the job. She continued up to the next floor and was happy to see that it, too, had undergone a miraculous transformation. Ducking into the master suite, she saw that all the fixtures were in place, the tile work was finished, and all the walls were up. More work would be necessary, but at last she began to feel hopeful that her renovation nightmare would soon be over.

The "Ode to Joy" ringtone trilled from the phone in her pocket. Tricia pulled it out and glanced at the number. Angelica, of course.

"Hi, Ange."

"You'll never guess who's here with me," Angelica said with forced goodwill.

"I saw her car park in front of your store."

"Yes! It's Mother. And she's *dying* to see you."

"I am *not*!" said a voice in the background.

Tricia sighed. "Is it *really* necessary for me to come over?"

"Oh, yes!" Angelica sounded just a teensy bit desperate.

"You will owe me for this."

"But of course," Angelica answered cheerfully without missing a beat.

"Why do I think this is *not* going to be a pleasant experience?"

"I'm making a pitcher of martinis the second we end this call."

"And I may need a double," Tricia groused.

"Me, too," Angelica said with false bravado. "See you in a minute."

The connection was broken.

Tricia replaced the phone in her pocket and sighed. At that moment, she'd prefer to face an oral surgeon than her mother. Twice in one year was far, far too much.

With a heavy heart, she left a *construction* zone and headed for what she hoped wouldn't be a *destruction* zone.

TWENTY-FIVE

 **Tricia let** herself into the Cookery, which was deadly quiet. She locked the door behind her and tiptoed toward the back of the shop, opened the door marked PRIVATE, and headed for Angelica's loft apartment.

This time, there was no welcoming committee in the form of her sister's dog, which seemed very unusual. It was quiet; way too quiet.

The door at the top of the stairs was unlocked, and Tricia opened it and stepped into the hall that led to Angelica's kitchen. "Hello!"

"In the kitchen," Angelica called.

Still no sign of Sarge.

Tricia entered the kitchen, looking around warily. "Where is she?" she whispered.

"In the bathroom," Angelica answered in kind.

"What kind of a mood is she in?"

Angelica merely shrugged.

Tricia looked over to Sarge's basket, to find him cowering. "What's wrong with the little guy?" Tricia said, and crossed the floor to crouch down beside him, letting Sarge first sniff her fingers before she petted him. The poor dog was actually trembling.

"I don't know. He took one look at Mother and took to his bed. He hasn't moved since."

Until that day, Sarge had never met a man or woman he didn't like. Well, except for the person who had kicked and nearly killed him—before Tricia had rescued him.

The sound of a door closing caused Tricia to stand, and she and her sister turned to face the hall. Sheila Miles seemed to glide toward them like some odd kind of apparition. She hadn't changed a bit since they'd last seen her in January, except for the sneer on her lips, which seemed to have deepened.

"Hello, Mother," Tricia said.

"Hello," Sheila replied without inflection.

"How about that drink?" Angelica asked, sounding a little desperate. "Tricia and I are having martinis. What would you like, Mother?"

"Mineral water."

"I'm afraid I don't have any."

"Of course you don't." Sheila looked around the kitchen with disdain. "Your home is very small, Angelica." Then she leveled her evil eye on Sarge. "And you have an *animal*."

Angelica bristled. "Sarge is *not* an animal. He's my companion."

Sheila raised an eyebrow. "If you could hold on to a man, you wouldn't *need* a companion."

"May I remind you," Angelica said in a dangerous tone, "that you are here after your philandering husband."

Sheila's gaze was just as critical. "I don't need *you* to point that out."

Tricia did not want to be a part of this discussion. Luckily, Angelica poured the drinks, handing one to her. They didn't bother to toast, and both sisters took a big hit of their very dry drinks.

A long silence fell. It was Tricia who finally broke the quiet. "Where will you be staying?" she asked her mother.

"Apparently it's a problem. I understand every room in the area is booked up for some silly event."

"Tomorrow the first annual Stoneham Wine and Jazz Festival begins. There won't be a hotel room available within ten miles," Angelica said.

Again Sheila looked around Angelica's kitchen, her gaze straying in the direction of the hall. "I suppose I could stay here."

"I only have one bedroom."

"You can sleep on the couch."

"I don't think so," Angelica said firmly.

Sheila frowned. "Then you'll have to stay with your sister."

Tricia felt her cheeks redden. The woman couldn't even bear to say her name.

"Tricia's home is undergoing renovation. *She* isn't even staying there."

"Well, where is she staying?" Sheila asked, as though Tricia wasn't even in the room.

"At the Brookview Inn, in one of the bungalows."

"Then she can move out."

"I've barely moved back in," Tricia protested.

"Trish!" Angelica implored.

Tricia glared at her sister, but she also understood her unspoken plea. *Let Mother have the room so that she will take Daddy back and GO HOME!*

Tricia let out a frustrated breath. "And where am I to stay?"

"On my couch," Angelica said wearily.

Nobody else wanted to sleep on it—why should she?

Angelica cocked her head and pouted—adopting one of Sarge's most pathetic expressions.

"Oh, all right," Tricia acquiesced. "But where am I going to put all my stuff?"

"In my storeroom."

Which wasn't secure. Frannie had the run of the place—and knowing what a gossip she was, Tricia didn't think she'd be above snooping into boxes and totes, either. Still, she could bring her personal items up to the loft and store the unimportant things on the floor below. Things like her clothes.

"Do we have to stand around the kitchen?" Sheila asked with scorn.

Tricia eased onto one of the stools at the kitchen island. "I love this room. The afternoon sun fills the space and feels magnificent."

"I agree," Angelica said, taking her usual seat.

Sheila did not sit.

"I suppose we should talk about Daddy," Tricia suggested.

Sheila glanced at the diamond watch on her thin wrist. "It's too late in the day to do anything about him. I'd best be checking into the hotel."

Which meant that first Tricia had to move out of her room. She pushed her drink aside. It could sit in the fridge for an hour or so.

"I'll call Antonio and arrange for him to have your things brought here."

Tricia stood. "Thanks. But I'd better go supervise." She turned to face her mother.

"I have no intention of sitting around a hotel lobby for an hour or more. I'll stay here. You can call as soon as the room is ready."

Tricia had to bite her tongue to keep from saying something she might regret. "As you wish, *Mother.*"

Angelica winced at the inflection Tricia used on that last word. "The inn has a wonderful restaurant. Or would you rather I whip us up some omelets for dinner?"

"I don't eat greasy food," Sheila said.

"Then maybe you would be happier at the inn's restaurant. They have lovely tossed greens. I'm sure Tricia would be more than happy to take you there, wouldn't you, dear?"

Tricia shot her sister a murderous look.

"I have my own car," Sheila reminded them.

"Then you could follow Tricia. I'm sure by the time you have dinner she'll be out of your room."

"*My* room," Tricia grated.

Sheila sighed dramatically. "I suppose I can do that."

"Let's go," Tricia said, sounding anything but welcoming.

"We'll talk tomorrow morning, Mother," Angelica promised as she followed her mother and sister down the passageway.

They all trooped down the stairs—except for Sarge, who still hadn't left his doggy basket.

Tricia retrieved her car from the municipal parking lot and pulled up on the opposite side of the street from the Cookery. Sheila did a U-turn and followed her to the inn.

Angelica must have done some fast phoning, for two of the bellboys were waiting outside the bungalow when she arrived. She opened the door, and within five minutes the inn's van was packed full of her stuff for the second time that day.

Sheila insisted they put her luggage in the room, accepted the key from Tricia, and then turned without a word—including a thank-you to any of them. Tricia's cheeks felt hot as she apologized to the bellboys, whom her mother had stiffed, and she vowed she'd make it up to them when they arrived at Angelica's place.

As Tricia got back in her car, she pictured that chilled martini glass with her name on it that sat in Angelica's fridge. After her mother's performance, she had certainly earned it.

The reception Tricia received upon returning to Angelica's loft was far more welcoming than what she'd been given an hour earlier. Sarge was back to being his old self, barking happily and wagging his tail so hard Tricia thought it might fly off. She gave him not one, not two, but *three* biscuits, and for once Angelica didn't complain.

"Tell me again what Mother did," Angelica said, wincing, as though despite the fact she'd asked, she didn't really want to hear the truth.

Tricia opened the fridge and retrieved her drink. "She stiffed them."

"Was it Bobby and Doug?"

Tricia nodded.

Angelica sighed. "They're probably two of the nicest guys on the planet."

"Don't worry; I took care of them."

"Thank you. What happened next?"

"Mother stalked off into the inn and I left. I'm sure she can take care of herself."

Angelica shook her head. "I'm *so* glad the staff doesn't know she's Nigela Ricita's mother. They might riot."

That would be an extreme reaction, but Tricia was sure that after a few days of the same kind of treatment, every member of the staff that came into contact with the Miles family matriarch would be disgruntled. She and Angelica were going to have to do some major damage control in the coming weeks.

"Let's talk about anything *but* our parents," Angelica suggested as she sautéed onions and bell peppers in a pan on the stove. They were the only fresh vegetables she had on hand.

"I think this makes the third egg-heavy meal we've eaten this week," Tricia said, and took another sip of her martini. What the hell; she was now in for the night, with no chance of a DUI in her future.

"We'll go vegetarian for the next couple of meals," Angelica promised. "That is, if I can ever get to the grocery store. I'm far too busy during the day, and now I've got this whole Mother and Daddy problem on my plate."

"*Our* plate," Tricia corrected her.

"Yes. And what are we going to do about it?"

Tricia shrugged. "Do we take her to Cherry's apartment, knock on the door and let Mother scream '*J'accuse!*'"

"While she hasn't come right out and said so, I truly believe she's going to take Daddy back."

"Because she loves him, or because she needs someone to bully?" Tricia asked.

"Oh, she's got *you* for that," Angelica said offhandedly.

"Thanks a lot," Tricia groused.

"No, really. From what we've pieced together, it sounds like she's spent the last half century bailing Daddy out. That's either love or masochism on her part."

Was their father a loveable rogue, or just a con artist? Tricia wasn't certain—and worse, wasn't sure she *cared* to find out.

"How's that toast coming along?" Angelica asked.

As if on cue, two slices of beautifully tanned bread popped out of the toaster. "Ready."

Angelica slid the perfectly puffed omelet onto a waiting plate and handed it to Tricia. "Here you go."

Tricia took the plate to her place at the island and sat down. She bypassed the butter and slathered raspberry preserves onto her slice of toast, while Angelica added a little butter to the pan, letting it melt before she poured more egg mixture into it.

"What's our next move?" Tricia asked as she cut into her omelet.

Angelica looked down at her feet, where a hopeful Sarge patiently sat. "As soon as we're finished eating, Sarge is going to need to be walked."

"No problem for me. I could use the exercise."

"Good. I wouldn't mind taking a walk through the village square to see how things are shaping up for the festival. Ginny e-mailed me a full report on everything that happened today, and I'm sure nothing is lacking, but I'd still like to take a look."

"Can we just walk through the square? Won't there be some kind of security?"

"Definitely. It was part of the contract we signed with each vendor. But we can at least walk the perimeter to see how things stand."

"That's fine with me," Tricia said, and took a bite of her toast. Lovely!

During their meal, the sisters chatted about the day's events—pointedly avoiding the subject of their parents—and after Angelica placed all the dishes in the dishwasher, she clipped Sarge's retractable leash to his collar and carried him down the stairs and out the door. Setting the dog on the pavement, they headed down the sidewalk toward the village square.

The twilight sky had dissolved into inky darkness, and the air carried a bit of a chill, but the square looked festive with bunting and streamers, which would no doubt be lit up the following night.

"What a beautiful evening," Tricia said as they crossed the road. They walked along the outside of the square, stopping at a fire hydrant for Sarge to relieve himself before moving on.

They must have lingered a little too long, for a beefy, uniformed security officer approached them.

"Can I help you ladies?"

"Just taking my dog for a walk," Angelica said cheerfully. She looked beyond him to the square filled with trucks and other equipment. "It looks like it's going to be a wonderful festival."

"And we aim to make sure of that. Granite State Security is patrolling the area. I'm sure you can understand that the festival sponsors and vendors have a lot riding on this."

"And we have no intention of interfering. We're just going to walk around the square and then head for home. And we won't leave a mess," Tricia said, brandishing a grocery bag.

"Thank you, ma'am. We appreciate that." He actually tipped his hat. "Have a good evening, ladies."

"You, too," the sisters chorused, and started on their way.

Tricia waited until they'd walked ten or twelve feet before speaking. "That's got to make you feel better."

Angelica nodded, distracted.

Tricia glanced at her sister, who seemed unusually quiet. "Is something wrong?"

Angelica sighed. "Mother and Daddy's marital problems couldn't have come at a worse time. Thanks to the festival, Chamber business, and other upcoming Nigela Ricita projects, I'm feeling really stressed."

"Is there any way I can help?" Tricia offered.

Angelica shook her head. "Thanks, but no. But again, let me encourage you to run for Chamber president. You've got *two* employees who are more than capable of taking over your shop in your absence. I really believe you'd be a tremendous asset to the business community, and I know I could trust you to carry on my legacy."

"I've been giving it some serious thought," Tricia admitted.

"And?" Angelica pressed.

"Because I *do* have good people at Haven't Got a Clue who can take care of my business if I have to be away, I think it might be a real possibility."

Angelica's grin was positively beatific. "Oh, I'm so happy to hear you say that. I was so worried that everything I've done might be tossed aside by someone coming in who isn't as forward-thinking as me."

"That thought has crossed my mind as well."

Angelica clasped Tricia's arm, giving it a squeeze. "You just might be an even *better* Chamber president than me."

"Okay, now you're teasing me."

"No, really. I think you could far surpass what I've done—but only if you're willing to give it a few years more than I can reasonably do. And, of course, you'd have my guidance, so how could you miss?"

Tricia smiled, shaking her head. Anyone else hearing that proclamation would have thought Angelica an egomaniac, but she trusted that her sister only had the Chamber's—and the village's—best interests at heart.

They rounded another corner, with Sarge trotting along at a brisk pace, pulling on the leash. Angelica pressed the button on the handle, giving the dog another five or six feet of line as she cast an eagle eye on the trucks and trailers that surrounded the square.

"I think I'm going to have to give Ginny a raise. Everything is exactly as it should be," she said, sounding extremely pleased.

But then Sarge stopped dead.

"What's up?" Angelica asked her dog, whose little black nose wrinkled. He gave a sharp bark.

"What's up, boy?" Angelica asked again.

Sarge put his nose to the ground and began to sniff around in earnest, dragging his mistress closer to one of the parked trailers.

"No, Sarge, no!" Angelica admonished, but her dog had other ideas. He strained against his leash, pulling her forward. "Oh, good grief," Angelica said, distress evident in her voice.

"What's wrong?" Tricia asked.

"Look!"

Tricia squinted in the feeble light and saw a pair of shoes protruding from under the nearest food truck that proclaimed it sold French crepes. Sarge nudged one of the shoes, but the foot attached to it did not budge.

"Oh, no," Angelica wailed.

"Looks like we'd better call nine one one," Tricia said grimly, then pulled out her phone, and wondered who belonged to the worn pair of work boots.

TWENTY-SIX

Chief Baker glared at the Miles sisters. "You two are definitely a menace to society."

"I beg your pardon," Tricia said, as angry as she'd ever been with her former lover. "We are *not* responsible for this man's death, nor any others!"

Baker shook his head and walked away from them.

"Grant, wait!" Tricia called, and followed him, leaving her sister behind. "I was wondering, when you and your men checked out Carol Talbot's home, did you come across any kind of collections?"

Baker eyed her warily. "What do you mean? Like stamps or something?"

"Definitely not stamps."

"What do *you* know about it?"

"The collection? Only that there was one."

Baker looked around, as though to see if anyone was in earshot, then leaned forward and spoke to her quietly. "There was an empty file cabinet in one of the bedrooms. We noticed that there were pictures missing from the walls, too."

"And jewelry?"

He shook his head. "We found a jewelry box under her bed. It appeared to be intact."

That piece of news brightened Tricia's day, albeit infinitesimally.

"It seems the Talbots collected vintage erotica."

Baker didn't blink. Had he known that the Talbots and the Shieldses were swingers?

"You may want to speak with Marshall Cambridge at Vamps down by the highway."

"Has someone tried to sell him the collection?"

"Not that he said. He just said Carol had been selling pieces of it to him, but I thought you should know about this."

"How long have you known about it?"

"Um, maybe a day."

"Why didn't you call me sooner?"

"I thought you might dismiss the whole thing. You don't like it when I find out and report something you don't know about."

"I never said that."

"Actions speak louder than words," Tricia said firmly.

"I'll consider what you've told me," Baker said. He looked away, then back to Tricia. "I have other people to speak to."

She nodded. What more could she say? She turned and rejoined her sister.

The medical examiner and crime photographer had both shimmied under the food truck to examine and photograph the corpse in situ, but so far nobody had mentioned who the dead man was, though—by the footwear alone—Tricia was positive the victim was a male of the species.

"I don't get it," Angelica said. "The security guard we spoke to spotted us and made sure we weren't up to no good. How could none of the guards have seen someone dump a body under the food truck?"

"The *crepe* truck," Tricia clarified. "I was going to eat there tomorrow night."

"The body was found *under* the truck, not *in* it. You can eat to your heart's delight," Angelica told her. She glanced at her watch and sighed. "How long do you think Chief Baker will make us wait *this* time?"

Tricia shook her head. "I have no idea. I wonder if they'd let us go sit on one of the benches. At least then we could take a load off our feet."

"And violate the sanctity of the guarded square? I doubt it." Angelica glanced to her left, and Tricia could see the guard they'd spoken to earlier in animated conversation with one of the other police officers, no doubt defending himself and the other guards, who'd somehow missed either a murder or someone stashing the corpse under their watch.

"Rigor mortis hadn't set in," Tricia said, keeping her voice low, "so the victim hadn't been there long."

"You touched the guy?" Angelica asked, aghast.

"I nudged his foot a little."

Angelica shuddered. "So who do you think it could be?"

"It has to be one of the suspects in Carol Talbot's murder," Tricia said adamantly.

"Good heavens! You don't think it can be Daddy, do you?" Angelica cried.

Tricia shook her head. "Not wearing those clodhoppers. Daddy's feet are much smaller, and he would *never* wear work boots."

Angelica frowned. "How about Jim Stark—or one of the guys working on your renovation?"

"I sure hope not," Tricia said. The thought of her renovation coming to a standstill was unthinkable. "Besides, what possible motive could any of them have for killing anyone?"

"Well, perhaps whoever is lying under that truck had nothing to *do* with Carol Talbot's death. What if this is just a random killing?" Angelica shook her head, and when she spoke again, her voice cracked. "At this rate, Stoneham will *never* get back its title of Safest Village in New Hampshire."

Tricia ignored her sister's last sentence and addressed the first. "I suppose it could be. A construction worker wouldn't have looked out of place during the festival's setup."

"Poor Ginny," Angelica lamented. "This could be disastrous for her *and* the first—and possibly only—Stoneham Wine and Jazz Festival. She's worked so hard. I don't want her spirit crushed by this."

"There's going to be a lot of gossip—and if you're smart, you'll make sure that Frannie isn't an instigator. But because Russ and the *Stoneham Weekly News* have been pretty much absent about reporting Carol's murder, it's likely there won't be as much fallout as in the past."

"Thank goodness for small mercies," Angelica muttered. "I'd better call Ginny and give her a heads-up. Will you take care of Sarge for a few minutes?"

"Of course."

Angelica handed off Sarge's leash and stepped away to stand behind one of the police cruisers, whose flashing blue-and-red lights illuminated the gloomy surroundings.

Tricia bent down to pat Sarge's head. "Everybody seems to be blaming us for finding the dead guy, but you are a good boy to have led us to him."

Sarge probably didn't have a clue what she was saying, but her tone was soothing, and he wagged his tail, looking self-satisfied. "I'll slip you a couple more doggy biscuits when we get back home," she promised him.

Straightening, Tricia noticed Chief Baker speaking with the crime photographer, who seemed to be passing off a cell phone to Stoneham's finest. Baker stared at the phone for long seconds, said something else to the photographer, and then charged toward Tricia. He halted and shoved the phone in her face. His voice was taut when he spoke. "Do you know this man?"

Tricia stared at the photo of the lifeless face and felt her stomach turn. "Good grief; it's Brad Shields."

Baker studied her face. "I'm assuming this is a genuine shock for you."

She nodded. "Of course it is. I have to admit, I thought he might have been the one who killed Carol Talbot. But his death means it might be . . ."

"Who do you suspect?" Baker demanded.

Although she had no real evidence to base her gut feeling on, Tricia blurted, "His wife, Ellen. I've heard rumors that there was hanky-panky going on between Carol and Dale Talbot and Brad and Ellen Shields. Wife-swapping."

"And where did you hear this?" Baker demanded.

"From one of their neighbors."

Baker nodded. "I think I can guess who." That meant Frannie had definitely shared her suspicions with more than just Tricia. Good—because Tricia did not want to be the one to out Frannie as the eyes and ears of the world.

"What do you know about the guy?" Baker asked.

"He played in the darts tournament last night at the Dog-Eared Page, and we spoke after the match, but other than that . . . not much."

"Then why did you suspect him?"

"I spoke to his wife yesterday at the big pharmacy in Milford. She and Carol had had a falling-out of late. I'm guessing that after Dale Talbot's death, Ellen's husband and Carol decided to carry on their sexual liaison, and Ellen wasn't happy about it."

"Why's that?"

"Just the way Ellen seemed to have turned against Carol. I mean, despite their past relationships, who really wants their spouse to be sleeping with someone else?"

Tricia had never known why Baker's marriage had broken up—he'd never spoken about infidelity—but she knew that he'd been devastated by its dissolution.

He nodded. "My next stop is to visit the deceased's home and break the news to his wife. It may be that I can't ask such pointed questions until at least tomorrow."

Thankfully, the chief seemed to have a modicum of compassion, because, despite what she suspected, Tricia didn't have a shred of evidence that Ellen harbored ill will against her husband and wanted him dead. On the contrary—she no longer wanted to *share* him. There was no other reason, that she knew of, why she'd kill him.

"Can Angelica and I go home now? You know where we'll be if you have any more questions."

He shrugged. "Sure."

Angelica was still on the phone as Tricia and Sarge approached.

"It's okay—it's going to be okay." She nodded. "Yes, don't worry about it. It'll still be a huge success. No, I'm not just saying that." She paused again. "Okay. I'll send an e-mail to your team as soon as I get back to my place. It's going to be all right." She listened some more. "Okay. Try to get some sleep. You have a lot to do during the next couple of days, and I'm sure the festival will be a huge success. Now, good night." Angelica stabbed the end call icon. "Whew."

"I take it Ginny wasn't pleased."

"No, and who could blame her? But I wanted the news to come from me and not someone else."

"Do you think the festival is doomed?"

"Of course not. It's going forward and will be a fabulous success," she said with authority.

Tricia didn't doubt her.

Angelica held out her hand for the leash. "Come on. Let's go home."

Tricia followed her sister across the street and back to her apartment. But before she entered the Cookery, Tricia looked over her shoulder to where the blue lights from the police cruisers continued to flash. Had she wanted Brad Shields to be Carol's murderer? What did his death mean? What if Ellen hadn't killed her spouse? There could only be one other suspect . . . but she didn't like the idea, and was determined not to embrace it.

TWENTY-SEVEN

There comes a time when you're just too old to spend the night on someone else's couch. Tricia Miles had come to that point. She missed her bed. She missed her cat. She missed being able to roll over. Sleeping in one position for so long—that is, when she *could* sleep—caused the muscles in her back to protest. So much so that she was up and making coffee just after five the next morning.

Sarge arrived in the kitchen soon after, telling Tricia he really needed to go outside. By the time they came back to the kitchen, Angelica was up. She'd showered, dressed, and even had applied her makeup, looking businesslike, and was stationed in front of her computer in the living room checking her e-mail. "Good morning," she called cheerfully. "Thanks for making the coffee. Did you sleep all right?"

"Not really," Tricia admitted, and shuffled into the kitchen in her bathrobe and slippers to grab her own cup of joe. She had hours and hours to kill before Haven't Got a Clue opened for the day.

Angelica scrolled through more items in her in-box, deleting as fast as she could maneuver her mouse.

"Don't you need to read them all?" Tricia asked.

Angelica shook her head. "Most of them I'm just cc'd on. I trust Antonio to handle the day-to-day problems of Nigela Ricita Associates. If it's important, he'll bring it to my attention."

Tricia dreaded asking her next question, but it had to be done. "What have you got on tap today?"

"I want to walk through the wine and jazz festival several times today, surreptitiously overseeing things, but not get in Ginny's way. I have Chamber business to attend to, and Frannie wants me to go over her list of stock requests for the Cookery. Oh, and Tommy and I have a meeting to plan next month's menu over at Booked for Lunch."

In comparison, Tricia's to-do list was pretty lame.

"I know this will be a difficult thing for you to do, but I'm afraid dealing with Mother is going to fall on you."

"Will Mother *let* me deal with her?"

"If she wants to find Daddy and confront him, it's either you or nothing."

That didn't make Tricia feel better. It wasn't at all an enjoyable experience to be saddled with someone who despised you. Something that hadn't been apparent to her until earlier that year.

"Think of it this way," Angelica suggested, "perhaps you and Mother will bond over this experience."

"How? My husband left me, but he never cheated on me."

"Are you sure?" Angelica asked.

Tricia thought about it. If nothing else, she felt certain that Christopher had never lied to her. "Yes."

Angelica nodded. "I wish my ex-husbands would have been as virtuous."

Tricia studied her sister's sad expression. Much as she *didn't* want to spend time with their mother, she also knew that on any given day Angelica was juggling ten times as much as she did. What she did for the village—employing scores of people who otherwise might not have meaningful work that paid the bills—and promoting Stoneham to the world at large, made Tricia feel like she wasn't contributing much to the village and its denizens. She loved owning Haven't Got a Clue; it would always be her first love. But could she walk in Angelica's footsteps and be another guiding force in Stoneham? She might not win if she ran for the post, but what if she did? And was there any other business venture she wanted to champion? Sort of. Currently, there wasn't a no-kill animal shelter in the area. She would have no qualms championing that cause.

Yes, there was far more Tricia could do to make life in her community better—if not for humans, then at least for their four-footed friends.

"You're smiling," Angelica accused.

"I'm thinking about what you said. Things I might want to pursue in the future."

Angelica positively grinned. "And I'll bet you'll be *fantastic* doing them. Now, sit down and tell all."

"Let's eat *and* talk."

"Sounds like a plan. I'm afraid I don't have all that much in my fridge right now, but we could cross the street for Booked for Lunch and find everything we need for a truly magnificent breakfast."

"I'm not dressed for that," Tricia said.

"Then *get* ready for the day. It'll give me a chance to go through the rest of my e-mails, and by that time, we'll both have worked up an appetite."

Tricia smiled. "You've got a deal!"

She drank the last of her coffee and set her mug down on the table before heading toward the bathroom, her head filled with scores of ideas. And yet . . . she still couldn't push the problem of Carol Talbot's—and now Brad Shields's—deaths out of her mind. And she knew that no matter what the day brought, the deaths of those two people were sure to plague her.

"Where is your sister?" Sheila Miles demanded after opening the door to her bungalow at the Brookview Inn when she found it was Tricia who stood before her.

"She's busy. She has an empire to take care of. Me? I've just got one measly store." Not that that was the way she thought of Haven't Got a Clue. But it was what she believed her mother thought of her only commercial enterprise.

"So I understand."

"I assume you want to be taken to Cherry's apartment."

"Cherry?"

"That's the name of the woman Daddy was with."

"Have you been there before?"

Tricia shook her head. "Angelica and I weren't really introduced to her."

"Where did your father meet this woman?"

"At a poker game."

Sheila didn't roll her eyes, but it looked like she wanted to. "Let's go. I want to wrap this up soon. My bridge group meets on Friday, and I want to be home by then."

And I would be more than happy to wave good-bye to you, Tricia thought. She gestured toward her car across the parking lot. "Shall we?"

Sheila grabbed her purse and locked the bungalow's door. "Let's get this over with."

They climbed into Tricia's Lexus and she started the engine, then pulled out of the lot. Once they made it to Main Street, she headed north.

What could they talk about? The weather? That seemed innocuous enough. But Tricia had other questions she wanted answered. Whether her mother would answer them was debatable. There was nothing to do but plow ahead.

"So exactly how long have you and Daddy been married?"

"What kind of a question is that?" Sheila demanded.

"An honest one."

"Why would you even ask?"

"Because Daddy said you'd been married fifty years, and Angelica is fifty-one."

"He must have made a slip of the tongue," Sheila asserted.

"Maybe. I guess it wouldn't be hard to find out."

"What do you mean?"

"I could always go back to New Haven and check the records at City Hall. Of course, it might be even easier than that. A lot of public records are now on the Internet," Tricia bluffed.

"They are?" Sheila asked, sounding none too pleased.

"Yes." She glanced askance at her mother, who looked distinctly unhappy. The timing of Angelica's birth may have been inconvenient, but there was no question that she and Tricia shared the same parentage. The Miles nose was a dead giveaway.

"Why don't you tell me about your wedding?" Tricia said.

"I told you about it years ago."

"No, you never did."

"I'm sure I did."

"It was a quiet affair," Tricia guessed. Yes. It would have to have been if Angelica had been born out of wedlock, or perhaps just a few months before the nuptials. And perhaps that might have explained why Sheila had insisted that Angelica and she be treated to such extravagant weddings. Had her mother been living vicariously through her daughters? Tricia had let her mother talk her into the big church wedding with the opulent dress, and Sheila had insisted that she have the six attendants and a guest list that had bordered on the obscene. It was during the whole planning process that she'd felt closest to her mother.

They drove in silence straight through the village. It was Sheila who broke the quiet. "It's rather pretty around here."

"Yes, it is. And a lot of the improvements during the past two years are because of Angelica's hard work as Chamber of Commerce president."

"Oh?" Sheila asked offhandedly.

"Especially the flowers along Main Street. Stoneham has come in the top five for prettiest village in New Hampshire for the last two years. One day we'll win it." Because they sure weren't even in the running for safest village, thanks to all the deaths that had taken place during the past few years within the village's boundaries.

Tricia stopped at the highway entrance and turned left.

"What happened to your hand?" Sheila asked.

"Sarge jumped up and knocked a pan of hot grease on it."

"Animals are dangerous," Sheila grumbled. "Your sister should get rid of it."

"Oh, no! He's a wonderful little dog. He didn't mean it, and it's not serious. It'll heal."

"It looks terrible. You might need plastic surgery. Did you see a burn specialist?"

"Just Angelica. She knows about these things. It's already a lot better than it was." Tricia almost added *"don't worry,"* but figured Sheila wouldn't anyway. Then again, she *had* asked about it. Could it be her mother didn't entirely despise her? She wasn't ready to make that leap of faith.

"How much farther do we have to go?" Sheila asked irritably.

"Not far. What are you going to say to Daddy?"

Sheila let out what sounded like a bored breath. "I'll probably remind him what a fool he is."

"That's not the way to win friends and influence people."

"Said she who was divorced."

"I didn't initiate it. And before his death, Christopher asked me to remarry him."

"Were you going to?"

"No."

Tricia momentarily glanced at her mother once again, but, as usual, her face was impassive. Sometimes she wondered if the woman had any feelings at all—other than negative ones. Or, if she was fair, perhaps her mother had dealt with so much pain in her life that she'd simply shut them off—or, more likely, refused to experience them. She hadn't considered that before. But that still didn't excuse the woman's treatment of Tricia for more than four decades.

They didn't speak for the rest of the journey—a very long five minutes—but finally Tricia pulled into the parking lot of yet another apartment complex outside of Milford.

"Shabby," Sheila commented. "Not at all your father's style."

"It may be that he's adjusted to a lower standard of living. From what he's said, he had to."

Sheila turned to look at her. "Do you think I should have given him money to maintain the lifestyle he'd become accustomed to?"

"That's between you and him."

"You wouldn't have given Christopher money after he left you. Why should I?"

"Christopher gave me a very generous settlement. Daddy made it sound like your separation was a mutual decision."

"It was not," Sheila said simply.

"I'm sorry to hear that," Tricia said truthfully. She'd been devastated that someone she'd trusted with her life could one day up and announce he was leaving—not only her, but his job, and moving halfway across the country, too. It had taken several years for Christopher to figure out that he wanted his old life—and her—back. He hadn't wanted to believe that she had moved on.

Would Sheila be able to accept it if John had decided to move on, too?

Tricia wondered if she was about to find out.

Sheila opened the car door and got out. Tricia followed.

"Which apartment is it?"

"Number three." Tricia started for the building's entrance, but Sheila held out a hand.

"I'll take care of this."

"Are you sure?" Tricia asked.

Sheila's gaze was blistering. Tricia now understood where Angelica had learned that burning glare.

Tricia hung back, watching as her mother entered the building, her back straight, her head held high. Was she going to beg her father to return to her? Somehow, Tricia couldn't see that happening.

She waited a minute before she advanced toward the steel security door, which didn't live up to its name, because she was able to crack it open without being buzzed in and without a key. She poked her head inside and listened. She could hear voices—one male, one female—reverberating in the two-story open atrium, but she couldn't make out the words. She closed her eyes and listened harder, but still, the words were just a muddle. Frustrated, Tricia retreated to her car.

She didn't have to wait long. Less than five minutes later, Sheila exited the building, her expression just as stoic as when she'd entered.

Tricia waited until her mother had gotten back in the car before she'd started the engine and engaged the air-conditioning before she spoke. "Well, what did he say?"

Sheila wouldn't look at her. "He'll think about it."

"About what?"

"Coming home."

"Do you really want him back, knowing that he's been with other women?" Tricia asked.

Sheila turned her icy gaze back to her daughter. "You may not believe it, but I actually love that old fool."

"What will you do if he doesn't want to come back to you?"

"I will deal with it," Sheila said acidly.

"When did he say he'd give you an answer?"

"I gave him an ultimatum. He has twenty-four hours. So it looks like I'm stuck here until at least tomorrow," she said as though that might be a prison sentence.

"Perhaps you might like to go to the wine and jazz festival. Angelica's daughter-in-law has put the whole thing together. She's done an amazing job. I think it would please Ange if you came."

"Daughter-in-law?" Sheila said.

"Yes, Angelica's stepson, Antonio, is the chief operating officer for Nigela Ricita Associates. The company owns quite a bit of the village and is a major player in its resurgence."

"Really."

"Yes. But there's just one thing . . . Angelica hasn't told the world at large that she's his stepmother. She would like to keep that quiet."

"Whatever for?"

"She has her reasons—as does Antonio."

Sheila shrugged. "Then I shall keep her secret."

"Thank you," Tricia said, and eased her gear shift into reverse, backed up, and then pulled out of the parking lot.

"Will I get to meet these people?"

"If you'd like. Antonio and Ginny have a daughter. She's absolutely adorable. Her name is Sofia."

"That's an Italian name."

"The baby was named after Antonio's mother. But her middle name is Angelica."

"Why doesn't Angelica want anyone to know about her relationship with this man and his family?" Sheila pushed.

"She has her reasons. That's all I can tell you."

"Keeping secrets, Tricia?"

"Yes. It seems to be a trait the Miles family shares."

Sheila's mouth drew into a straight line. She made no comment in that regard. "When I went to the restaurant for breakfast this morning, I heard talk about another murder in the village. There was talk—about you, too."

Tricia steered toward Stoneham, considering how she wanted to reply to that statement. "Sarge, Angelica's dog, sniffed out the dead man when we took him for a walk last night."

"Oh, I heard it was *you* who found him. That you make a habit of such things."

Word did get around.

"People exaggerate."

"It sounds foolish and dangerous."

Tricia didn't bother to give an explanation. Chances were Sheila wouldn't listen or would just find yet more fault with her. She changed the subject. "What would you like to do for the rest of the day?"

Sheila sniffed. "I suppose I could see Angelica's shop and restaurant."

"It's more of a café. She also owns a share of the Sheer Comfort Inn, which is very nice."

"She seems to be quite successful. A *lot* more successful than you."

"I guess that depends on one's definition of successful. Angelica is driven."

"And you're *not*?" Sheila asked.

"I like to think we both are—but in different ways."

"How do you two get along? When you were younger, you couldn't stand each other."

Tricia had to bite her tongue. It seemed to her that for years, Sheila had pitted the sisters against one another. That was no longer the case. Tricia and Angelica were now best friends. There wasn't anything Tricia wouldn't do for Angelica, and she had no doubt that her sister felt the same way.

"We understand one another. We're family." Tricia braked for a red light. "There's nothing that could ever come between us."

"Really?" Sheila asked, as though the concept of unconditional love was totally foreign to her.

"Yes. Angelica's even been teaching me to cook."

"And how is *that* going?" Sheila said, and Tricia looked to her right to see her mother eyeing the gigantic blister on her hand.

"Not bad, actually. I'm planning a dinner party when my renovation is complete, and I plan to cook everything I offer my guests."

"Your grandmother liked to cook," Sheila admitted, "though God knows why."

"Because it turns out there's a certain satisfaction about feeding those you love."

"And who do *you* love?" Sheila asked, although it sounded almost like an accusation.

"Lots of people. Angelica, Antonio, Ginny, who was my former assistant, Sofia, and Grace and Mr. Everett."

"Who?"

"Mr. Everett is one of my employees. He and his wife are very dear to me."

Sheila curled her lip. "Fraternizing with the help is just unacceptable."

"No, it isn't. Mr. Everett is a wonderful man. I kind of look at him as my surrogate father."

"You *have* a father," Sheila reminded her.

"Whom I've rarely seen for the past ten or more years," Tricia reminded her. "You two made yourselves pretty inaccessible by moving to South America."

"The weather was pleasant, and until recently, it was a nice place to live."

"Until Carol Talbot was murdered—and Daddy became a suspect—we didn't know he had a criminal record."

"Your father's a murder suspect?" Sheila asked, aghast.

"Oh. Didn't Angelica mention that?"

"No, she did not! Why is he a suspect?"

Oh, dear. Was this the time to mention that Carol and her father had been lovers?

"Um, it seems Daddy and Carol had a little tiff at my bookshop the night of Carol's death."

"What did they fight about?" Sheila asked, her voice sounding shaky.

"Daddy was looking for a place to stay and asked if he could stay with her?"

"Why would he ask a perfect stranger if he could stay with her?" Sheila demanded.

"It seems they knew each other."

"When did they meet?"

"When Daddy came to visit in January. It seems they became friends."

"How close a friend?"

Tricia wasn't brave enough to risk looking at her mother. "Pretty close."

"I see," Sheila said, her voice as hard as Tricia had ever heard it.

Tricia didn't want to pursue that subject. "Angelica and I were pretty upset to hear about Daddy's past."

"It's not something I'm proud of," Sheila said.

"It seems Daddy may not have changed his ways." Tricia braked as they entered the village.

"In what way?"

"Back in January, he left the village owing many of the merchants money. And he took some valuable items from the Sheer Comfort Inn. Angelica made good on his debts, but she was devastated over the theft."

When she next spoke, Sheila's voice was again shaky. "I think I've heard enough."

Yes, and Tricia had been the bearer of bad news. Was that likely to cause her mother to dislike her even more? It wasn't something she could do anything about.

"It's nearly lunchtime. What do you want to do?"

"Please take me back to the hotel."

"I could call Angelica and the three of us—"

"I'm not up for company right now. I need to digest all that you've told me."

"I understand," Tricia said as the Lexus rolled down Main Street at a rather sedate speed. Traffic had certainly picked up in the hour or so they'd been gone. "The wine and jazz festival starts this evening. Angelica and I are planning on attending. As I mentioned, we'd like you to come with us."

"What would I do at this festival?"

"If nothing else, drink wine and listen to some jazz."

"I haven't been to a concert in ages."

"Then it sounds like this could be right up your alley."

Tricia rounded the corner and drove to the Brookview, pulling into the parking lot and stopping as near to the bungalow as she could. She eased the gearshift into park.

Sheila unbuckled her seat belt, grabbed her purse, and exited the car, walking around it. Tricia was about to take off again when Sheila paused and turned. She motioned for Tricia to roll down her window. "I'll let one of you know if I'm up for company later this evening."

Tricia nodded. "Okay." There didn't seem to be anything else to say.

Sheila turned, and Tricia waited until her mother had entered the bungalow and closed the door behind her before she backed out of the lot and headed for the exit.

Sheila hadn't said no to the invitation. Was there a chance Tricia and her mother might have more conversations of a civil nature? And now that Sheila had found out that her husband had been unfaithful to her twice—and maybe more—during the previous five months, how would this impact all their lives?

Tricia wasn't sure she wanted to know.

TWENTY-EIGHT

Tricia was shocked that it took nearly fifteen minutes for her to drive from the Brookview Inn to Haven't Got a Clue, and then she was unable to find an empty space in the municipal parking lot and had to park several blocks away. It wasn't that she minded the walk, but it could become inconvenient if she had to park so far out for the rest of the festival. Perhaps she'd try to snag a parking space tomorrow morning and just not move her car until the event ended.

The heavy traffic brought with it many potential customers, and Pixie spent a good part of the day ringing up sales while Mr. Everett bagged the purchases. They staggered their lunches so that there'd be two of them in the store for the entire afternoon—not that Tricia went anywhere other than the basement office to attend to the regular business dealings that needed attention. It was almost closing time before she returned to ground level.

"Wow—this was certainly a great day for sales," Pixie said as they prepared to close the store for the day. "It was almost as good as a Saturday in December, and there was hardly any noise from the construction guys upstairs. Maybe that means you'll soon be moving back in."

"I sure hope so. Camping out on Angelica's couch isn't exactly a laugh riot."

"You girls need to do some real *fun* stuff. Like make s'mores or something. Watch romantic or scary movies. Paint each other's toenails and talk about men."

"I'm afraid we're a little too old for that, Pixie."

"Really? Are you both dead below the waist?"

"Pixie!" Tricia admonished.

"Okay, sorry. I'm just sayin'. 'Cuz I'm *not*. Fred and me, we're lookin' forward to our honeymoon. Not that we ain't done the dirty before now. But now it'll be different." Her grin was positively infectious. "I'm getting hitched, and I still can't believe my good luck."

Tricia smiled. "As long as you keep your goal of making each other happy, you guys will do fine."

Pixie nodded. "I never thought I'd fall in love. Finding a great guy like Fred was something I didn't think would ever happen to me."

Suddenly Tricia found herself feeling just a little envious. And then she thought of her own failed marriage, and the fact that her parents were on the outs. There were no guarantees in life. But somehow she had a feeling that Pixie and Fred were destined to make it until death did they part.

"So, are you goin' to the jazz festival?" Pixie asked.

"I'm planning on it."

"Great. Then maybe we'll see you there. Although I gotta admit, I'm attracted to the food-truck rodeo more than the wine or the music."

"Yes, there's at least one of them I want to try. I'll look out for you. How about you, Mr. E?"

"Grace and I wouldn't miss it. Ginny has worked so hard to set things up, we want to celebrate her achievement. But we won't stay out too late," he assured Tricia. "We don't want Miss Marple to be alone for too long."

"Thank you, Mr. Everett," Tricia said, smiling.

Pixie gathered up her purse and headed for the door. "See you later, Tricia."

"You bet!"

"I shall see you later, too, Ms. Miles," Mr. Everett said, and followed Pixie out the door.

The phone rang. Tricia picked up the heavy vintage receiver. "Haven't Got a Clue—"

"Trish, it's me," Angelica said.

"What's up?"

"I had a call from Mother accepting your invitation to come with us to the festival tonight."

"I must say I'm a little surprised by that."

"Me, too. Parking around here is a nightmare. Luckily I had the foresight to arrange for the Brookview to shuttle guests to the festival. She's supposed to show up on my doorstep any moment now. Are you available?"

"Ready and waiting."

"Great. See you outside my shop in, say . . . a minute?"

Tricia laughed. "You've got it."

The sisters hung up and Tricia gathered up her purse. She lowered the blinds and did a quick walk around the shop to make sure the back entrance was secure, and then turned the OPEN sign to CLOSED. Locking the door, she headed outside. She took a look to her left and saw the Brookview's shuttle van inching along Main Street. Tricia moved to stand in front of the Cookery, and when the van finally got that far, it paused, opening its doors and letting out a stream of people,

Sheila among them. The others headed for the village square, but Sheila caught sight of Tricia and walked over to meet her.

"Oh, what a pretty blouse," Tricia said in greeting.

"It's old," Sheila said bluntly.

"It's still pretty," Tricia said. She'd rather see the best than the downside of things.

The Cookery's door opened, and Angelica emerged. "There you two are."

"You're not bringing Sarge?" Tricia asked.

Angelica shook her head. "Much as I'd like to, it wouldn't be fair to him. All that noise and commotion. If I want to stay late, it's not far for me to return home to let him out." She turned to her mother. "Oh, what a pretty blouse."

Sheila managed a weak smile. "Thank you."

Tricia forced an ironic smile. When it came to her mother, she couldn't win for losing. "Shall we go to the square? We don't want to miss Ginny's welcoming speech."

"Oh, no," Angelica agreed, and gestured for her mother and sister to start down the sidewalk.

"What's so special about this Ginny person?" Sheila asked.

"Ginny?" Angelica asked. "I told you; she's my stepson, Antonio's, wife. She's just a doll. So sweet, and mother to their adorable little girl, Sofia. I'm her *nonna*."

"You are not," Sheila declared. "They are *not* your blood kin."

Tricia could see that Angelica's smile was rigid. "Blood or not, Antonio *is* my son. Ginny *is* his wife, and Sofia *is* my granddaughter. I don't care what their biological heritage is. We are family," she said in her no-nonsense voice.

"I love being an aunt," Tricia said. "And Ginny, who was my former assistant, looks up to me as her big sister. I never got to play that role before. I like it. I like it a lot."

Sheila shook her head ruefully, but made no further comment.

The three women marched down the sidewalk, waited for the light to change before they crossed the road, and then waited again on the other side. The village square was already teeming with people, all clustered around the restored gazebo, which had been partially demolished three years before when a light aircraft had crashed into it—killing not only the pilot but the speaker who'd been addressing the crowds on Founders Day—an event which had not been celebrated since.

Angelica threaded her way through the crowd, leading Tricia and Sheila toward the gazebo, where Ginny stood with her back to the crowd, conversing with several people Tricia did not recognize, while a trio consisting of a bass, a drummer, and a pianist waited to perform.

"That's Ginny," Angelica said, pointing her out for Sheila. "Isn't she just darling?"

Sheila frowned. "Not especially."

Ginny was dressed in dark slacks and a white blouse, and her long red hair had been pinned up—no doubt to keep her cool on this rather muggy evening—and Tricia thought she looked utterly charming with a long strand of jet beads hanging around her neck. She knew they had been a gift from Angelica, and Ginny wore them often and proudly.

Ginny turned, and Angelica waved. Ginny held a hand up to shield her eyes, caught sight of them, and waved enthusiastically.

"I'm just so proud of her I could cry," Angelica gushed.

"Proud, shmoud," Sheila muttered.

"Yes, I am," Angelica asserted. "Ginny pulled this event together in an extremely short space of time, vetted the acts, negotiated the contracts, and supervised an unfriendly team. It's a very big deal indeed."

"Why isn't she home taking care of her daughter?" Sheila countered.

"Like you did with Tricia?" Angelica said accusingly.

Sheila positively glowered.

Ginny approached the microphone, tested it, and then addressed the considerable crowd.

"Hello, Stoneham!"

The crowd—of mostly people unknown to Tricia—roared with approval.

"Welcome to the first annual Stoneham Wine and Jazz Festival, which is sponsored by Nigela Ricita Associates. Let's give them a big hand."

The applause was loud and appreciative. Tricia glanced at Angelica, who positively beamed.

"Our other sponsors tonight are Haven't Got a Clue, our magnificent vintage mystery bookstore—"

Tricia allowed herself a smile.

"The Stoneham Chamber of Commerce; the Sheer Comfort Inn; the *Stoneham Weekly News*—"

That startled Tricia, especially after Russ's most recent declaration of poverty.

"And the Have a Heart romance bookstore. Let's give them a wonderful round of applause."

And so the audience did.

"We've also got some terrific food trucks, featuring Asian-fusion cuisine, crepes, every kind of chicken wing under the sun, artisanal mac-and-cheese, and just about every other thing you could hope to eat, and, of course, we've got twelve representatives from some of New Hampshire's best wineries—so grab your complimentary wine glass and sample their flights. And all the while, bask in the lilting tones of some of the best jazz on the East Coast. And first up to entertain you is the Winston Freeman Trio, featuring Winston on piano, Jonny Martin on bass, and Charley Taylor on drums. Let's give them all a big hand."

And once again the audience stepped up to Ginny's bidding. She raised her hands over her head, clapping enthusiastically, and the musicians jumped into their first tune, Dave Brubeck's "Take Five."

For those in front of the bandstand, the volume was deafening. Covering their ears, Tricia, Angelica, and Sheila hurried away from the large speakers to save their hearing.

They wandered over to where the bulk of the food trucks were parked, but before Tricia could suggest they get something to eat, she caught sight of a familiar figure dressed in a green golf shirt and tan slacks.

Daddy! What was he doing there? And why did he have to bring Cherry? The sparks were sure to fly now—if not downright explosions.

Tricia caught her sister's eye and nodded in the direction of the couple. Angelica saw them and grimaced, then wasted no time turning their mother in another direction and shouting, "Let's check out the crepes truck." They started off, but then Tricia saw that John had seen them and was marching straight toward them as though to intercept. She waited until he caught up with her.

"What are you doing here?" she demanded

"It's a free country. I came to hear the jazz and drink the wine. What's your excuse?" he asked tartly.

"The same."

"Well, great. I see your mother deigned to lower her standards more than a notch to be here tonight. Why don't we just have a nice family reunion?"

"You just want to rub Mother's nose in the fact that you brought another woman."

"I did not. Cherry brought me, isn't that right, dear?"

"Sure thing, honey," Cherry said, chomping on a piece of gum. She wore a pair of white slacks and a loud print shirt of massive fuchsias on a white background, which clashed terribly with her magenta hair.

"Cherry, would you mind giving my father and me a few minutes to talk?"

"Sure thing, honey. I'll meet you by that wine stand over there. Okay?"

"Yes, dear," John said. He watched her go, his gaze fixed on her ample bottom, and positively grinned. Sheila was skinny as a rail. Did Tricia's father prefer women with curves?

She put the thought out of her mind and focused on the here and now. "I take it you've made up your mind not to reconcile with Mother."

"Why should I? She just wants to bully me—like she always has. Well, I'm tired of it. I've been on my own for almost six months now, and I *like* it. I like doing what I want to do when I want to do it. I like playing cards with the boys. I like eating what I want to eat when I want to eat it and without scathing looks."

"How will you support yourself?"

"The same way I have since I left your mother in January. Gambling. I did real well yesterday, thanks to the tip I got from that fella at the bookshop."

Tricia gasped. "Mr. Everett?"

John shook his head. "No. That author guy who was at your bookstore last week."

"Steven Richardson?"

John nodded.

"When did he tell you about the poker game?"

"Yesterday. He called me at the Brookview right after you left to go to the drugstore. Then he picked me up and drove me to the game."

But that didn't make sense. Richardson had asked Tricia on more than one occasion where he could find and talk to John—how would he have known John was staying at the Brookview?

"Had you spoken to him before that?"

"Sure. On the night Carol got killed. I bummed a ride off him to get to Fred's apartment."

"How soon after you left the signing did he give you the lift?"

John shrugged. "Five, maybe ten minutes later."

"Did you go straight to Fred's apartment?"

John shook his head. "He said he needed gas. We stopped at a station on the highway."

No wonder Baker had eliminated Richardson so fast. If he hadn't been able to produce a receipt, it would have been easy enough for the chief to check out his credit card purchases, which would have instantly cleared him of Carol's murder. That still didn't explain *who* had done the deed.

It couldn't have been her chief suspect—Brad Shields—because he'd been murdered, too. Whoever killed Carol had to have killed Brad, too.

Had to have? Or had *two* killers been responsible for the deaths?

"Come on," John said, interrupting Tricia's reverie, and took off after his wife and oldest daughter.

For a man who'd recently suffered a heart attack, John strode through the crowd with amazing speed. Why couldn't he have just accompanied Cherry to the wine stand—or was he itching for a fight with Sheila?

Angelica and Sheila stood before the crepes truck, whose sign chronicled the various permutations on offer. Sheila did not look impressed. Instead of going up to stand beside his wife to subtly let her in on his presence, John strode right up to her, put a hand on her shoulder and yanked, nearly pulling her off her feet.

Sheila pivoted. "How dare you." Then she saw just who had manhandled her. "What are *you* doing here?"

"I just went through that with the Princess. Why are *you* here?"

"Because they *made* me come," Sheila cried.

"Is that true?" John demanded.

"No!" Angelica said, looking as puzzled as Tricia felt.

"I suppose you're here with that *woman*."

"Why shouldn't I be? She's very nice. She *appreciates* my company. She doesn't whine about me. She doesn't order me around."

"And how long have you known this person?"

"A day."

"I'm sure by the end of the week she'll have figured out who you *really* are and will walk away, as I did."

"*I* did the walking," John reminded her.

"Well, I certainly didn't go looking for you."

"Oh yeah? That's not what Peter Collins told me."

Sheila bristled at the mention of the name.

"Who's that?" Tricia asked.

"The private detective your mother hired to find me. No matter where I went, he kept showing up."

"I don't believe you."

"Believe it. He might be good at tracking down people, but he's terrible at keeping a low profile."

Sheila's cheeks grew a livid red. She had *let* him go—but she had kept her eye on him, as well.

"And then you showed up at Cherry's apartment yesterday, practically begging me to return."

"I *never* beg," Sheila grated. "I don't know why I even bothered. Obviously you're not worth my time." She turned. "Angelica, let's go get some wine."

"What about me?" John called.

"Go back to your girlfriend," Sheila sneered.

John just stood there, watching, as his wife of half a century stalked off.

Tricia hung back with her father. "What did you accomplish by that?"

"I put her in her place."

"All you did was make her angry—or should I say angrier at you. Don't you realize what this all means?"

"No, what?" he snapped.

"She loves you. She really *does* want you to go back to her."

"I wouldn't go back to her if she was the last woman on Earth. I wouldn't go back to her if she offered me *two* million dollars."

Tricia started. Did that mean Sheila had offered him *one* million bucks?

"What are you going to do now?"

"Go find Cherry and get a drink—and not wimpy wine. I want a *real* drink."

Tricia watched as her father stomped off in the direction of where they'd last seen Cherry. Since the only adult beverage on sale at the festival was wine, that had to mean he would head for the Dog-Eared Page. Maybe that was a good thing. It would give both her parents a chance to cool down.

Tricia turned back and followed in her mother's and sister's footsteps.

Sheila was obviously upset, for she practically chugged her glass of wine.

"I got you one, too, Tricia," Angelica said, handing her the glass of white.

"Thanks."

"Where did Daddy go?"

"To find Cherry."

"You mean to hook up with her, don't you?" Sheila accused.

Tricia was shocked to learn her mother even knew that term.

"Why don't we all calm down and enjoy the wine and the music," Angelica suggested, sounding far more cheerful than her expression conveyed. "Look, there's a bench over there. It's far enough away from the speakers that we won't all go deaf, and maybe we can have a nice chat."

"About what?" Tricia asked.

Angelica opened her mouth to reply, but then seemed to have no answer. Instead, she took a hearty sip from her own glass. "Come along, Mother," she said, then hooked arms with her and led her toward the bench. That was when Tricia saw a familiar face in the crowd, belonging to someone who lounged against one of the square's maple trees. It was her turn to stalk off in another direction.

She stopped in front of the man, suddenly almost as angry as her mother had been moments before. "What did you hope to gain when you set my father up with poker games and misled me about his whereabouts?"

"Nothing," Richardson insisted, raising his hands as though in surrender, but then he looked away and shrugged. "Okay, maybe I did that."

"Why the pretense?"

"I wanted excuses to talk to you. You're a very attractive woman."

Somehow that didn't ring quite true—especially since he'd avoided her for more than a day after Carol's murder.

"What are you really doing here in Stoneham?" Tricia demanded.

"I told you. I came for your signing and to talk to Carol Talbot. It's too bad she died before I could get what I needed for my book."

"And what was that? A grandstand ending?"

Richardson said nothing.

"You may have an alibi for Carol's death—but what about Brad Shields?" she bluffed.

"Why would I want to kill him?"

"He was very protective of Carol. They had a years-long relationship. When her husband died, he wanted to leave Ellen and live with Carol, but she was no longer interested in continuing their liaison. She felt guilty. It drove her to drink—and she nearly lost her job because of it." Okay, as far as Tricia knew, that was a complete fabrication, but she was on a roll.

"You're delusional," Richardson said.

"No, she's not," came a voice from behind them.

Tricia looked over her shoulder and saw Ellen Shields standing behind her, hands on her hips and looking almost as angry as Tricia felt.

Ellen continued, "We thought about swapping partners for good, but then Dale died. I couldn't bear the thought of Brad moving in with Carol and me being alone."

"So you killed him?" Tricia asked.

Ellen's mouth dropped open, her expression one of outrage. "Of course I didn't."

"Then who did?"

Ellen's gaze swung toward Richardson.

The author's expression was skeptical. "You're living in a fantasy world. What motive could I have had for killing someone I didn't even know?"

"As Tricia said: a grandstand ending for your miserable excuse for a book."

Richardson scowled. "You're not addressing who killed my golden goose."

Ellen let out a breath. "It was Brad," she admitted in almost a whisper.

"But why?" Tricia asked, confused.

"Because he found out about her *fling* with your father."

Tricia blinked in disbelief. "When?"

"Minutes before he killed her near that bar."

"How do you know he killed her?" Tricia asked.

"Because I followed him that night. He was obsessed with her—she wasn't even pretty—but he *wanted* her," Ellen practically sobbed, and seemed unaware that some of the concertgoers were now actively listening in. "I saw him drag her onto the darkened patio. I saw him come out alone. I didn't know what to do. And then I saw you and your sister coming down the sidewalk."

"What about the book? How did Brad get a copy of *A Killing in Mad Gate*?"

Ellen glanced at Richardson. "Carol told Brad some author was hounding her, wanting to dig up her past and humiliate her. She knew that even when you pay your debt to society, you're never really forgiven and that there's always someone out there who wants to bring up every bad memory."

"You felt sorry for her?"

"I don't know if I'd go that far. Brad went to one of *his*"—she nodded in Richardson's direction—"book signings in Boston."

"I never met the man before last week," Richardson declared.

"Brad waited until after the signing and bought a signed book."

"Why?" Tricia asked, still confused.

"Because he was a fan."

Richardson smirked. "I do have more than a million of them."

The smug bastard. But Tricia also believed what Ellen had said—that she was looking at a murderer.

"Carol had also told Brad that this *man*"—she said the word as though it was an epithet—"was hounding her because of her past. That made him curious."

"What about the collection?" Tricia asked.

"Brad took it the night of Carol's death," Ellen admitted. "What was left of it. He was afraid Dale or Carol had taken pictures of us during our swaps."

"Where is it now?"

"I don't know. But I know that this *man*"—again she glared at Richardson—"knew about it. He offered to buy it from Brad."

"I did nothing of the kind. Your claims are ridiculous."

"I'm sure Chief Baker will want to talk to you about Brad's death," Tricia pointed out.

"I didn't kill Shields, so I have no doubt I'll be exonerated—that is, should you push your absurd agenda," he told Ellen.

"That's exactly what I intend to do."

Richardson's mouth twisted into a caricature of a smile as he suddenly advanced toward Ellen. He stopped before her and bent down to grab his pants leg. Then he stood and, with no warning, lunged toward the woman.

Tricia leaned forward, but couldn't understand what was happening until Ellen fell back onto her rear end. Richardson straightened, whirling on Tricia. Before she could react, he grabbed her by the waist with his left hand, wrenched the wineglass from her right hand, and smashed it against the tree. Then he yanked her forward.

"Keep your mouth shut and you won't get hurt," he grated.

Tricia strained her neck to look behind her and saw Ellen doubled over, a patch of crimson staining her shirt.

Had Richardson just stabbed her?

The author yanked Tricia along, pulling her through the village square. She knew that she needed to do *something*, but what that something was she wasn't sure.

And yet, Tricia wasn't about to let this horrible man—someone she once thought she'd like to get to know, someone she'd kissed—get the better of her.

Anger swelled within her, and she dug in her heels and stopped dead. "The hell with you," she declared.

Richardson brandished the broken wineglass. "Are you sure you want to make a stand right here, right now?"

"You just stabbed Ellen. You killed her husband. There's no way you're letting me go."

"You've got that right," he muttered, digging his fingers into her side until Tricia winced. "Move!"

"No!"

Their faces were mere inches apart, and Tricia met Richardson's gaze, his expression one of pure malevolence. In that moment, Tricia experienced true terror. This man was a cold-blooded killer—and now he was determined to snuff out her life as well.

But then the background music was drowned out by a banshee wail. A missile in the form of a woman barreled toward Richardson, knocking him off his feet. Then another human projectile from the opposite direction was suddenly there, pushing Tricia aside with the strength of a Patriots linebacker.

On the ground, the three bodies thrashed around, the woman screaming as she punched Richardson over and over again. "How dare you—how dare you threaten my daughter!"

It was then Tricia realized who the woman was—her mother!

"Mother, Daddy!" she hollered as the two of them continued to pummel the author.

Angelica was suddenly beside her, waving her arms and hollering. "Help! Help!"

In no time, a crowd of people rushed forward. A couple of men made a grab for Sheila's flailing arms, trying to yank her away, but she fought with the strength of a mother tiger protecting her cub, while John held Richardson pinned to the ground by the shoulders.

"Mother, Daddy—stop!" Tricia cried.

The music abruptly ended, as a bunch of uniformed security men rushed onto the scene, assisting the bystanders who struggled to haul Sheila and John off Richardson.

"What's going on?" the security chief demanded.

"I'll sue! I'll sue!" Richardson hollered, and rubbed at his already swelling left eye.

"Get an ambulance. This man stabbed Ellen Shields!" Tricia cried, pointing back toward the tree where Richardson had smashed her glass, but she could already see that there was a crowd surrounding Ellen. The sound of a wailing siren cut the air. Someone must have called 911.

"These people are crazy!" Richardson bellowed, staggering to his feet, his face mottled where Sheila had punched him.

"He had a broken glass—he was going to cut my daughter!" Sheila hollered, and rushed forward, hauling Tricia into a startled hug. "I'm so sorry, baby—I'm so sorry. And I'm so damn glad you're safe." She began to cry—great, heaving sobs. John was suddenly there, enveloping his wife and daughter in a bear hug. And, like Sheila, tears streamed down his anguished face.

Tricia wasn't sure what to say and simply reached up to pat her mother's back.

Angelica suddenly loomed into Tricia's view, looking sheepish. "Well, this was unexpected."

It certainly was.

TWENTY-NINE

The festival's second act didn't begin their set for more than an hour after Ellen Shields had been stabbed. That had given Ginny and the sound crew more than enough time to tweak the decibel level to a more tolerable level, with the use of recorded music to fill the gap. By that time, an ambulance had taken Ellen to the hospital in Milford, and Chief Baker had arrived on the scene, shoving Richardson in the back of one of the police cruisers while he tried to get coherent statements of what had happened from all the participants and witnesses.

It looked like it was going to be another long evening.

Tricia, Sheila, John, and Angelica shared one of the park benches, with Tricia sandwiched between her parents, both of whom held her hands for dear life. It made the burn on the back of her hand throb with every beat of her heart, but she wasn't about to tell either of them to let go. Some part of her had been waiting for this moment her entire life.

A worried Antonio pushed Sofia's stroller past the assembled Miles family for what must have been the tenth time, but not close enough for John and Sheila to hear the baby's squeals of "*Nonna*!" every time she saw Angelica.

"Why do we have to wait so long?" Sheila grumbled. "What's taking the police so long to question everybody? It's an open-and-shut case."

Tricia raised an eyebrow at her mother's choice of words. "That's just the way the police work. They need to make sure they collect all the evidence so that when Richardson comes to trial he'll face the maximum penalty."

"Which he deserves. Do you think that poor woman will be all right?" Sheila asked, in another surprising show of empathy.

"I sure hope so," Tricia said.

"I heard one of the paramedics say her vitals were good, so that's a hopeful sign," Angelica said. "I still can't believe Richardson would be so reckless to assault her and try to kidnap you in such a crowded venue."

"Thank goodness he did, otherwise Ellen and I might *both* be dead," Tricia said.

"You're safe now, and that's all that matters, Princess," John said.

"Yes," Sheila agreed, and squeezed Tricia's hand even tighter, which really *hurt*. Still, she forced a smile.

"I'm glad we're all safe. Once the police let us leave, maybe we could go out to dinner and talk. We have a lot of things to discuss," Tricia said, not the least of which was her mother's sudden change of heart. Or was it? She had seemed concerned to learn about Tricia's injured hand, and they'd had several civil conversations earlier that day. Had there been other evidence, however slight, that under her decades-old resentment her mother had some feelings for her youngest daughter that Tricia had never noticed?

Antonio made another circuit, trying, but not succeeding, to look nonchalant.

"Why does that young man with the baby keep passing by?" Sheila asked, sounding slightly irritated.

"Because he's worried," Angelica said, and sighed.

"About who?"

"Tricia and me."

"Who is he?"

"My son, Antonio."

"He's *not* your son," Sheila said once again.

"Yes he is! That little redheaded girl is my grandbaby."

"Grandchild?" Sheila repeated.

"I'm her great-auntie," Tricia said, reminding their mother of their conversation earlier that day.

"How come I didn't get to meet them back in January?" John asked.

"I told you about him in Bermuda. You never asked to meet him, and I didn't volunteer to introduce you to him because . . . because . . ." Angelica had to swallow a few times before she could finish. "Because I'd never let anyone hurt my son and his family, and I wasn't sure you'd be entirely kind to him."

"Why wouldn't we?" Sheila asked.

Angelica turned her gaze to her sister. Sheila looked at her youngest daughter, and her eyes filled with tears, but then she cleared her throat and straightened. "It may interest you to know that since your father and I parted I've been going to counseling."

"You have?" Tricia blurted. Talk about unexpected.

"Yes. I have a lot of work left to do, but I've been working through issues that have haunted me for years."

"Really?" Angelica asked.

"I'm—I'm shocked," John said, and by his expression, he truly was.

"It's not something I want to discuss further here in the park, but . . . my therapist wondered if we all might like to have a session or two with her. I was afraid to mention it to any of you because . . ." But that's where she ran out of an explanation.

"It might be very painful—for all of us," Tricia stated, "but I'm willing to try."

"Me, too," Angelica agreed.

Three pairs of eyes swung in John's direction. He shrugged. "I've put fifty years into this marriage—I guess I'm willing to at least *try* to save it."

"What does this mean?" Sheila asked.

"Maybe that finally we're a family," Angelica said.

"What do you think about that, Princess?" John asked.

Tricia shook her head and forced a smile. "That it's about time."

Resigned, the four of them sat on the bench for several long minutes.

Antonio made another circuit, but this time Angelica waved him over to join them. He pushed the stroller closer to them, his expression tight. "Mother, Daddy, I want you to meet my son, Antonio."

Antonio offered his hand, shaking John's first. "I am pleased, finally, to meet you, sir." He bowed slightly before offering his hand to Sheila. She hesitated, and then she, too, shook it.

"And this is my *bambina*, Sofia."

"*Nonna*! *Nonna*!" Sofia called, raising her arms to be picked up.

Angelica scooped her out of the stroller and kissed the child's cheek. The baby instantly grabbed for her necklace and laughed.

Sheila's smile was faint. "You and Angelica used to do that when you were babies."

Had she just admitted to a pleasant memory from Tricia's childhood? Perhaps there was hope for this family after all.

ANGELICA'S SUMMERTIME ZUCCHINI RECIPES

Zucchini Sausage Casserole

2 pounds zucchini, coarsely grated
1 pound hot or sweet ground Italian sausage
2 onions, chopped
3 garlic cloves, chopped
1 cup heavy cream
1 cup fresh bread crumbs
5 large eggs, lightly beaten
2 to 3 cups grated sharp cheddar cheese
salt
freshly ground pepper
hot sauce

TOPPING
6 tablespoons butter, melted
¾ cup fresh bread crumbs
½ cup grated cheddar cheese

Preheat the oven to 350°F. Grease a wide, 2-quart baking dish, or coat it with nonstick spray. Put the grated zucchini into a colander to drain for about 30 minutes or wrap it in a clean tea towel and gently squeeze it to remove the excess liquid. Place the zucchini in a large mixing bowl.

Heat a large skillet and add the sausage. Cook until the sausage starts to brown, stirring to break it up. Pour off all but about 3 tablespoons grease. Add the onions and cook until soft, about 5 minutes. Stir in the garlic and cook 1 more minute. Add the zucchini to the sausage mixture. Stir in the cream, the bread crumbs, the eggs, and the cheese. Add salt, pepper, and hot sauce to taste. Pour the mixture into a baking dish. The casserole may be refrigerated at this point for up to 2 days or frozen for up to 3 months.

For the topping, combine the butter and the bread crumbs. Sprinkle evenly over the casserole. Bake, uncovered, until hot through, about 30 minutes. Sprinkle the top with the ½ cup of cheese and return to the oven just until the cheese is melted and lightly browned.

Yield: 6 servings

Zucchini Soup

1 tablespoon butter
2 tablespoons olive oil
1 small onion, finely chopped
1 garlic clove, thinly sliced
kosher salt
freshly ground pepper
1½ pounds zucchini, halved lengthwise and sliced ¼-inch thick
⅔ cup vegetable stock or low-sodium chicken broth
1½ cups water

In a large saucepan, melt the butter in the olive oil. Add the onion and garlic; season with salt and pepper and cook over moderately low heat, stirring frequently, until softened; 7 to 8 minutes. Add the zucchini and cook, stirring frequently, until softened; about 10 minutes. Add the stock and the water and bring to a simmer; cook until the zucchini is very soft, about 10 minutes.

Working in batches, puree the soup in a blender until it's silky-smooth. Return the soup to the saucepan and season with salt and pepper. Serve it either hot or chilled, garnished with julienned zucchini.

Yield: 4 servings

Zucchini and Bacon Quiche

1 (9-inch) refrigerated pie dough round
¼ pound sliced bacon, coarsely chopped
2 medium zucchini (¾ pound total), halved lengthwise, then cut crosswise into ⅛-inch-thick slices
½ teaspoon salt, divided
¾ cup heavy cream
¾ cup whole milk
¼ teaspoon black pepper
3 large eggs
1 cup (4 ounces) Swiss cheese, coarsely chopped

With the oven rack in the middle position, preheat to 450°F. Fit the pie dough into a 9½-inch deep-dish pie plate and lightly prick all over. Bake according to package instructions, then transfer the crust in the pie plate to a rack. Reduce the oven temperature to 350°F.

While the crust bakes, cook the bacon in a large, heavy skillet over moderately high heat, stirring occasionally, until just crisp. Transfer the bacon with a slotted spoon to a paper-towel-lined plate, reserving the fat in skillet. Add the zucchini and ¼ teaspoon salt to the fat in skillet and sauté over moderately high heat, stirring frequently, until the zucchini is tender and starting to brown, then transfer with a slotted spoon to a plate.

Heat the cream, milk, pepper, and remaining ¼ teaspoon salt in a 1- to 2-quart saucepan until the mixture reaches a bare simmer, then remove from the heat.

Whisk together the eggs in a large, heat-proof bowl, then gradually whisk in the hot cream mixture until combined. Stir in the bacon, zucchini, and cheese together and pour into the piecrust. Bake until the filling is just set, 25 to 30 minutes. Transfer the quiche pan to a rack to cool slightly before serving.

Yield: 6 to 8 servings

Zucchini Bread

3 cups shredded zucchini (3 medium)
1⅔ cups granulated sugar
⅔ cup vegetable oil
2 teaspoons vanilla extract
4 large eggs
3 cups all-purpose flour
2 teaspoons baking soda
1 teaspoon salt
1 teaspoon ground cinnamon
½ teaspoon ground cloves
½ teaspoon baking powder
½ cup coarsely chopped nuts
½ cup raisins, optional

Move the oven rack to low position so that the tops of pan will be in the center of the oven.

Preheat the oven to 350°F. Grease bottom only of a loaf pan, 9 x 5 x 3 inches, with shortening. In a large bowl, mix the zucchini, sugar, oil, vanilla, and eggs. Stir in the remaining ingredients. Pour into the pan. Bake for 70 to 80 minutes, until a toothpick inserted in the center comes out clean. Cool for 10 minutes in the pan on wire rack. Loosen the sides of the loaf from the pan; remove from the pan and place top side up on wire rack. Cool completely before slicing. Wrap tightly and store at room temperature up to 4 days, or refrigerate for up to 10 days.

Yield: 1 loaf (approximately 12 slices)